MUSIC OF THE DISTANT STARS

Recent Titles by Alys Clare

The Hawkenlye Series

FORTUNE LIKE THE MOON
ASHES OF THE ELEMENTS
THE TAVERN IN THE MORNING
THE ENCHANTER'S FOREST
THE PATHS OF THE AIR *
THE JOYS OF MY LIFE *

The Norman Series

OUT OF THE DAWN LIGHT *
MIST OVER THE WATER *
MUSIC OF THE DISTANT STARS *

*   *available from Severn House*

MUSIC OF THE DISTANT STARS

Alys Clare

This first world edition published 2010
in Great Britain and in the USA by
SEVERN HOUSE PUBLISHERS LTD of
9–15 High Street, Sutton, Surrey, England, SM1 1DF.
Trade paperback edition first published
in Great Britain and the USA 2011 by
SEVERN HOUSE PUBLISHERS LTD.

British Library Cataloguing in Publication Data

Clare, Alys.
  Music of the distant stars. – (Lassair mystery)
  1. Fens, The (England)–Fiction. 2. Great Britain–
  History–Norman period, 1066-1154–Fiction. 3. Detective
  and mystery stories.
  I. Title II. Series
  823.9'2-dc22

ISBN-13: 978-0-7278-6941-8 (cased)
ISBN-13: 978-1-84751-272-7 (trade paper)

All Severn House titles are printed on acid-free paper.

Severn House Publishers support The Forest Stewardship Council [FSC],
the leading international forest certification organisation. All our titles that
are printed on Greenpeace-approved FSC-certified paper carry the FSC
logo.

Mixed Sources
Product group from well-managed
forests and other controlled sources
www.fsc.org Cert no. SA-COC-1565
© 1996 Forest Stewardship Council

FSC

Typeset by Palimpsest Book Production Ltd.,
Falkirk, Stirlingshire, Scotland.
Printed and bound in Great Britain by
MPG Books Ltd., Bodmin, Cornwall.

For Richard, Tim, Holly, Davey and Lisa,
and happy memories of a birthday dinner that
saw the birth of a wizard,
14th October 2009

The poem on page 163 is by
Richard Stuart-Pennink

ONE

D awn.
As I crept out of Edild's house, careful not to wake my exhausted aunt, I glanced up and saw the first faint, silvery light beginning to extinguish the stars. I have lived in the fens all my life, but there are some moments when the immensity of the vast skies can still take my breath away, and this was one of them.

It was very early, for Midsummer Day had only just passed and the nights were short. I fastened the door behind me, again ensuring I did not make a sound. For many nights now, Edild had barely slept, and I knew she would make herself ill if she did not rest. When I left, she was lying curled up like a cat on the hearth. She would have hated me to say so, but she was snoring; quite softly and musically, but nevertheless snoring.

Isn't it funny how we all vehemently deny something that probably every one of us does?

I had made my preparations the previous evening before I went to bed. Edild had explained exactly what I must do and, once she had convinced herself that I was up to the task, she had seemed very relieved that in the morning it would be me, not her, who would slip out at first light to do what had to be done. As for me, I was both thrilled because my aunt and teacher had deemed me worthy, and tense with anxiety about the grave responsibility entrusted to me.

I crept into the shadow of the little outhouse next to where the hens were penned up for the night. By touch, I located the shallow dish of water in which I had placed my flower garland and retrieved it. I checked in my leather satchel to ensure that all the other objects I would need were safely packed, then, taking a few deep breaths in an attempt to slow my racing heartbeat, I set off along the track that led out of the village.

Like my aunt, the majority of Aelf Fen was still fast asleep. I heard not a sound, and I saw not a single small, flickering light. I stopped for a moment, looking down the road to where my parents' house stood, at the opposite end of the village, and I knew instinctively that my father was awake. I concentrated hard, visualizing his familiar, beloved face that now wore the signs of grief, and I sent him my love. We are close, my father and I, and I am quite sure he received my silent message of support.

Then I hitched up my satchel, steadied the flower wreath on the palm of my hand and went on my way.

I had perhaps a mile to go; possibly a little more. As I walked, keeping up a good swift pace, I tried to ignore the shadowy places under the clumps of willow and alder and concentrate on the faint path that wound this way and that ahead of me, as clear to my eyes as if it had been cast out of moonlit silver. I am a dowser and, besides having the knack of finding underground water sources and lost objects, I have discovered that in some inexplicable way I can see hidden tracks and pathways that are all but invisible to others. Recently, I had even managed to locate a safe way across the waterlogged fens, but I was under severe stress at the time and I'm not at all sure I could repeat the achievement.

The track I was following that morning was ancient; as ancient as our family's habitation of Aelf Fen. Sixteen generations ago, Faol the Wolf Warrior took to wife Ligach the Pearl Maiden of the Fens, whose line had been fen folk since the beginning of time. Ligach's revered ancestor Aelfbryga spoke with the spirits, and they showed her the secret way to Aelf Fen. They taught her magical skills, including how to build an artificial island out in the black waters of the mere. I had long known this – we treasure our past and our bards keep it alive for us, telling us the tales of our ancestors so that they are almost as familiar to us as our living kin – but, when first I was told of it, I well recall how surprised I was to learn that Aelfbryga's island still existed. It was my destination this morning. Haunted by the spirits, seeming to vanish at times into the mist on the water and then reappear in a sudden shaft of sun or moonlight, it is a place so full of magic that it never fails to raise the hairs on the back of my neck and send shivers right through my body.

I was close to the island now. I was still excited, still anxious. In addition, I was now terrified.

Suddenly, my feet seemed to freeze to the ground and I could not move. I stood on the narrow path, my heart thumping so hard that it hurt. I could hear my teeth chattering, although the thinly-lit morning was not cold and I was snugly wrapped in the lovely shawl that my sister Elfritha had made for me. My fear threatened to master me. Aelf Fen was far behind me, too far for any cry of mine to reach the ears of any drowsy villager. The path still glowed faintly, but on either side the land was clothed in its thick-leafed summer foliage, providing far too many places where someone bent on harming me could hide.

I was not afraid of ill-intentioned humans, however. The entities I dreaded had no need of hiding places, for they were, I was quite sure, perfectly capable of invisibility. They could creep up on me without my suspecting a thing, and the first I would know was when icy fingers clutched at my throat and supernaturally strong arms thrust my head down into the black waters till I drowned and went to join their grey, shimmering company . . .

With a great effort I commanded myself not to be so fanciful and cowardly. I was there for a purpose: a very special, very important purpose. I had a task to fulfil, which had been entrusted to me because I had been deemed worthy, and that was a great honour. Was I going to turn tail and run back to the village, knock on my aunt's door in a melt of tears and moan that I couldn't do it – oh please, *please*, don't make me – because I was too *scared*?

No. I wasn't.

I had faced danger before, more than once. Someone had tried to drown me in the sea and I had survived. I had attacked an armed man and had the scar on my face to remind me. I thought about these occasions, and slowly my courage began to come back. I managed one step, then another. Soon I was walking on towards the artificial island. Moving slowly, yes, but nonetheless going in the right direction.

The reeds and rushes of the fenland vegetation on either side of the path thinned, and I could see out across the water. Daylight was waxing strongly now; it would not be long before the first thin arc of the sun came up in the eastern sky. Ahead of me, in the west, night still had command; the three great stars – Vega in the constellation of the Lyre, the Swan's Tail in the Swan, and Altair in the Eagle – shone out brightly, forming the familiar and beloved summer triangle. Pausing briefly to twist round and hold up my face towards morning, I turned and walked on.

Now I could see the stakes that marked out the path to the island. Our ancestors drove them down deep into the black mud, fixing bracing struts between them on which the sawn lengths of timber were laid, making a secure way across the water. The timbers and the bracing struts are taken away when not in use and, unless you knew, you would not appreciate the secret purpose of the stakes, for they are set at random intervals, they are of different lengths and emerge from the water at a variety of angles to the surface of the mere.

The struts and timbers were there now because we needed access to the island, and we would continue to do so for many days to come. This was our burial island, where the most revered of our people were interred. My great-grandfather Leofric and his wife Aedne were there, lying together for all eternity in the same grave. Beyond the slight hump that marked the precious place lay Ceadda, the Keeper of Swans, and Vigge, who died defending Edmund, King of the East Angles. Over on the far side of the island, where land melted into water, were the most ancient graves, among them Beretun the Cunning Man, and Yorath the Young Wife, who married her teacher. It was our lasting sorrow that many of our greatest warriors did not lie among their kin; my father's two uncles, for example, Sagar Sureshot and Sigbehrt the Mighty Oak, died at Hastings and their bodies were never found.

There was a new grave on the island, a snug little furrow

dug in the rich black earth and covered over with a flat slab of stone. Within lay a small body wrapped in linen and strewn with the flowers of early summer. Prayers had been said for the deceased, and more pleas would be added in the days to come. Gifts had been put in the grave alongside the body for, despite the priests of the new religion, we adhere to the old ways and send our dead on into the afterlife with the possessions they most treasured during their life on earth. I had come this morning with a fresh flower garland to arrange on the stone slab over the place where the wrapped head of the corpse lay. I had also brought the symbols of earth, air, fire and water, for I intended to summon the spirits of North, East, South and West to aid me in my prayers. As I set my feet on the timbers that seemed to float on the dark water, in my mind I went over what I was going to say and do.

I was concentrating so hard as I approached the stone slab over the grave that at first I did not appreciate that anything was wrong.

'—and take to rest the soul of our beloved . . .' I was muttering aloud.

Then my eyes succeeded in getting the horror they were seeing through to my brain. I stopped in mid-sentence and let out a cry of fear and dismay.

Someone had moved the stone slab.

We had left it so that it neatly and completely covered the grave. Now it was askew; only slightly, but enough that there was a dark corner where you could see right down into the grave.

I was shivering, filled with unreasoning abhorrence at the thought of that recently-dead body lying there so close to me. With the stone slab out of alignment, I could have reached into the grave and touched the cold flesh . . .

'Stop it!' I commanded myself, my voice loud with distress. 'That is the body of someone you loved very dearly. It isn't some fearful *object*, to make you shudder!'

The trembling slowly stopped. As panic receded a little, another frightful worry occurred to me: why had the slab been moved? Oh, *oh*, what had they *done*?

Without thinking what I was doing, I was on my knees, pushing the slab so that the gap increased. As soon as I could, I lowered my head and stared into the grave.

The linen-shrouded corpse was still there, and the precious belongings lay around it. The flowers had not been touched and had a little life left in them.

But there was a very vital alteration to the grave's contents. We had left there one body, small and thin. Now there were two.

My Granny Cordeilla was dead.

We had all known it was going to happen but, as we always do with those we love, we prayed in our different ways for a miracle. Well, I don't believe Granny prayed for any such thing; she seemed to know her time on this earth was coming to an end, and she approached death with a calm serenity and a slight sense of curiosity. 'I'm tired, Lassair child,' she said to me in one of her last moments of lucidity. 'I've had a long, hard life and now I'm ready for a rest.' She must have seem the unshed tears in my eyes, for all that I tried to turn away, for she took my hand in hers – her grasp, so weak where once it had been so strong, almost undid me – and whispered softly, 'No weeping, child. You'll miss me and you'll be sad for a while, but there's no tragedy in the death of an old woman. It's the way of things.'

With that she lay back on her pillows and went to sleep. Over the next day and night her sleep deepened and we watched as she slipped away. Then we stood around her body, our hands joined, and we wept.

My father – her son – had seen the change in her before any of us, and this quite irked my aunt Edild, my father's sister, because she's meant to be the healer and my father is an eel fisher. It quite irked me too, I have to admit, because I am Edild's apprentice and, like her, ought to have spotted the signs. In our defence, neither of us had seen Granny as often as my father, for Granny had lived with him, my mother and my siblings, whereas I live with Edild in her neat little house on the other side of the village. However, even if we'd observed Granny all day and every day, I'm not sure if we'd have picked up whatever subtle signals my father had seen; it's probably a mother–son thing. Of Granny Cordeilla's five children, he was her favourite, and that was probably why she'd chosen to live with him and his family instead of with Ordic, Alwyn, Edild or Alvela. As for my father, he is an undemonstrative man, but we all know his emotions run deep and true. He would have done anything for his mother, and his grief at her death was none the less for being hidden. My mother, sensible woman that she is, let him alone. She understands my father very well; better, probably, than Granny did, but it would be a brave person who said so in my father's hearing. To have said it in Granny's hearing would have been tantamount to suicide.

Anyway, whatever it was that my father saw, he'd kept it to himself . . . or, more likely, Granny had sworn him to secrecy. Some time later – a few weeks, according to my father – Granny had a fall. Then she had another one. This time, when she came round from her swoon, or whatever it was, she did not know where she was. She recognized us, although she muddled up some of our names, but she seemed to be seeing things that were invisible to the rest of us. She urged my brother Haward to find a bale of straw to sit on and get a good place so that he could watch the travelling jugglers and tumblers. She kept telling my mother that *they* were listening to our conversations and we must be careful. Then she had another fall, banged her poor head and lay insensate on her cot for three days.

When she woke up she was herself again. She commanded my father to summon all her children, grandchildren and great-grandchildren – most of them were already there, hovering around my parents' little house and not really knowing what to do with themselves – and called all of us to her bedside in turn, in order of age, so that she could speak privately to us. Well, I don't suppose she had much to say to my niece and my nephew, since one is a toddler and the other a baby, but the rest of us were with her for some time. I've no idea what she said to everyone else, but when it was my turn, she made me sit down beside her cot and, her deep eyes fixed on my face so that I did not dare move a muscle, said quietly, 'Lassair, child. Yes.' She nodded and then paused, watching me closely. 'When I was a girl I was sent to live with my uncle, Leir the Bard.'

I knew that already. Granny was a wonderful bard herself, always much in demand when we all sat round the fire in winter and there wasn't much to do through the long hours of darkness, and she had told me many times that her great fund of legends, myths, stories and the all-important record of our family's history and the doings of the ancestors were taught to her by her uncle Leir, after whom my youngest brother is named. 'Yes, Granny, I—'

She held up her hand to silence me. 'When he died, my uncle Leir summoned me to his deathbed. I was older than you, child, with a family of my own, for Leir was a long-lived man. He called me for one purpose, and it was not to say his fond farewells.' There was a twinkle in Granny's eyes as if somewhere deep inside she was laughing. 'Can you think what it was?'

I believed I could, but I hesitated to say so because it would have sounded big-headed and I'd have felt a fool if I'd been wrong. 'Er—' I began.

With a flash of her old impatient self Granny said, 'It's no time for false modesty, child. I'm dying, and I've still got two of your brothers and Goda's pair to see yet. Come on, say what you're thinking.'

I took a breath to steady myself. 'You want me to become a bard.' There. I'd said it. I felt my face, neck and throat flush with the sudden rush of hot blood.

'No, Lassair,' Granny said softly.

I hung my head, shame flooding me. How had I dared to presume to take on Granny's role, to think I could fill the shoes of one such as her? Why—

'Look at me.'

I made myself meet Granny Cordeilla's eyes. They were crinkled up in a smile, and she was looking at me with such love that a sob broke out of me. Her hand made a small movement where it lay on the clean linen sheet and, realizing what she wanted, I took it between mine. Hers was cool.

'So warm,' she murmured, her fingers entwining with mine. Then she said, 'You do not need to *become* a bard, Lassair. You have a very good memory, and all the skill you will require runs in your blood, for you are my granddaughter and Leir the Bard was your kinsman.' She paused, a faraway look on her face as if she saw things I could not see. 'Every one of us,' she went on, 'Leir, me, you, all the other extraordinary storytellers, singers and poets in the family, are descended from Ligach the Pearl Maiden of the Fens, the most famous bard of all time. *Her* talent was bestowed on her by the gods,' Granny added with pride thrumming in her voice, 'and she sang before kings.'

I could not speak. Yes, I'd had an inkling that Granny was going to say it was up to me to take on the bard role, but I'd thought it was because, out of all the family, it was I who clamoured most frequently to hear her tales. I'd never dreamed I would be commanded to take my place as the latest in this long family line of illustrious ancestors.

It was quite a lot to take in.

Granny squeezed my fingers again, then let me go. 'You'll get used to the idea,' she said briskly. Then, wrapping her shawl more closely around her thin shoulders, she flapped her hand in dismissal and told me to send in my brother.

I only had one more conversation with her after that. Then she died.

I don't know how long I stood there staring down into Granny's grave. It felt like an age, but I don't suppose it was very long really. I couldn't stop myself from speaking to her, calling out to her, even though I knew she couldn't hear me.

'Granny, I'm sorry, I'm so, so sorry!' I sobbed. 'We should have stayed with you, then this – this *desecration* wouldn't have happened! Oh, who did this to you?'

I paused, my grief overcoming me. It was such a recent loss, and I was still raw, for I had loved my Granny Cordeilla very much. Doing everything just right had been a consolation; the funerary rites had eased the pain, as I imagine is their purpose. But, oh, now this awful thing had happened, and everything was spoiled, we'd have to—

It was a sort of miracle, I suppose; I heard – or thought I heard – Granny's voice.

It's not your fault, child, she said, softly but firmly. It sounded as if she was speaking from a long way away, and almost at once I realized I wasn't hearing through my ears but right inside my head. *Stop standing there howling and pull yourself together!* That was typical Granny, so much so that I smiled and a sort of snorty laugh broke out of me. *Funeral rites are for the living,* she went on decisively, *and although I'm grateful for what you have all done, it is not that important, certainly not enough for you to get in such a lather about.*

'Not important?' I cried, amazed and shocked. 'But—'

Don't interrupt, Granny said. *Child, think about what* is *important.*

I thought. 'Your grave has been violated,' I began, 'and—'

Nonsense, Granny interrupted. *That doesn't matter, as I'm no longer there.*

Shock after shock; whatever did she mean, she was no longer there? Did that imply that none of them remained with us, all those beloved, honoured ancestors?

I swear I heard Granny sigh. *Lassair, we will never leave you,* she said patiently. *But listen, child! What did you see in the grave with me?*

'Another body,' I whispered, the horror flooding through me all over again.

Yes, quite, Granny said testily. I thought she added, *At last!*

'But it's got no right to be there in your special place!' I protested. 'This is *our* island, for our people!'

Death is death, Granny answered. *This poor soul died too soon, and the corpse has been hidden here. That is not right, Lassair.*

'Died too soon,' I repeated softly. 'A corpse hidden in someone else's grave, where but for the small mistake of leaving the stone slab slightly out of place, nobody would ever have found it . . .'

Because, of course, if someone had slipped a body in with Granny then it was very likely that the poor dead soul hadn't died of natural causes in his or her own bed. It was eminently likely that this was a murder victim, and that the killer had cruelly and cynically used my Granny's grave as a convenient hiding place.

I had found the body. It was up to me to act.

I pushed the slab back in place, placed my flower wreath over Granny's head and then, in some haste, I'm afraid, said my prayers and made my pleas for her soul.

Then I packed up my satchel, fastened it and, gathering up my skirts and clutching my shawl, fled across the wooden walkway and raced back to Aelf Fen.

TWO

only saw one person on my headlong flight to the safety of home. I was about halfway back to the village. I'd just run past a clump of willows when I heard the sound of someone weeping; a man, I thought. The sounds were gruff and full of pain.

I am a healer, or at least I am training to be one, under the tuition of my aunt Edild and a strange man called Hrype, who is a cunning man and the father of my friend Sibert. Even trainee healers know they must not ignore those who suffer. I stopped and, very cautiously, approached the willows.

'Who's there?' I called softly.

The weeping ceased abruptly. Nothing happened for a few moments, then two thick-leaved branches parted and someone crept out.

It was a man, or I suppose that is what you would call him, for although he is fully grown and perhaps eighteen or twenty years old, his mind is that of a child. His body is misshapen under an over-large head, and his poor face is lopsided. I knew who he was; I had good reason to. I held out my hand, smiling, and said, 'It's all right, Derman. It's me, Lassair. Come with me and I'll take you home. Have you had breakfast?' He risked a quick glance at me, his deep-set eyes furtive, drew the back of one hand across his nose and shook his heavy, lolling head. 'Then you must be hungry,' I went on briskly. 'Come on, we'll walk fast, then you'll have something to eat all the sooner!'

Talk of food distracted him, as I hoped it would. For the length of time it took to reach the village, we amused ourselves describing what we most liked to eat. Not that he contributed much to the conversation, for his stock of words is paltry and those he does know he pronounces oddly, as if his tongue were far too large for his mouth. By the time I led him up to his door, he was smiling again, and the only reminders of his tears were the streaks of dirt on his face and the snot coming out of his nose.

Derman is a cross we are going to have to bear, for it looks as if he is going to become part of our family. My brother Haward is finally sweet on a girl, and we all have a shrewd idea that there could be a marriage before too long and a new bride in the house. It's high time Haward was wed; he is nineteen, and although he has a kind heart, gentle ways and a handsome face, he has never sought out the pretty girls with the rest of the young men of the village because of his stammer. It wasn't just that people made fun of him – although, of course, they did – it was also that if he ever met a girl he liked, some other lad would have charmed her with his silken tongue and led her away while poor Haward was still struggling to say *h–h–h–h–hello*.

Zarina isn't like the other girls, either in our village or any other in the vicinity. She isn't really like anyone. She's got hair so black it almost looks blue, and her eyes are a greenish-gold colour that changes according to what she's wearing. Her skin is smooth and silky, the colour of pale oak wood. She's only a year or so older than me, but she seems ancient, somehow, as if she's seen a lot and has had to learn how to look after herself. Haward met her at the Lammas Fair, where she was in the company of a group of travelling entertainers. It was unclear whether or not they were her kin, but either way she had no compunction about staying behind when they moved on – she'd met Haward by then – and now she lodges with an elderly widow in the village and spends her days doing laundry. If – when – she marries my brother, she'll make an interesting addition to the family.

Zarina, however, comes at a price, and that price is her brother Derman. I don't know how Haward feels about his prospective brother-in-law, for we have not spoken on the subject. Knowing Haward as I do, I imagine he will readily make room in his life for poor Derman if it means he can marry his beloved Zarina. My brother is full of what the

Christians say characterized Jesus Christ: a sort of all-encompassing loving kindness that accepts people for who and what they are. Had Derman been evil, malicious, spiteful or sinful, it might have been a different matter, but what ails him is not his fault – Zarina says he was born that way – and Haward is not likely to hold such misfortune against him. If Haward and Zarina marry – and I am all but sure they will – then the family and the rest of Aelf Fen will just have to make the best of it and accept Derman, even if he does look like a gargoyle and frighten little children. Zarina has implied that he cannot support himself and, as she is apparently the only living relative who cares whether he lives or dies, it is up to her to take charge of him. I suppose we'll get used to him, given time.

I handed Derman into the care of his sister – our knock on the door must have woken Zarina, for she answered it with loose, tumbled hair, a sleepy expression and a tattered old shift clutched loosely around her body, and even under those circumstances she looked absolutely lovely – and, waving aside her thanks, I hurried away.

Edild was already up. She was stirring the breakfast porridge as I arrived and I noticed bread and a pot of honey on the table; she knew I would not have broken my fast before I set out, and clearly she wished to have food ready for my return.

One look at my face told her something was wrong.

'What?' The single word cut the tense silence in the tidy, fragrant little house.

Swiftly, I told her. Her face went pale, and her eyes widened in shock. Without another look at the carefully-prepared meal that lay waiting for us, she grabbed my arm and dragged me back along the track to the burial island.

We did not speak as we hurried along. Sometimes we ran, then we would slacken our pace for a while and reduce it to a fast walk. When we crossed the planks on to the island, both of us were red-faced and sweaty. I knew, even before Edild laid a restraining hand on my arm, that this was no way to approach my grandmother's grave. We helped each

other, Edild rearranging my hair and I hers, each of us
straightening the other's robe as best we could. Edild took
a large, folded square of linen from her sash, and we both
wiped our faces. By now our breathing was almost back to
normal; my aunt took my hand, and together we stepped
up to the stone slab.

We each took a corner and pushed hard. The slab moved
quite readily; I recalled that earlier I'd managed to put it
back in its rightful position by myself, and it was, naturally, much easier with two. Then we stared down into the
grave.

I heard Edild mutter something – a prayer, an incan-
tation, I did not know – as gently, lovingly, her hand
dropped on to Granny's brow in a caress. Then, the due
observance of the grave's rightful occupant accomplished,
Edild turned to look at the interloper. Kneeling right
beside her, I now took in the details that my horrified
eyes had slid past the first time.

The second body was quite short, wrapped in a length of
grubby cloth that looked like cheap, coarse linen. The cloth
seemed to have been knotted clumsily around the body's
waist, for it made a bulge that was not in keeping with the
narrow shoulders and the slight build. Was it a youth or a
young woman? It could have been either . . .

Edild was carefully unfastening the linen, concentrating
on the head. Soon she had uncovered the hair – which was
a chestnut shade, long, glossy and curly – and then the face.

The young woman had been comely. Not beautiful,
perhaps, for her cheeks were round and her mouth was wide
and full. I knew, from that very first look, that this girl
would have been fun. Young as she was – she must have
been about my age, and I was just seventeen – already there
were laughter lines around her eyes and the suggestion of
dimples in her cheeks. Alive, she would have been the sort
of girl who smiled readily and convulsed into giggles at
the least excuse.

And now she lay dead in my grandmother's grave.

I swallowed the sob that threatened to burst out of me
and made myself concentrate on what Edild was doing.

She had gathered up the folds of linen at the head of the corpse and, in response to her nod, I did the same at the feet. Then, very carefully, we raised the body and laid it on the ground beside the stone slab.

Outside the narrow confines of the grave, it was much easier to remove the enshrouding linen. Quickly, Edild untied the knots that bound it and folded it out of the way. Now we could study the girl's clothing. She wore a gown of faded red, beautifully sewn with embroidered borders at the neck and cuffs, the colours of the silks chosen by an expert eye. The gown was not new, for not only had the fabric faded but, in addition, it was too tight for her. Her full breasts strained against the cloth, and she had recently let out the waist, where bright-red darts showed up to indicate she had altered the seams. Her hands lay folded over her stomach, and I was about to point out to Edild something I had just noticed when I was struck by something far, far more important.

I raised my eyes and looked at my aunt. She, too, had seen; I knew it from her face.

'Two people lie dead here on the grass, Lassair,' she said quietly.

I nodded, too sad to speak.

The young woman had been pregnant.

I was sent back to the village for help, leaving my aunt sitting on the ground beside the young woman and the child that swelled her belly. As I hurried away I could hear Edild's sweet, soft voice in a lament. It was a comfort, if only a small one, for had it been me lying there, I could think of nobody I'd rather have to plead for me with those who take in the souls of the dead.

I dried my tears and forced myself to walk faster. I had a job to do, and there was no time for sentiment.

I wanted very much to run for my parents' home. I no longer lived there – it was more practical to live with Edild, in the place where we both worked – but all the same, I saw my parents and my brothers regularly. Particularly in the recent days since Granny's death; mourning her as we did, it seemed that we had all moved closer, as if to try to fill the huge gap she had left. I would have given much, just then, to be able to fly to my home and throw myself in my father's strong arms while my mother made me something soothing and comforting to eat.

I could not do that. Instead I turned off the track to the village and headed for Lakehall.

Lakehall is where the lord of our manor lives. His name is Lord Gilbert de Caudebec, and he's fat, easy-going and not very bright. He is married to Lady Emma, whose intelligence far outstrips that of her husband. Fortunately for us, she's a good woman. Lord Gilbert and Lady Emma have two little children, and there's a rumour going around in Aelf Fen that she is expecting a third. The rumour is accurate. Healers get to know these things, although of course neither Edild nor I would dream of breaking a professional confidence.

The villagers do not, in the normal way of things, see very much of either the lord or the lady. If we have business at the manor, we speak to the reeve. His name is Bermund, and he is a fair but withdrawn man of early middle age and unprepossessing appearance, being very tall and thin with a sort of poky, pointy face. My little brother Squeak says he looks like an anxious rat. As I hurried into the courtyard, Bermund was emerging from one of the outbuildings.

He saw me, stopped, sniffed and said, 'Yes? Is it about the eels?'

My father, as I have said, is an eel catcher and so, seeing me, I suppose it was a natural assumption. There's no reason why Bermund should have remembered that I no longer live under my father's roof and am a healer.

'No, sir,' I said. I took a deep breath. 'There was a body in my grandmother's grave. I found it – her – early this morning.'

It seemed to take him a moment to understand what I was telling him. Just when I was wondering if I ought to have explained that the body wasn't my grandmother's but a second one, not put there by us, he spoke.

'Do you know the corpse's identity?'

I had to admire the way he went straight to the point. 'No,' I replied. 'As soon as I'd made the discovery I ran back to fetch my aunt – that's Edild, the healer?' He nodded impatiently. 'She came back with me to the grave – it's on the island out in the mere.' Again that quick nod, almost as if Bermund were saying, *Yes I know, get on with it.* 'Together, Edild and I lifted the body out of the grave, and Edild unwound the shroud. It is – it was – a young woman, about sixteen or seventeen, with chestnut hair and wearing a red gown. She—'

The flash of recognition in Bermund's narrow eyes was unmistakable. He held up an imperious hand and said, 'Wait.'

I waited.

Not, however, for long. After only moments, Lady Emma appeared at the top of the stone steps that led up into Lord Gilbert's hall. She looked very distressed, her face pale and her cheeks wet with tears. She beckoned to me, and as I crossed the courtyard and ran up the steps to stand beside her, she reached out and took my hand.

'Oh, Lassair, tell me what you told Bermund!' she pleaded.

'I found a—' I began.

'No, no!' she cried sharply, then instantly said, 'I apologize. I did not mean to shout. I meant, tell me what this poor girl looks like.'

I repeated the description I had just given, adding details such as the high quality of the workmanship on the red gown, the willing tendency to laughter I'd read in the face, the gloss on the chestnut hair.

As I spoke, I sensed Lady Emma begin to slump. I shot out my arms – I am wiry and pretty strong – and caught her as she fainted.

They couldn't send for Edild, for I explained to them that she was still out on the island. Instead they had to make do with me. I did my best to put aside the shocking drama of the morning's tragic discovery and concentrate on my patient. Lord Gilbert and Bermund had carried her to a couch at the far end of the hall, and I sent them off on errands: Lord Gilbert to fetch a warm blanket and make sure the nursemaid kept the children out of the hall, Bermund to the kitchen for cold water.

When we were alone I leaned down to Lady Emma, who was coming out of her faint. Seeing me, her eyes widened in alarm and she tried to sit up. Gently, I pushed her back.

'You're quite all right,' I said. I knew what she was going to ask before she had even framed the words; it's the same with almost all pregnant women. Speaking right into her ear, I added, 'So is the baby.' I felt her relax with relief. 'You did not fall down the steps,' I explained, 'so there was no danger.'

'I did not fall?' she echoed, her eyes searching my face. I shook my head. 'I caught you.'

She said nothing, but her hand shot out and clasped mine.

Lord Gilbert came puffing back with a lovely warm, soft, woolly blanket, which I told him to drape over his wife; it helps people, I find, if they think they're doing something useful. I watched him as he looked down at her. It was clear both that he loved her dearly – which was hardly surprising – and also that he knew she was pregnant, for he shot a fleeting glance at her stomach, raising his eyebrows, and swiftly she nodded, a radiant smile crossing her face.

Bermund returned with the cold water – it really was icy cold, as I discovered when I soaked a piece of clean linen in it; he must have drawn it fresh from the deep well outside the kitchen – and then he stepped back, looking worriedly down at Lady Emma. I sensed she wanted nobody but her husband just then – oh, and me, I supposed – and, turning to him, I said very politely and respectfully, 'I think Lady Emma needs to rest, sir.'

He took the hint. He bowed to the lord and lady, nodded curtly to me and turned to go. Before he did so he looked at Lord Gilbert in enquiry, and Lord Gilbert said, 'I will send for you very soon, Bermund. Meanwhile, get someone over to Alderhall and find Sir Alain. I must speak with him.'

Bermund bowed again and hurried away.

Sir Alain? Alderhall? I did not recognize the names. Not
that it mattered just then. I wrung out the linen cloth and
gently bathed Lady Emma's cheeks and forehead; her faint
had made her sweat, and her face was hot and flushed. I
looked up at Lord Gilbert and back to Lady Emma and,
nerving myself, said, 'It's clear that you, my lady, know
who the poor dead girl was. Could you – I mean, would it
be all right if you told me?'

It was certainly not my place to ask such a thing, and I
was quite prepared for Lord Gilbert to command me to
mind my own business and get out before he threw me out.
But he is, as I've said, easy-going. In addition, he is neither
cruel nor particularly unreasonable, and I had, after all, just
saved his pregnant wife from falling down a flight of stone
steps. Perhaps he felt I had earned an explanation.

He sighed, then looked at his wife. She said softly, 'Tell
her, Gilbert.'

He turned back to me. 'We believe we do indeed know her
identity, and her death grieves us both, for in the short time
we have known her we have grown to like her.' He paused
and cleared his throat. 'She is an affectionate, cheerful,
amusing little thing, and the children love her, for she is
generous with her small amount of free time and always ready
for a cuddle or a game.'

It sounded as if the dead girl had been employed at the
manor as a nursemaid, which was odd because I thought
they already had one. Then I remembered something;
something I had noticed immediately before Edild had
uncovered the evidence of the girl's pregnancy. Oh, I thought
now, *oh*, but it explained the beautiful embroidery and the
well-made gown, as well as the dead girl's presence at
Lakehall.

'She was a seamstress!' I exclaimed.

They both looked at me in astonishment. Lady Emma
said tentatively, 'How – er, how did you know that?'

I wished I could say I had gazed into my scrying ball
and seen a vision of the dead girl bent over her sewing, but
it would have been a lie. 'I saw her hands,' I said. 'In particular, her left forefinger. It was covered in tiny pricks and

there was dead skin loose on the tip.' When you sew, if you are right-handed, the needle repeatedly stabs into your left forefinger. It doesn't hurt, really, unless you make a mistake and push the needle too hard, but it always leaves its unique mark.

'I see,' Lord Gilbert murmured. 'Very observant, I must say.' He looked at me, and I saw both respect and resentment in his expression. Typical of his sort, he did not really like observant women. With the exception of his wife, he probably found all clever women a threat.

Lady Emma took his hand and said something softly to him. His expression cleared and he managed a smile. 'We're grateful, er—'

'Lassair,' said Lady Emma.

'We're grateful, Lassair, that you came straight to us with this terrible news,' he said. 'What more can you tell us?'

I collected my thoughts and then described as succinctly and accurately as I could what my aunt and I had found and what we had done.

I could tell that Lord Gilbert was affected by my tale. He started to speak, and his voice broke with emotion. He paused, and I realized that he was struggling to control himself. 'This girl – her name is Ida – is, as you say, a seamstress, in the employ of my cousin, the lady Claude de Seés, who is at present staying with us as she prepares for her wedding. My cousin is, indeed, busy sewing her trousseau. Her marriage linen,' he added helpfully, although in fact I knew the word. 'Hence, er, hence the need for a seamstress to assist her.' He stopped, frowning. 'She – er, Ida was reported missing this morning. She eats breakfast in the servants' hall, but today she did not turn up. The others waited for a while to see if she had overslept and would soon come hurrying along out of breath and worried because she was late – she loves her food, you see – but she did not. In the end, one of them went to rouse her, but she was not there.'

'Where does she sleep?' Not with the other servants, it appeared, or they would have noticed her absence when they'd woken up.

Lord Gilbert glanced quickly at Lady Emma, and I sensed

that for some reason he was discomfited. 'My cousin, the lady Claude, is very protective of her trousseau. Quite understandably,' he protested, although I had made no remark, 'for she is a wealthy woman and has amassed household and personal linens of great value, all most beautifully sewn, I have no doubt, although I have not myself seen any examples of the work, nor, indeed, would I expect—'

Lady Emma came to his rescue. 'My husband's cousin is very aware of the need to take every precaution against theft,' she said, and I noticed that her carefully neutral tone did not give away what she thought of Lady Claude's behaviour. 'For this reason, she insists that all work on her trousseau is performed in a small room, whose door is kept locked. She also insists on the presence of someone to watch over the precious items at all times, this person being Ida.' She looked down at her hand, which still clasped Lord Gilbert's. 'We arranged a truckle bed in there for the poor girl. I believe she was adequately comfortable. Certainly, she did not complain. She was always ready with a smile and a bright remark.'

I was starting to dislike Lady Claude. I had heard sufficient tales of the way some lords and ladies treated their servants and, in truth, locking a girl into a small room each night so that her presence would safeguard a pile of linen was not bad at all by the standards of the times. It was just that I kept seeing that pretty face, all ready for laughter. The thought of Ida shut up all by herself, away from everybody else and missing any fun that might be happening, was all but unbearable.

Not that I dared say so. I cleared my throat and straightened my back, determined not to give away my private feelings. I also resolved not to mention Ida's pregnancy; it seemed that she had not been married and, if the lords and ladies here at the hall did not know of her condition, then I wasn't going to be the one to tell them. Let the poor girl keep her secret.

'Your aunt has remained with – with the body?' Lord Gilbert said gruffly.

'Yes. She felt that the dead girl should not be left alone.'

'Quite right, quite right,' Lord Gilbert rumbled. He glanced towards the door through which Bermund had disappeared. 'Where is he?' he muttered. 'What can be taking him so long?'

I decided to risk my luck once more. 'You said he was to fetch someone called Sir Alain?' I said, making it a question.

Lord Gilbert's brows descended in a frown. It was Lady Emma who answered. 'Yes. Sir Alain de Villequier.' A Norman, then. Of course. 'He's recently been appointed our local justiciar.'

I did not know what she meant. Now was not the moment to find out, however. I stored the words *local justiciar* away in my head.

'We shall await his arrival,' Lord Gilbert announced. 'Then you, girl, you will take him out to the place where you found her.'

He had, I noticed, spoken of Ida all the time in the present tense. Now, as he spoke of the place where she lay dead, it seemed that finally the truth was catching up with him. Ida was dead; she lay on the fresh summer grass beside my grandmother's grave.

As I watched, Lord Gilbert's hazel eyes filled with tears. Belatedly, he covered his face with his hands, and I heard Lady Emma make an inarticulate sound of distress. They had both cared for Ida, I thought. She might have been no more than a sewing girl in Lord Gilbert's cousin's employ, but she had made her mark on this household. The children had loved her because she had played with them, cuddled them, and, I had no doubt, had also told them funny stories, tickled them, and made them laugh. Hearing of her death had made Lady Emma swoon, and now as her husband faced up to the fact that Ida was gone, he had given in to his sorrow and wept.

They were all going to miss her.

THREE

Wherever they had expected this Sir Alain de Villequier to be, it became clear that he wasn't there. We waited for him to come, Lord Gilbert, Lady Emma and I, and after a while the wait became uneasy, then embarrassing. For all of us; lords and ladies do not normally spend any length of time with lowly people such as I, and, as for me, I was steadily growing more and more aware of my dishevelled appearance. Edild and I might have tidied each other up sufficiently to approach my Granny's grave, but standards in Lord Gilbert's hall were considerably more elevated.

We all exchanged several furtive glances, and I knew they wanted rid of me as badly as I wanted to go. Finally, Lord Gilbert had had enough. He got up from Lady Emma's couch, strode across the hall and launched himself through the doorway through which Bermund had disappeared.

With his departure, much of the awkwardness vanished. Lady Emma looked up at me and murmured, 'Oh, dear.' Then, to my surprise, she smiled.

I smiled back; she has that sort of face. No matter what mood you're in – and just then mine wasn't very good, given all that I'd been through since I got up – it's hard not to be affected by Lady Emma's smile. 'I'm sorry I'm still here,' I said. It was a daft remark, but Lady Emma was quite disarming and I'd said exactly what I was thinking.

'It's hardly your fault, Lassair,' she said. 'My husband asked you to stay, so that when Sir Alain arrives, you can take him out to where you found poor Ida.'

It was tactful of her to have said Lord Gilbert had *asked* me. I'd have said *ordered* or *commanded* was nearer the mark.

I looked at her, and I guessed by the sadness in her face that she was thinking about the dead girl. I wanted to turn her thoughts elsewhere, but I wasn't quick enough. Before I'd had a chance to come up with some innocuous remark, she spoke again.

'Did she – oh, I know I should not ask you this, but it's all I can think about. Lassair, did Ida suffer?'

I met her eyes. 'I cannot say, my lady.' That was true; there had been no time to find out how the girl had died. By now Edild probably had a good idea, for she would not have wasted this long period of waiting by the body.

'Could it possibly have been a dreadful accident?' Lady Emma asked. 'She might have tripped and fallen into the grave, perhaps banging her head as she fell . . . Oh, no.' Her face fell, and there was no need for either of us to say it: if Ida had met her death by accident, who had wrapped her in the shroud and replaced the stone slab over the grave?

I watched Lady Emma closely. I could see the distress rising in her. She was muttering under her breath, one hand clutching at her throat, the other on her belly. My impression was that her health was reasonably robust, but it doesn't do to take any chances, especially when a woman is in the early stages of pregnancy. I reached down to the small leather bag that hung from my belt, mentally reminding myself of the small store of herbs that I usually carry in it. Yes; I had what I needed.

'My lady,' I said softly, 'will you permit me to make a comforting drink for you? I have a remedy with me that is calming and promotes rest.'

She shot a look at me, and I had the impression that her first instinct was to refuse. Perhaps she wished to remain fully alert because she wanted to hear more news of Ida as soon as there was any. But then she slumped back into her pillows and nodded. She picked up a bell that was on the floor by her couch and rang it, sending the servant who quickly answered its summons to fetch hot water and a mug. I made up a mild sedative, and soon Lady Emma slipped into a doze.

I settled myself on the floor beside her, leaned back against the couch and let my head sink down on to the soft woolly blanket. Time passed, and in the still silence of the cool hall, I almost fell asleep myself.

There was a sudden commotion outside in the courtyard. The sound of a horse's hooves, then loud male voices. I detected anger. Then someone hushed the speakers and I heard heavy footsteps coming up the steps. Getting hurriedly to my feet, I stepped forward to meet Lord Gilbert as he came puffing into the hall, Bermund at his side. Behind them was a man I had never seen before.

I studied him. He was a big bear of a man, tall and broad. He was younger than Lord Gilbert; around the mid-twenties, I guessed. His light-brown hair was worn long but, unlike many young men who followed the new fashion set by the king and his intimate circle, Alain de Villequier had neither flowing beard nor elaborate moustache. He wore a blue robe cinched with a handsome leather belt with a gold clasp and carried a short hunting knife in a scabbard at his side. He had been riding hard – hunting, perhaps, for the knife was stained – and his light cloak was thrown back. His face was rugged rather than handsome, the mouth wide, the light eyes crinkled at the corners. There was a vitality about him that was very attractive, and I guessed that he was a man whom people liked and who made friends readily.

His first words supported this; he swept down in a graceful bow before Lady Emma, who had woken up as the men entered the hall, and very charmingly apologized for having taken so long in reaching Lakehall. 'As I have explained to Lord Gilbert,' he added, 'I took advantage of the beautiful morning light and went hunting.' He gave her a rueful look, like a small boy caught stealing a pie, and she smiled at him and said he was forgiven.

I realized something else about Sir Alain: he was a flirt.

Then he turned to me. 'This must be Lassair,' he said.

He knew my name! That was a surprise, for I am never sure that Lord Gilbert does, even though he's heard it several times. Sir Alain, on the other hand, had only been told of my existence a short time ago.

I bowed to him. 'Yes, sir.'

'You discovered the body?' His tone told me nothing;

he sounded like what he was: a man given the task of investigating a death, whose personal feelings on the matter, whatever they might be, were irrelevant.

'I did. She – the dead girl – had been wrapped in a shroud and placed in my grandmother's grave.'

'What were you doing there?'

'I had taken fresh flowers to place on the stone slab that covers the grave.' I decided not to mention the prayers with which I had hoped to invoke the guardian spirits. This man was undoubtedly a Christian and, whatever his private sentiments, in his official role he had to follow the Norman line.

'And you noticed that this slab had been moved?'

'I did.'

'So you looked down into the grave?'

'Yes.'

'Why?'

I hadn't expected the abrupt question. I tried to think back; what had been in my mind? 'I believe,' I said slowly, 'that I feared whoever had moved the stone might have somehow harmed or damaged my grandmother's body. She is but recently dead, sir, and I loved her dearly.'

To my surprise and shame, for I thought I was in control of myself, tears formed in my eyes. I lowered my head.

Sir Alain might have been a newly-appointed official whose responsibilities, presumably, included finding out how the dead girl had died, but still he had room for compassion. I heard a quick movement, and suddenly he was right beside me. He touched my shoulder and said quietly, 'Nobody has considered your feelings, have they? We are all so preoccupied with this death that we have not spared a thought for the poor young woman who went to pray for her grandmother and instead made such a terrible discovery.'

I wiped my eyes, sniffed and said, 'Thank you, sir, but I am all right.'

I looked up to find that he was studying me. 'You will be as soon as we can send you back to your family,' he remarked. Then he stepped away from me and said decisively, 'Come with me now and show me where the grave is, then you may go home.'

I raised my chin and met his eyes. 'Very well, sir.'

He went on looking at me for a moment, and I thought I saw the hint of a smile. Then he turned to Lord Gilbert, bowed deeply and, spinning round, strode out of the hall. I wondered if I ought to wait to be formally dismissed, but Lord Gilbert, obviously distressed, frustrated and bemused, waved an impatient hand and sent me on my way.

Out in the courtyard Sir Alain had already mounted. I stared at his beautiful horse. She was a bay mare, and she had a star-shaped mark on her brow. Her black mane and tail flowed free, and her coat gleamed with health. I was going to have to run hard to keep up with her, and my heart sank, for I had already covered quite a distance that morning and I was weary.

Sir Alain must have seen my face. He leaned down and held out his hand. 'Come on, she can carry two, and you're a slim little thing,' he said.

I took his hand, and he swung me up behind him. I settled just behind the rear board of the saddle, frantically trying to arrange my skirts to preserve my modesty. He put his heels to the mare's sides, and she sprang away, causing me to give out a yelp and fling my arms round Sir Alain. 'No need to stop my breathing!' he said with a laugh, and I eased my grip. Then I realized that the mare had settled into her stride – an easy, loping canter – and I no longer felt I was about to fall off. Embarrassed, very glad he could not see my hot face, I removed my hands from his firmly-muscled waist and held on to the back of the saddle.

I leaned forward to call out directions, and very quickly we had covered the ground and the stakes marking the walkway across to the island appeared in the distance. He drew rein as we approached, and I slid down off the mare's back. He dismounted more slowly, gazing out across the dark waters of the mere.

'What is this place?' he asked. His voice was soft, almost awed.

'It is an artificial island. It was built a long time ago as a safe place in times of threat. It is—' But I had said enough. This was the secret place of my family, my kin, my ancestors. He might be charming and likeable, but he was still a Norman and therefore potentially an enemy.

'Your grandmother is buried over there?' He nodded over the water.

'Yes. Shall I show you?'

'Go on.'

I led the way across the planks. I could see Edild, standing quite still at the head of the grave. The young woman's body, once more covered with the coarse linen, lay beside it. I wondered if Edild was in a light trance and thought I ought to warn her of our approach.

'That's my aunt Edild,' I said loudly. 'I went to fetch her as soon as I'd made the discovery, and she offered to wait here while I went for help. She's—'

Edild turned to look at me. 'No need to shout, Lassair,' she said quietly. 'I heard you coming when you were still some way off.'

'Edild, this is Sir Alain de Villequier,' I said, flustered. 'Sir Alain, my aunt Edild.'

'Good morning, sir,' Edild said calmly, as if she greeted important Normans every day of her life.

'Good day, Edild,' Sir Alain replied.

She made a graceful gesture, indicating the grave. 'That is where the dead young woman was placed.' She pointed to the body on the grass. 'My niece and I removed her from the ground so that we could unwrap the shroud and see who she was. We did not recognize her.'

Sir Alain knelt down in the grass and very gently folded the linen away from the dead face. He stared at her for some moments. His back was turned to Edild and me, and I could not see his expression. After a while he stood up, cleared his throat and said, 'Her name was Ida. She was a seamstress in the employ of Lord Gilbert's cousin, the lady Claude, who has recently come to our area and is staying at Lakehall.'

I'm not sure, but I thought I saw him pass a hand over his face before he turned around to us. I knew then that this dead Ida had cast her spell over him as well, just as she had done over Lord Gilbert and Lady Emma. He, too, had cared about her; he, too, would miss her.

Impulsively, I said, 'She must have been such a lovely girl.'

He looked down, and I could not see his expression. 'Why do you say that?' His voice sounded gruff.

Because you're all grieving over her death, I could have told him. But it wasn't my place to make such an intimate remark, and instead I said, 'I studied her face, and she looks like somebody who laughed a lot and brought sunshine into other people's lives.'

He turned away from me and stared down at the dead girl. He looked at her for some moments. Then he said heavily, 'She did. She—' It was as if he, too, had suddenly recalled our relative positions in the world, for whatever he had been going to say, he bit it back. I thought he made an effort to control himself – I saw a sort of shudder go through him – and then he said curtly to Edild, 'Well? Have you studied the body? Have you anything to tell me concerning how she died?'

Edild and I exchanged a quick glance – I could tell she was as taken aback as I was by Sir Alain's abrupt change in demeanour – and then she stepped forward and crouched down beside the body. 'I have,' she said neutrally. She beckoned – to him, I believe, but I, too, took it as a summons – and Sir Alain and I knelt down either side of her.

My aunt began to speak, and straight away I felt calmer, for her voice had taken on the tone that it adopts when she is teaching me something new. I dare say she did it purposefully, for she must have sensed how unsettled I was by that morning's discovery and she would have wanted to soothe me. It was only later that I realized she also wanted me to be fully alert so that I did not miss anything.

'Death was by strangulation,' she began, moving the long hair away from the dead girl's neck with a tender hand. She pointed, and I saw the deep purplish-red mark around the throat. It had bitten deep into the soft flesh. Below it, the skin was white. Above it, the dead face was a different colour, as if stained with dark blood. I wondered why I hadn't noticed before; I had, I supposed, been too busy staring at the features in that face made for fun and laughter.

'What—' Sir Alain coughed and tried again. 'What was she strangled with?'

Edild pointed again. 'A thin length of plaited leather, I believe. In some places there are the marks of a regular pattern. See?'

I spotted what she meant. Someone must have wrapped a plaited thong round the girl's throat, strangled her and then removed it. Unless—

Sir Alain had had the same thought. 'You have not found such a thing, I imagine.' He sounded as if he already knew we hadn't, and no doubt he realized Edild would have shown him straight away if she had.

'No,' she confirmed. 'The killer must have taken his weapon away with him.'

'And the shroud?' He picked up the edge of the linen in which the body had been wrapped.

'It appears to be an old piece of fabric,' Edild said, 'something previously used for a different purpose, for there are seams in it. It's been torn so as to make a long strip.'

'Did the killer bring it with him, knowing he would have need of it?' Sir Alain said. 'Or did he tear up his shirt and use that?'

Edild was smoothing the fabric. 'It is too long for a shirt,' she said. 'My guess is that the killer prepared it earlier and brought it here, knowing he would have a body to wrap.'

Sir Alain did not speak. I wondered why. I was bursting with questions, but then I was not in the habit of trying to discover how people had met their death and perhaps he was; the things I was so desperate to know were probably clear as daylight to him.

'He came here knowing he was going to kill her, then,' I said, trying to prompt a reaction.

I got one. Sir Alain spun round to me and said sharply, 'Why do you say that?'

'Because, although anybody might have a piece of plaited leather on them, not many people carry lengths of linen except their clothes, and Edild thinks there's too much fabric in the shroud for a shirt.'

I sensed him relax. 'Well reasoned,' he said with a quick smile. 'Yes, you speak with good sense.'

Then I had another thought. 'Maybe Ida had the cloth with her!' I exclaimed.

Both Sir Alain and Edild glared at me. Edild could be forgiven, for she did not know and must have thought I was being foolish. I would, however, have expected Sir Alain to see the relevance. 'You just said, Sir Alain, that Ida was a seamstress,' I said. 'She was helping Lady Claude prepare linens for her marriage, so maybe she'd brought some sewing out here to do while she sat in the sunshine.'

'But this cloth is old,' Edild pointed out.

'Yes, but she could have been using it as a practice piece,' I said eagerly. 'You know, perfecting some new stitch before she sewed it into the object it was intended for?'

'Hmm,' said my aunt. She did not seem convinced.

Sir Alain was about to speak but, too carried away by my own argument, I did not let him. 'Perhaps this lady Claude is a perfectionist and very fussy about her linens, so Ida felt she had to make sure her work would be acceptable and had to practise on this old linen. Perhaps Lady Claude is—'

'Your speculation is interesting,' Sir Alain said, interrupting my flow of words. 'However, we can readily test your theory. Edild, have you noticed any fresh stitching on the shroud?'

Edild gave me a glance in which pity and irritation were perfectly mixed. 'No.'

Sir Alain turned back to me, eyebrows raised as if to say, *Well*?

'Perhaps she hadn't started yet!' I cried desperately. 'Perhaps she was just threading her needle when he jumped on her! Perhaps—'

But I had run out of possibilities. I don't know why I was so keen to believe Ida had supplied the fabric for her shroud. It might have been because the alternative – that her killer had been so cold-blooded in his meticulous preparations that he had taken it with him – was just too harsh. For the second time that morning, I realized I was weeping.

My aunt made a soft sound and put her arms around me.

I leaned against her, taking comfort from her warmth, her nearness and her love. She said, quite crossly, 'Sir Alain, Lassair has borne enough. Please let me take her home, for there is nothing more that she or I can do here.'

I thought she had gone too far. Whatever a local justiciar might be, I was sure they did not permit the likes of Edild to speak to them so curtly and, in effect, tell them what to do. Possibly Sir Alain did not realize this, for, far from being angry, he jumped up, helped Edild and me to our feet and said, 'Of course. I am sorry. Lassair – go home now, rest, and if I need to speak to you again, I will come to find you.'

I felt we ought to go before he changed his mind and got cross after all. I grabbed Edild's hand, muttered, 'Come on, then,' and led her away.

I risked a glance behind me as we hurried back over the water. He was standing where we had left him, staring down at Ida's body. His head was bent, and I thought his hands were clasped in front of him.

He looked as if he were praying.

FOUR

Edild tended me solicitously for the remainder of the day. There was plenty of work to be done – we are usually kept busy, even in the middle of summer – but she insisted that I do nothing more arduous than wash out empty bottles and make them ready for new preparations and remedies. I would rather have done what I usually do, which is to take my share of the less demanding conditions that are presented to us by the villagers, because being forced to concentrate on something more exciting than bottle-washing would have taken my mind off Ida's round, pretty, dead face. Still, Edild had her reasons. She keeps telling me that a healer must turn all her mind to every single patient, even those with something mundane like corns or a crop of boils, and she probably suspected that today I would have found it difficult. She'd have been right.

Catching her between patients – she was washing her hands in a bowl of warm water scented with lavender oil, and the smell was delicious – I said, 'Edild, what's a local justiciar?'

She paused, then resumed her washing and said, 'King William has, I believe, a new system for promoting law and order. Apparently, he wishes to ensure that justice is done out in the more remote parts of the kingdom, and to this end he has appointed men to judge the graver misdemeanours, attend meetings of the shire courts, observe how rulings are given out and, in general, ensure that the law is upheld.'

She did not ask why I wanted to know. I decided to tell her, anyway. 'Alain de Villequier is our local justiciar.'

She gave me a serene smile and said, 'I know.'

I did not bother demanding how she knew. My aunt seems to have the ability to pick information out of thin air; either that or she is exceptionally observant and just keeps her eyes and ears open. Instead I said, 'Do you know anything else about him?'

Just then there was a very timid tap on the door. It sounded as if Edild's next patient had arrived. My aunt looked at me, sympathy in her eyes. 'I can see you're burning with impatience, but you'll have to wait,' she said kindly. 'As it happens, I do know more about Alain de Villequier, and I promise I'll tell you later.'

I took myself out to the barrel in the yard behind the house to resume my bottle-washing. I could hear muttered words from inside the house, but deliberately I made myself deaf to what was said; it's another part of my healer's training. Instead, I filled my mind with a question: what did my aunt know of our new justice man, and how on earth had she found it out?

When the two of us had finished work for the day and were sitting outside on the bench in the shade of the three young birch trees behind Edild's house, sipping one of her cool, refreshing concoctions, at last my patience broke and I said, '*Well*?'

She smiled. 'Wait a while longer, for the person who provided the information is on his way.'

I waited. After a short while, there was the sound of quick footsteps on the path that leads around the house and Hrype appeared. He gave me a nod by way of greeting, paused behind my aunt and briefly touched her shoulder, then sat down on the end of the bench and accepted a mug of Edild's cold drink.

My aunt and my friend Sibert's uncle Hrype are lovers. Nobody knows this except for the two of them and me. I discovered their secret last autumn, through some unusual circumstances that I won't describe now. Around that time I also discovered that Hrype is not in fact Sibert's uncle; he's his father. Both these fascinating facts I have kept to myself. If Hrype and Sibert choose to present themselves to the world as uncle and nephew, instead of father and son, that is their business. Regarding Hrype and Edild, I love my aunt dearly and would not hurt her for the world and, if the truth about her relationship with Hrype became

known, it would cause her – and others – great distress and
pain. I would not say I am *fond* of Hrype exactly; he is too
strange and powerful for an ordinary mortal like me to have
such a normal emotion regarding him. Another reason for
keeping these secrets, which are his too, is that he'd probably turn me into a two-headed toad if I didn't.

Hrype has begun to teach me about some very deep, dark
magic. My respect and my fear of him are growing all the
time.

That evening I watched them together, my aunt Edild and
Hrype the cunning man. Now that I knew their secret, their
feelings for each other were plain to see, or perhaps it was
that, knowing I knew the truth, they allowed their guard to
slip a little. Either way, it was both a pleasure and a pain to
see the way his eyes filled with tenderness as he looked at
her; the way she stroked a lock of hair away from his lean
face with a hand as gentle as a mother's with a sleeping baby.
A pleasure because it touched my heart to see Edild looking
so happy. A pain because I understood the difficulties they
faced; also because observing a pair so devoted to each other
reminded me of the man I love, who had slipped out of
my life the previous autumn and left me with no hope that
I'd ever see him again. Except for something my aunt had
said . . .

I brought myself back to the present with a lurch; Hrype
was speaking to me. 'You wish to know about Alain de
Villequier, Lassair?' he asked.

'Yes.'

'Listen, then, and I will tell you what I know.' He
stretched out his long legs, crossing them at the ankle, and
fixed me with his silvery eyes. 'He is a man who moves
close to the king's intimate circle. He is not within it, but
his own circle touches it.' He leaned forward and drew a
diagram in the dusty ground: a small circle surrounded by
five other, larger circles, the edges of which touched against
the small one. 'This is King William, with his personal
elite,' he said, pointing to the inner circle. 'These are the
groups of his close associates –' he indicated the five larger
circles – 'in each of which there is a leading figure who

reports directly to one of the elite. Alain de Villequier, who comes from a powerful and prominent Norman family, is in one such group. The king's trust in him is sufficient that he has appointed him justiciar for our area and has provided him with a small but handsome manor house, Alderhall, where Sir Alain will live while he is with us.'

'Edild explained what "justiciar" means,' I said.

'Good, then I shall not repeat her. This business of the dead girl in Cordeilla's grave will be a test for him. The king will be kept informed as to how he handles the enquiry.' I felt a shiver of sympathy for Alain de Villequier; such a challenge, with the spectre of King William looking over my shoulder, would have terrified me into petrifaction.

'Sir Alain has much to gain if he is efficient and brings this matter to a swift conclusion,' Hrype went on, 'for as well as the king, there is a future mother-in-law to impress.'

'Sir Alain is to be wed?' I asked.

'He is. The young lady's father was long a bedridden invalid, and died some years ago, but it has always been her mother whose opinion really counts, for it is she who holds the strings of the purse.' He paused. 'The mother is a very wealthy woman.'

He frowned, apparently gathering his thoughts, and neither Edild nor I interrupted. 'Alma de Caudebec, the young lady's grandmother, married a great Norman baron, Bastien de St Claire. He was awarded a grand estate in the Thetford Forest, close to the place where in ages past the ancestors mined for flint. Alma bore her baron a single child – a daughter, Claritia – who wed Gaspard de Seés, the younger son of another, much less prominent, Norman family; their earthly comfort was dramatically heightened by the addition of her wealth, but they remain socially insignificant. Claritia and her husband had two children, both girls. Our Sir Alain's family have much need of money, and I would guess that it was made plain to him from boyhood that he must marry wealth. A match was arranged between him and Claritia's elder daughter, Geneviève, and negotiations were well advanced when the girl fell into a fainting fit from which she has never fully recovered.'

I glanced at Edild and met her eyes. I imagined that, like me, she was going through her medical knowledge – in her case, so much greater than mine – to see if she could hazard a guess as to what had caused this fit and why its effects should persist.

'Fortunately for both families,' Hrype went on, 'each of whom has their reasons for desiring the match, there is another, younger, sister. She—'

'Why do the girl's family want this marriage with a man who is far from rich?' I put in.

Hrype raised an eyebrow. 'Because they want the de Villequier name,' he said. 'They have discovered that wealth is not enough. When it is in the hands of a name not recognized by the great magnates of the land, it buys material goods, but not position.'

'So he comes from a famous family?' I persisted.

'He does. The name resonates through Norman halls of power.' I would have liked to know more and was poised to ask another question when Hrype, who seemed to read my mind, shot me a glowering look and I subsided. 'There was still a problem to be surmounted, however,' he said, 'because the younger daughter is very, very devout and had set her heart on entering a convent and dedicating her life and her body to the service of God. When her mother told her that she could not have her dearest wish and instead was to marry Alain de Villequier, she, too, fell into a faint, although in her case recovery was somewhat swifter. She tried everything she could think of, even going as far as shaving her head and adopting the habit of a nun, but her mother was adamant.'

I felt a surge of sympathy for this poor girl. I am quite interested in the Christian religion, and I appreciate how people love the charismatic, compassionate, suffering figure of their saviour, but I cannot imagine dedicating my life to him at the cost of everything that normally lies in wait for a woman. Earthly love, a husband, children. My sister Elfritha is a nun, in the convent at Chatteris. I know that she is blissfully happy, despite the hardships of the life. I also know it is not for me. However, to want with all your soul to be a nun and be forced into marriage instead would, I imagined, be as bad as wanting to marry and being shut up in a convent.

'In the end the girl bowed to her mother's wishes,' Hrype was saying, 'although they say that the concession was partly starved, partly beaten out of her.' He frowned. 'Claritia has, apparently, a heavy hand.'

'Where is she now?' I asked. 'Have they locked her up in a high tower in case she runs away?'

Hrype smiled. 'No. She has given her word at the altar that she will marry Alain de Villequier, and her word is good enough. She is, as I have said, very devout. She will not break an oath sworn before God.'

It was, I thought, cunning of her mother to have made the girl swear her oath in church. It was devious, somehow, to use the strength of the girl's feelings against her. I decided I really did not like the sound of this Claritia.

Hrype was speaking. To my amazement I heard the word Lakehall.

'*What*?' I demanded. 'What's that about Lakehall?'

'It is where the lady is staying,' Hrype said. 'She lodges with her kinsman Lord Gilbert.'

Of course! I'd thought fleetingly when Hrype had mentioned the name of the young lady's grandmother that it was somehow familiar. 'So Lord Gilbert's grandfather and the girl's grandmother were brother and sister,' I said slowly, working it out, 'making her and Lord Gilbert second cousins.'

'Yes,' Hrype agreed. 'With his future wife living for the moment at Lakehall, where she is staying prior to the wedding to allow her to become acquainted with her husband, all the more reason for Sir Alain to be given the task of investigating the death of the young seamstress.'

Information had been coming too fast. I held up my hands, muttering, 'Wait, wait!' It did not take me long; I just had to bring together two strands of the story, which I had thought ran separately. 'So Sir Alain is to wed Lady Claude,' I said, 'for she is the woman you've been speaking of – the wealthy heiress who wanted to be a nun, but has to

marry because her mother wants the power of an ancient
and revered family name.' Hrype began to answer, but I
hadn't finished. 'Lady Claude has come here to meet Sir
Alain, and it's her seamstress, Ida, who accompanied her
to Lakehall to help her sew her trousseau, who has been
killed.'

Hrype waited with exaggerated patience to see if I was
going to say more. When it became clear that I wasn't, he
said, 'Well done, Lassair.' There was a definite note of irony
in his voice.

Edild had not spoken for some time. She had sat there
absorbing Hrype's story and only now did she stir. 'You
are well-informed, Hrype,' she observed.

'Yes,' I agreed, 'how do you come to know all this?'

He took one of Edild's hands in both of his, gently caressing
the back of it with his long fingers. Then he turned to look
at me. 'I heard several weeks ago of Sir Alain de Villequier's
appointment,' he replied, 'and I thought that, since he would
come to be a prominent figure in the vicinity, I ought to
discover what I could about the man. I went to see a good
friend of mine who lives in Cambridge.' He glanced at me,
a flash of mischief in his eyes. 'Gurdyman is a wizard, Lassair.
He has the power to stare into the scrying glass and divine
the secrets of men's lives and hearts.'

I did not know whether to believe him. The idea of a magical
wizard living in the urban sophistication of Cambridge was
somehow hard to accept but, on the other hand, Hrype certainly
did know some very odd people . . .

'Have pity on her, Hrype,' Edild murmured.

He grinned, suddenly looking much younger and almost
carefree. 'Very well. Gurdyman is in truth a sage, a wise
man who spends his days hunched up over ancient manu-
scripts, trying to winkle out the wisdom of the past. He
is also very astute and, for a man of such an academic
temperament, surprisingly well informed about the doings
of the great and the good of our land. The de Villequier
family's history is well known to him, as is that of the
de Caudebecs.'

I wondered why a Cambridge sage had been prompted to learn so much about a bunch of Normans. Hrype answered my question, even though I had not spoken it aloud.

'I was not entirely in jest when I said Gurdyman was a wizard,' he said softly. 'He is profoundly wise in the Old Ways and therefore potentially an object of interest to our new masters. It always pays, young Lassair, to know your enemy. Gurdyman's knowledge of the Normans is probably as great as that of King William himself.'

Your enemy. His words chilled me, not because they told me anything I did not already know – the Normans have been ruling over us for more than twenty-five years now and, although we have no choice but to bow down before their ruthless and chillingly efficient authority, nevertheless in our hearts they are still the enemy. No; what caused my attention to falter is that it is to one of them, a Norman, that I seem to have given my heart. The man I love is, on his own admission, close to the central power that now rules in our land.

It hardly mattered, though, *who* he was, if I was never going to see him again . . .

There was a touch on my arm, and I came out of my sad reverie. Edild was looking at me, concern in her eyes. 'You are very pale, Lassair,' she said. 'You should sleep now, for the day has been long and full of distress for you.'

She was right. All of a sudden I felt so weary that it was all I could do to stand up. 'Please excuse me, then,' I said politely. 'I will go and prepare for bed.'

I wanted to visit the jakes and wash my face and hands before I undressed. In addition, it was nice if my aunt and Hrype had the chance to say goodnight without a witness. I took my time and, when I had finished, I strolled down the track for a few paces, sensing the small rustlings of the evening as the wild creatures settled down for the night. I looked up at the sky. The stars were appearing even as I watched. It was a beautiful sight.

Suddenly I was vitally alert, my eyes, ears, even my skin, sensing all around me and fear coursing through me like flame. I had heard an unexpected sound: someone was singing.

I don't know why it alarmed me so much. Yes, it was a plaintive, sad song, so full of despair that it would have moved me to tears had I not been so afraid. It was not exactly a song; more a chant, and I am very familiar with chants. My Granny Cordeilla taught me that it is often easier to remember the endless lines of a long narrative if you put in some rhythm and some rhyme, and from there it's only a matter of time before you start singing.

What was worrying about this lament – it could not have been anything else – was that I did not recognize the voice, the notes of the chant nor the words, and I knew therefore that the singer was nobody I knew; nobody who belonged in Aelf Fen.

What was really frightening was that, although I stared all around me, I could not see anybody. The singer was invisible.

I wanted to flee, but I could not. It was as if the sounds I was hearing, which seemed to flow over me and draw me into the strong emotion behind them, had fixed me to the spot. Against my will I listened to the words. It was very strange, but it was as if I could not hear them individually; I could only perceive the meaning they strove to impart. The chill of coming night seemed to flow up out of the ground into my feet, up my legs and into the warm centre of my body, and as the chant went on I felt as if my soul was being drawn out of me, up, up, away from the good, solid earth and into the darkening sky, heading for the stars . . .

Then I heard a door quietly close and the sound of firm footsteps on the path behind me. Abruptly, the singing stopped.

Hrype called out, 'Sleep well, Lassair.'

I dragged myself together and managed a reply. Even to my own ears, my voice sounded shaky. Hoping he would attribute this to my fatigue – he had stopped and was eyeing me curiously – I made myself smile. 'I'll be quite all right tomorrow,' I said.

He smiled back. 'You'd better be,' he remarked. 'It promises to be a challenging day.'

Wondering what he meant – it sounded ominous – I
hurried back along the track to Edild's cottage, let myself
in and very carefully closed and fastened the door.

FIVE

My sleep was filled with weird dreams, and in the morning I did not feel all that rested. Edild informed me that our duty today was to lay out the dead girl's body. It is one of the services that Edild performs for our village, and she has been training me so that I can follow in her footsteps when she is too old. I knew I could not avoid the task – I know full well I must do whatever my aunt tells me – but the thought of preparing poor Ida's body for the grave was quite dreadful.

Edild must have noticed my reaction. Instead of querying it, which would have been pointless as we both knew I had no choice but to do as I was told, she said calmly, 'We are not expected at Lakehall until midday. I can manage without you this morning, so why don't you go across the village and see your mother?'

I bolted the last of my porridge and leapt up. It was early yet, and if I hurried, I might get home before my father left for work.

Some time later, I was sitting beside my mother in our family's house. There had been barely enough space for us all when we'd all lived there, for at our most crowded we had numbered eight plus a baby: my father, my big, blonde mother, my Granny Cordeilla (not that she ever took up much room), my sisters Goda and Elfritha, my brothers Haward and Squeak (his real name's Sihtric, but hardly anyone remembers that) and the baby, Leir. Now that my sisters and I all lived elsewhere – I with Edild, Elfritha with her nuns and Goda, the eldest of us (and I have to say the least agreeable) with her husband and two little children in Icklingham, a few miles away – my parents shared the house only with their three sons and, although Leir is a baby no more (he is four), there would still be room enough for Haward's bride.

I don't think any of the family had thought yet how it would be living with Derman.

This morning just my mother was at home. I had caught my father as he was leaving, my disappointment assuaged a little by the warmth of his hug and his quiet words of comfort, just for me, spoken softly in my ear. My mother, too, was red-eyed; Granny Cordeilla had been a good mother-in-law to her, and the two had been close.

'I know she was small and had few possessions,' my mother said, twitching a stray strand of long, pale hair neatly behind her clean white headdress, 'but the house just seems so empty without her.'

I felt the same. I was rapidly learning that it's not the actual space a person occupies that matters; it's the extent to which their character expands to fill a house.

I squeezed my mother's hand. 'It's hard for you and the men folk,' I said, 'since you have to live with the constant reminder that she's not here any more.'

My mother wiped her eyes. 'Yes, that's true, but there's a comfort in being here, because she's still with us.' She frowned. 'Well, she's not, of course, but—' She shrugged, apparently unable to put the feeling into words.

'I know,' I whispered. I had just caught a glimpse of Granny Cordeilla, sitting up on her little cot eyeing us brightly and waiting her chance to get a word in, just as she always did when I came to visit. The fact that her cot had been dismantled and ceremonially burned, as is our custom, and that Granny herself was dead and in her grave, did not appear to have made any difference. I hugged my mother's large body to me and winked at Granny over her shoulder. Granny winked back.

Presently, my mother disentangled herself from my arms, gave me a quick but affectionate peck on the cheek and said, 'Enough of tears! Let's talk about something else.'

I took a last look at Granny, already fading into the planed planks of the wall behind her. She would be back, and we both knew it. Then I settled down beside my mother and said, 'What shall we talk about?'

As if she had been waiting for this invitation, she said

instantly, 'Haward's going to marry her,' and I knew precisely what was on her mind.

'That's good,' I said. 'Zarina's a fine woman, and she loves Haward sincerely. She'll make him happy.'

In my eagerness to reassure my mother, I had spoken without thinking. Instantly, my mother pounced: 'How can you possibly know?'

I could not tell her. Could not begin to explain how Hrype had started to teach me the rudiments of rune lore and how, unable to resist the temptation, I had slipped away with my own crude set of symbols, succeeded in putting myself in a light trance and asked the question burning in my mind: *will she make my loving, vulnerable brother Haward a good wife?* The answer had come, swiftly, unequivocally, and I had read it both in the fall of the runes and in the succession of images that had seared through my head.

I could not tell my mother this. Far more crucially, I could not tell Hrype, for he had specifically warned against the perils of a novice such as I asking personal questions. The pounding, throbbing, sick-making headache I had endured all the next day was my punishment. If Hrype had noticed – and he probably had – he must have decided there was no need for him to add anything.

'I just feel she's the right woman for him,' I said now. It was a weak answer, but seemed to satisfy my mother.

'I do too,' she said, the frown deepening. 'I shall welcome her here, just as Cordeilla welcomed me, and I shall do as she did and endeavour to overlook what differences Zarina and I may have and concentrate on what binds us.'

'But?' I knew there was a *but*. I also knew what it was.

My mother gave a faint, defeated shrug and said simply, 'Derman.'

I waited, gathering my thoughts. Then I said, 'What does Zarina say? Is it definitely the case that where she goes her brother goes too?'

'I don't *know*!' My mother spoke sharply, but I knew her frustration was not with me. 'I said Haward's going to marry her, but in truth I believe he hasn't actually asked her yet.' A soft smile lit her face. 'He told us all two days ago that he was going to. It was so sweet, Lassair, almost as if he were asking our permission.'

That was just like my brother. I could follow his thought process: he'd have reasoned, very fairly, that his parents and his brothers were going to have to share their house with the new wife and so would have wanted to ensure they were happy at the prospect. Naturally, it was better for everyone if people liked each other. Houses in our village are pretty small. There is nowhere to get away from an uncongenial fellow inhabitant, as all of us had known all too well when Goda had still lived at home.

'Perhaps we should just wait and see,' I said tentatively. 'Maybe Zarina has a plan. There could be family we haven't heard about who could take Derman.' My mother began to protest. 'Yes, I know she said they were alone in the world, but maybe there's someone who's *like* a relation, but not actually kin. What about those travelling entertainers that Zarina was with when first she came to the village? It's possible, surely, that Derman may go back to them?'

My mother looked singularly unconvinced. 'It's possible, I suppose, but not very likely. You see, Lassair,' she added in a burst of confidence, 'it's been the problem all along, the one thing that's come between Haward and Zarina: what to do about Derman. If there was an easy solution such as you suggest –' I'd never actually said it would be easy, but I let it pass – 'then I'm sure Zarina would have said so, got on with implementing the arrangements and she and Haward would have been wed these many months past.'

'Hmm, yes, perhaps,' I murmured. My mother was right, and logic agreed with her assessment. The trouble was, my rune-casting and the visions it had sent me were at variance with what she said. In the glimpses I had seen into Haward's future with Zarina, there was no sign of Derman.

Again, it was not something I could tell my mother.

'How is he?' I asked.

My mother shrugged. She knew who I meant. 'The same, only more so.' She ran a hand over her face. 'You know when you brought him home yesterday morning, when you'd found – er, found what you found?'

'Yes.' I could scarcely believe it had only been the day before. 'I came across him as I was hurrying back to the village. He seemed upset.' Considering it now, I wondered what he'd been doing out there all by himself and what had distressed him. 'I thought Zarina kept a close eye on him,' I said. 'Did he slip out, do you think?'

'Yes, she tries not to let him wander about on his own,' my mother agreed, 'although she's not always successful. He does like to go off by himself, and sometimes he's gone all day.' She frowned worriedly. 'He can be quite frightening if you don't know him – the way he looks, I mean, poor boy – and there's always the possibility that if he strays too far from the village he'll encounter some gang of bullies who will have cruel sport with him.'

Yes, Zarina had good cause for keeping her brother where she could watch over him. 'So she didn't know he'd gone out yesterday morning?'

My mother hesitated. Then she said, 'It's not the first time. He – Zarina thinks something very unfortunate has happened.' A delicate pink flush spread up the smooth, pale skin of her pretty face, and I wondered what on earth was coming. 'Derman has taken a fancy to someone,' she said, staring down at her hands in her lap.

'To a girl?' It should not have surprised me for, although Derman has the mind of a child, his body is that of a man, and he undoubtedly had a grown man's urges.

'Of course a girl!' my mother said sharply.

'Is that so bad?' I asked gently.

My mother's eyes filled with tears. 'What future can there be in such an infatuation?' she said. 'Poor boy, what girl or woman is going to look kindly on one such as he?'

'If she's gentle with him, and understands his limitations, it might be all right,' I persisted.

My mother made an impatient sound. 'Lassair, for someone who thinks she's so clever you can be very *dense*,' she fired at me.

I started with surprise – did I think I was so clever? Yes, perhaps so, but had I let my mother see? Apparently, I had.

But already she was apologizing. 'I should not have said

that.' She took my hand again. 'It's not you I'm so upset about. It's just that . . . that—'

'That I'm here to take the blows you wish you could aim at somebody else,' I finished for her. 'Don't worry, I understand.' I reached out and hugged her. 'So, Derman thinks he's in love, and he's been sneaking out from under Zarina's vigilance to gaze at his lady love with moonstruck eyes.' Deliberately, I tried to diminish it. I met my mother's gaze, raising my eyebrows and silently repeating the query: is that so bad?

'He could be so very hurt,' my mother said quietly. I remembered Derman's heart-wrenching sobs; perhaps the lady had already rejected him. 'And,' she added, lowering her voice, 'suppose he turns violent if he doesn't get what he wants?'

'Violent?' I had not associated slow, bumbling Derman with violence. Now, thinking about it, I wondered why not. His mind was like a child's – how easily we all came up with those unthinking, dismissive words – but he was very far from being a child. Squeak was a child; well, he was eleven now, so he was fast growing to manhood, but when he was little he was not at all like Derman. He might not have known much – children don't – but there had never been any doubt that he was intelligent. As for Leir, even at four years old it was clear he was a bright boy. Whereas it was all too plain that no spark of intellect burned behind Derman's deep, dull eyes. If he loved some village girl and she turned him down, no matter how gently and kindly, what would he do?

A sudden horrible suspicion bloomed in the corner of my mind, waxing fast until it was all I could see. I turned to my mother and read the same awful thought in her eyes. I clung to her and whispered, 'What should we do?'

She held me close, her strong arms around me. I could feel her trembling. Then she said, 'You told me you are to go with Edild to lay out the body.'

I nodded. 'Yes. I should be going – Edild will be wanting to set out soon.'

My mother held me at arm's length, staring intently into

my face, her light-blue eyes fierce with purpose. 'If it's as we fear, then someone will have seen him,' she said. Suddenly, she was strong, her concern for her family overriding her dread. 'Don't say anything – don't admit you know who he is, and whatever you do, don't tell them.'

'No, no, I won't,' I promised.

'Keep your wits about you,' my mother went on. 'Listen carefully; try to detect the slightest finger of suspicion pointing in his direction. If they do think he—' But she could not go on. Mutely shaking her head, she let me go.

I wanted more than anything to go straight to the house where Zarina lodged and ask to speak to Derman, then make him tell me where he had been before I'd found him. To ask him what he had done. I resisted the urge. I walked quickly back to Edild's house, and shortly afterwards we set out for Lakehall.

As we walked I sensed my aunt's eyes on me. 'Are you all right?' she asked.

I nodded. Much as I love my aunt, I always feel restored by a visit to my parents' home. I looked up and caught Edild's swift assessing look. Although she made no comment, I felt her support. The task ahead was going to be a severe test for an apprentice healer but, with my aunt watching over me, I knew I could do it.

They were expecting us up at the hall. Bermund was waiting, and without a word he led us across the courtyard and around the side of the manor house, along a narrow passage between outbuildings and up to the door of a small lean-to set against the rear wall of the kitchen. The kitchen door was ajar, and I could smell food cooking. There were voices engaged in light conversation. I heard a burst of laughter, quickly suppressed as if whoever it was had just remembered there was a dead body on the other side of the wall.

Bermund opened the door of the lean-to and ushered us in. 'It's cool here,' he said shortly. There was no need of further explanation. 'When you're done, send one of them to find me.' He jerked his head in the direction of the voices in the kitchen. 'I'll bring the coffin on the cart and take her to the church crypt.'

He had, I noticed, said *take her*, where many people, referring to a body, would have said *take it*. Bermund too, it appeared, was not without feelings for Ida.

It was strange, I mused, how we who had never known Ida in life were building up such a clear picture of her through the emotions, words and actions of those who had.

Edild stepped up to the body, laid out on a trestle table. 'Thank you,' she said gravely, turning to Bermund.

He nodded, spun round and left the room, closing the door after him.

My aunt and I set about our task.

We made her look lovely, not that it was hard to do. Her face was expressionless, like some stone effigy, but her handsome, regular features somehow retained a vestige of her living essence. We removed her garments and washed her, and I noticed how tenderly Edild bathed the rounded belly and the full breasts. I thought Ida had been about four months pregnant, for the swelling in her womb was not very pronounced. I had observed how sometimes a woman's breasts fill out dramatically before she even suspects she is carrying a child, and this seemed to have been the case with the dead girl.

'It is midsummer,' Edild murmured, 'and I judge that this child was conceived in February, perhaps early in March.'

I would have to find out if Ida had been here at Lakehall then. Before I could stop myself, other questions began racing through my mind. If she had, was she already the object of Derman's hopeless love? Had he seen her, desired her, waylaid her and forced himself on her? Oh, but such a thing was abhorrent, and surely Ida would have protested, shouted out at her rape, demanded that justice be served on her attacker? But perhaps she had understood he could not help it and had taken pity on him, not wanting to make his miserable life any worse. Oh, but what of the infant she carried? Would it have grown up like its poor, pathetic father and been a child all its life? Ida, oh, Ida, what did you think? How could you bear to—

My concentration had lapsed with my wild thoughts, and I dropped a bottle of lavender oil. Quick as a flash Edild's hand shot out and caught it. She looked me straight in the eye and said sharply, 'You are no use to me like this, Lassair. I know this is not easy for you, but if you cannot pull yourself together, I shall send you home.'

My aunt is very rarely cross with me. The fact that I had richly earned the reprimand made me feel even worse.

We worked side by side in silence until we had finished our task. Edild wrapped the last length of the shroud around Ida's head, covering the glossy, curly hair. Then she bent down, whispered something I did not hear and kissed the stone-cold brow. She eased the end of the white cloth across the dead face, tucking the end in securely. I had packed up the oils, perfumes, wash cloths and towels that we had used into Edild's leather bag and now she held out her hand for it. I gave it to her. She smiled at me and said, 'You have done well.'

Then we stepped outside into the sunshine.

We had been summoned to see the lord and lady before we left. Vowing not to allow my emotions to get the better of me again, I followed Edild's straight back into the hall. Lord Gilbert and Lady Emma sat on one side of the great hearth. Opposite them sat another woman, younger than Lady Emma, whom I guessed must be Lady Claude. Edild had stopped and was standing before the lord and lady. Invited to speak, she said that Ida's body was now freshly enshrouded and ready for burial. I noticed she did not mention the pregnancy. Perhaps, like me, she had decided that if Ida had not revealed her secret, then neither should we.

I slipped into her shadow, from where I felt it was safe to study Lady Claude de Seés.

I thought she was a few years older than me, perhaps in her early twenties, although her uncompromising appearance made her age hard to determine. I recalled what Hrype had said, that she had wished to become a nun. A woman with such a vocation would naturally not have wasted her own or anyone else's time making the best of herself while she searched for a husband. Looking at her, I realized that she was clad as if she had achieved her ambition, for her gown, although beautifully made of soft silk that had a sheen on it only found in the costliest fabric, was of unrelieved black. Around her face she wore a tightly-fitting headdress not unlike those worn by the nuns of Chatteris. It covered her forehead down to just above her eyebrows and curved round either side of her face, joining at the jaw with the wimple around her throat. She wore a heavy, jewelled crucifix around her neck, the cross hanging over her flat chest.

She was pale and the skin of her face was coarse; even from where I stood I could see enlarged pores in the flesh either side of her longish nose. Her eyes were light and the lashes all but invisible. Her mouth was small and, although she was young still, already small lines radiated out from her upper lip, almost as if someone had once sewn it to the lower one.

So this was the woman who was to marry Alain de Villequier. Fleetingly, I wondered if he would have agreed to the match if he had set eyes on her beforehand, no matter how much his family needed her wealth, but I did my best to suppress the unkind thought. I wished him joy of her. I wished them joy of each other.

I heard my name spoken. Edild turned and held out her hand. 'Lassair here found the body,' she was saying, 'as Lord Gilbert and Lady Emma already know, my lady.'

She was addressing Lady Claude. My hand grasped firmly in Edild's, I now found myself being presented to her.

She looked me up and down with her pale eyes. I could see she was nervous, for her hands were twisting in her lap, the fingers busy at some object . . . It was a small velvet bag, also black, that hung from her belt. I wondered what treasured object was inside, for her to clutch at it so in this time of trial.

I reminded myself that she had just lost her seamstress. I put aside the antipathy I felt for her and, bending my head in a bow, said, 'My lady, I am so sorry for your loss.'

She made a soft sound and closed her eyes. She too, it seemed, felt the death of Ida grievously. There was silence for a few moments as we waited for Claude to speak, then she cleared her throat and said, 'Ida was a most gifted seamstress. I do not know how I shall manage without her.'

Lord Gilbert was her second cousin, I had been told, and he was also her host. Even so, it seemed that he could not allow Claude's comment to go unremarked. He got up, crossed over to her and, bending down with an exhalation of breath – he had put on even more weight recently – he whispered something in her ear. She stiffened, frowned deeply and drew herself away from him. Again he bent close to her, presumably repeating whatever he had said, and this time some of it was audible: '. . . mourn her for herself, even if you do not!' he hissed.

'This is such a tragedy, for us all!' Lady Emma, looking embarrassed, spoke up suddenly and over-loudly in an attempt to cover her husband's words, but it was too late. Edild and I had heard, and Edild had shot me a horrified look.

Lord Gilbert stumped back to his seat and a very awkward silence fell. Lady Emma was the one to break it. 'As we told you, Lassair, Lady Claude is to be married,' she said brightly, 'to Sir Alain de Villequier, whom you met here yesterday.'

'Yes, my lady,' I mumbled.

Silence again. Then Lord Gilbert tried: 'Ida was helping my cousin to sew her trousseau.'

Yes, I thought, *you told me that yesterday too.* I felt very strongly that Edild and I ought not to be there, but nobody appeared to know quite how to dismiss us. I noticed that Lady Emma kept glancing at the main door, the one that lead out into the courtyard. After a short time I heard footsteps and understood why. Sir Alain de Villequier strode into the hall.

He bowed to the lord and lady, nodded to Edild and me and hurried to his future bride, swooping down beside her and taking her hands in his. 'Claude, my dear, I am sorry to have been so long,' he murmured. 'I was detained.'

She had edged away from him slightly and was holding herself very stiffly. 'It is of no matter, sir,' she replied politely. 'I have been adequately entertained by my cousin and his wife.'

'I should have been here to look after you at this dreadful time,' Sir Alain persisted, his voice pitched low, but nevertheless audible. 'You have lost your seamstress and your friend, and all we here who knew Ida, albeit briefly, are aware how deep the grief must go for you who were so close to her.'

He was sitting beside her on her bench now, his arm around her thin waist as he tried to comfort her. Again she seemed to slide away from him, and I wondered if she might be embarrassed at his attentions. He meant well, I could see that, but perhaps it was not done to show your emotions so blatantly in the lord's hall.

At last her reluctance penetrated even Sir Alain's well-intentioned determination, and abruptly he stood up. Then he turned to look at Edild and me and said, 'I wished to speak to you both, which was why I asked Lord Gilbert to keep you here until I arrived.'

He wanted to speak to us! Instinctively, I prepared myself, although I am not sure what it was I feared. But it was not what I had thought. Instead of starting to bark out questions – which, before this tense, taut audience, it would have been very hard to answer – he stepped forward, took my aunt and me by the arm and, turning us neatly around, ushered us towards the door. 'I shall escort you back to the village,' he announced, 'and we shall talk as we go.'

The three of us reached the door, turned to bow to the lord, the lady and to Claude, and then we were outside, hurrying away across the courtyard and off down the track.

SIX

I t was quite apparent that he had wanted to get us on our own, for why else would a man of Sir Alain's standing offer to escort the two of us back to our house? Quite what his intention was, he did not immediately make clear. We would just have to wait, for it would be improper for the likes of us to ask a man of his position what he wanted with us.

He relaxed visibly almost as soon as the three of us had gone out through Lord Gilbert's impressive gates. As we strode off down the path to the village, he turned to Edild and said, 'So, you are the village healer.'

'I am.' Her answer was dignified, and clearly she saw no need to elaborate.

'And Lassair here is your assistant?'

'She is my apprentice.'

He looked from one to the other of us. We were dressed for work – well, we had just been working – and both wore white aprons over our plain gowns, our hair covered by neat kerchiefs. We are often told we are alike, and I suppose that the garb emphasized our similarity. 'You look more like mother and daughter,' he observed.

Neither of us responded.

We walked on for a few paces, and then he said, 'About Lady Claude.'

Edild shot me a glance, and I raised my eyebrows in reply. We waited. Watching Sir Alain closely, I could have sworn he blushed slightly. Then he said, 'She is very shocked by Ida's death. When she knew she was to marry me, it was arranged that she should come here to meet me and stay for these weeks before our wedding with her cousin, Lord Gilbert. She had no hesitation in bringing Ida with her, so impressed had Claude become by Ida's skill with her needle.'

I badly wanted to ask a question, but was not sure if I dared. He might appear relaxed with us, but if I stepped over that invisible but very high fence that divided a man like him from a girl like me, he would no doubt freeze me and clam up, and then we would learn no more. Ask or stay silent? Ask.

'When did she come to Lakehall, Sir Alain?' I asked meekly.

He smiled down at me. 'When did she come?' He appeared to have to think about it. 'Let me see, it must have been a month ago – perhaps a little less.' I thought I had got away with it, but then his eyes narrowed slightly and he said, 'Why?'

I had prepared an answer. 'Oh, I was just wondering why we in the village didn't know she was there. Sometimes when Lord Gilbert has important guests, some of us are summoned to serve them in some way. But Lady Claude was here to work on her trousseau, and she brought her own seamstress with her, so had no need to call on any of us.' I gave him my best ingenuous, wide-eyed, not very bright look, hoping he'd take me as a simple village girl who had taken a hopeless fancy to him.

He did. He was, as I've already said, a flirt. He had been astute enough to ask why I wanted to know when Lady Claude had arrived, but, like many attractive men, he was susceptible to a young woman's admiration. He was still looking at me and so, maintaining the pretence of the smitten young maid, I gave him a shy little smile and modestly lowered my eyes.

I had learned what I wanted to know. Ida had already been pregnant when she'd come with her mistress to Lakehall.

'You must understand about Lady Claude,' Sir Alain was saying. 'She dearly wanted to be – that is, her life has not taken the course she originally envisaged. Dutiful daughter that she is, she has bowed to the wishes of her mother and agreed to marry me.' He hesitated. 'Both our families greatly desire this union.' And Edild and I both knew why, even if Sir Alain did not explain. 'Lady Claude—' Again he hesitated. Then his words emerged in a rush, and I knew what he was trying to do. 'She brought Ida here to her death.

She feels so very guilty. If she sounded unfeeling back there
–' he nodded in the direction of the hall – 'it's only because
of the shock of what has happened and her quite natural
sense that, had she not selected Ida as her seamstress, the
poor girl would still be alive.'

As an apology for the lady, it was well reasoned, and I
ought to have been convinced. My estimation for this man
rose considerably, for he was gallantly defending his future
wife's actions. More than that, he had agreed that she would
be his wife, yet all that I had seen of the two of them –
admittedly not much so far – shouted out that they were
vastly different people and their chances of happiness slim.
Still, as I well knew, people in their level of society married
for many reasons, and love rarely featured at all.

I was unconvinced by his words, though, because I had
also heard what Lord Gilbert had to say of his cousin. I
had formed a clear and not very flattering impression of a
purse-mouthed woman who treasured her precious linens
above the comfort of her sewing girl, forcing Ida to sleep
locked away in the sewing room to guard them. And, of
course, I had met the lady. Whatever Sir Alain might say,
I had already made up my mind about Lady Claude.

I became aware that Edild was speaking, saying something courteous and, I thought, insincere about Lady Claude's
distress and its cause, and offering her professional help if
it became necessary. I made myself listen.

'That is very kind, Edild,' Sir Alain replied. 'I will pass
on your offer to Claude.' He fell silent, frowning, then said,
'I wished to speak to you concerning the simpleton who
has been dogging Ida's footsteps.'

My heart gave a lurch, and I could feel its hard, fast
pounding right up in my throat. All my terror for Derman,
for Zarina, for my own family, came surging back. It was
all the more powerful because Sir Alain's well-meaning
defence of Claude's behaviour back in the hall had allowed
it to fade to the back of my mind. My awful suspicion that
Derman might be responsible for Ida's death would surely
be visible in my eyes, so I kept them down and surreptitiously eased my kerchief forward over my face.

'Simpleton?' Edild echoed the word, making it plain by her tone that she queried its use.

Sir Alain waved an impatient hand. 'I do not know what you would call him,' he said tersely. 'He's a big lad, shambling gait, large head, loose mouth. Little intelligence, so they say.'

'He is an unfortunate who was born lacking wits,' Edild said coolly. 'He is in the care of his sister, who lodges with a village washerwoman. He helps with some of the heavy work. His name is Derman.'

She did not say, as I'd hoped she would, *he is quite harmless*. Oh, perhaps she, too, had her suspicions . . .

'Derman,' Sir Alain repeated. 'Well, it appears that your Derman fell for Ida. I am told that he saw her out collecting wild flowers and followed her back to Lakehall. That was two or three weeks back, and since then he has appeared regularly at the hall, lurking outside the gates in case Ida should appear. He makes – he used to make little posies for her, clumsy things of a few grass stems woven together with a couple of flowers stuck in. He'd leave them outside the kitchen door, although oddly enough nobody ever saw him there or worked out how he got in without anyone noticing him. Both the courtyard gates and the smaller, rear entrance behind the kitchen are always watched in the daytime, then locked and bolted at night.' He shot Edild a glance. 'He is sly, your *unfortunate*.' He emphasized the word she had used.

Edild did not speak for some moments. Then she said calmly, 'If, as you say, Derman had fallen in love with Ida, then surely you cannot be suggesting that he *harmed* her in any way?' She managed to make the suggestion sound quite absurd.

Sir Alain had the grace to look abashed. Then, rallying, he said, 'The man is not like the rest of us. How can anybody say what he would or would not do? If he felt Ida had rejected him, he might well have attacked her.'

Edild shook her head firmly. 'I think not, Sir Alain.'

He muttered an oath. Then, grabbing both Edild and me by the arm, he urged us on towards the village. I knew where we were going, and my heart started hammering again. I wished there was some way I could rush on ahead and warn them, but, as if he knew my intention, he held me fast.

Inexorably, the distance between us and the humble little house of the washerwoman grew less.

Sir Alain banged on the door – which, it turned out, was ajar and not fastened. It fell open at his pounding, revealing a small room crammed with a disorder of objects, with a narrow bed in one corner and a cot opposite the hearth. Both beds were too small for a big man like Derman, and I guessed that he slept in the lean-to on the side of the house. He would bluster about in this confined space like a maddened bull, knocking over the cooking utensils, the crudely-made stools, the bundles of kindling beside the hearth, the display of personal possessions beside the bed in the corner. The cot was the only orderly space in the room, and I knew instinctively that it was where Zarina slept.

There was another little door at the rear of the room, and it, too, was open, giving on to a narrow path that wound away to the water's edge. I could see two figures out there: on the bank was the rounded shape of the washerwoman, kneeling down and rubbing hard at whatever item was receiving her attention, her large bottom up in the air. I could hear her humming to herself as she worked. The other figure was slim, straight-backed, graceful, and walking up the path towards the house.

We all stared at Zarina, and she stared right back.

She wore a gown of the coarsest cloth, and over it she had tied a sacking apron. The hems of both gown and apron were soaking wet, and there were splashes all over her front. Her hands were red and raw; in places the flesh had cracked open. I could not see that detail just then, but I knew all about Zarina's hands. I made the remedy myself.

Her throat rose gracefully from the rough neck of her gown. Zarina always holds herself like a dancer, and just one look at her reminds you of her past, when she lived and worked with the troupe of entertainers. Her luscious hair was wound in a plait and pinned on top of her head; rarely among us, she never covers her head. Her golden eyes and her fine-boned face were illuminated by the sunlight, her firm, pale-oak skin glowing from her exertions.

I thought she looked lovely. Sir Alain's sudden indrawn breath suggested he thought so too.

Zarina came into the house and deposited the bundle of dry, folded linen she was carrying on to her cot. She greeted me, nodded to Edild and looked enquiringly at Sir Alain. He took a step towards her and said, 'Your name?'

'I am called Zarina.' Her voice was quite deep, her tone assured.

'You have a brother, Derman?'

She hesitated. Then she nodded.

'Where is he?'

'I do not know.'

Sir Alain muttered a curse. 'But he lives here, or so I am told.' He looked around.

'Derman does indeed live here,' Zarina said. 'He sleeps in the lean-to.'

'So where is he?' Sir Alain repeated. He sounded angry.

Zarina raised her chin. 'I have not seen him since yesterday evening.'

Was she telling the truth or was she trying to protect her brother? I searched her face, trying to decide.

'Explain.' Sir Alain's single word bit through the tense atmosphere.

'Derman went to bed as usual yesterday evening after supper. We eat and retire for the night early, for our day's work is hard. This morning he did not appear for breakfast and so I went to call him, thinking he had overslept. He was not there.'

'His bed had been slept in?' Sir Alain demanded.

Zarina shrugged. 'It is hard to say. Probably, yes.'

'So he ran away some time during the night . . .'

Quick as a flash Zarina pounced. 'Who says he has run away? All I said was that I had not seen him today.'

He stared at her, after a moment grunting his agreement. 'Very well. If he comes back, I want to see him. You can find me up at Lakehall. I am Alain de Villequier.'

'I know who you are, sir,' Zarina replied levelly. 'When my brother comes home, I will send word.'

I had to admire her. She had neatly altered *if* to *when* and, by saying she would send word, she had subtly implied that she had no intention of presenting either herself or her brother to Sir Alain at the hall.

Sir Alain seemed about to speak. I wouldn't have blamed him if he'd issued a harsh reminder of his and Zarina's relative places in the hierarchy. Apparently thinking better of it, he spun round, ducked under the doorway's low lintel and strode away.

Zarina maintained her straight-backed pose until he was out of sight. Then she fell into my arms.

Edild watched as carefully I helped Zarina to her cot, sitting down beside her, her hand in mine. Then she said, 'Where is he, Zarina?'

She shook her head. 'Truly, I do not know!'

'But there is something you do know that you did not reveal?'

Zarina met her eyes. 'Of course!'

Edild smiled faintly. 'Go on.'

Zarina's hand was clutching convulsively at mine. Her grip was strong, and it hurt. 'Lassair brought him home early yesterday,' she said. Edild shot me an accusing glance, and I recalled that, what with everything that had happened, I'd forgotten to tell her. Or maybe something in me had stopped me, as if the fact of explaining to Edild where I'd found him and what I suspected made what I feared more real. 'He'd been crying,' Zarina was saying. 'I gave him some food, then tried to find out what had upset him. He refused to tell me at first, then he started sobbing and saying something about a dead girl and how she was lying in the grave, and then he began this awful howling, as if he were in pain, and I made him drink some of that stuff you gave me.' She looked up at Edild, and I guessed she was referring to a sedative of some sort. It would be useful to have a sedative if you had to deal with a big, strong child-man like Derman.

'He slept then?'

'He dozed, but he was very restless. Then he got up and came to help me till it was time for dinner. He ate a bit, although not much, then he went to bed.' She stifled a sob. 'That's the last I saw of him.'

Edild now crouched down so that her eyes were level with Zarina's. 'A young woman is dead,' she said gently. 'Her name was Ida, and she was a seamstress working for a relation of Lord Gilbert's, who is staying with him up at the hall. It's said that Derman took a fancy to Ida, that he used to lie in wait for her and left her little offerings. He—'

'Yes, I know,' Zarina said calmly. 'Well, I knew there was someone, although I didn't know who. I've talked it over with Haward and his mother. They're both very worried too.'

Edild's eyes bored into mine. I could hear her voice in my head: *something else you didn't see fit to tell me!* I was going to have quite a lot of explaining to do. Then, turning back to Zarina, she said, 'Where do you think he has gone? Is there any place you know of where he goes if he's upset?'

Zarina shook her head. 'It's very unlike him to venture far away from me,' she said. 'It's how I guessed about this girl he fancied – because he started disappearing. I followed him one day and spotted her, and when I challenged him he admitted it.' She shook her head again, more slowly. 'All I can think of is that he's gone to the places he used to see her. Maybe he doesn't understand she's dead and is trying to find her. I was going to go and look, soon as this lot's done.' She indicated a basket of dirty laundry awaiting her attention.

Edild rose to her feet. 'We will go, Lassair and I,' she announced.

Zarina looked up at her, gratitude flooding her face. 'Will you? That's most kind, and I'm very grateful.' I made as if to rise, but she clutched my hand. 'Wait!' she hissed.

'Edild, I'll catch you up,' I said to my aunt. She raised a questioning eyebrow but, bless her, did not object. I watched her walk away, then whispered, 'What is it, Zarina?'

'I'm very worried, Lassair!' she whispered back.

Shocked, I said, 'You really think he could have harmed Ida?'

'No, no, I know he couldn't have done any such thing!'
Her protest was heartfelt, but then she was his sister and
had apparently spent her life looking after him.

'What is it that worries you, then?'

She sat quietly for a moment, staring into the distance.
Then she said, 'You know Haward wants to marry me?'

'Yes, and I'm *very* glad,' I replied.

She smiled. 'Thank you. But it's not as simple as him
asking and me saying yes. There's Derman.'

Yes. There was Derman. 'What does he think about the
marriage?'

'He's not—' She stopped herself. I don't know why, but
I had the distinct impression she had just bitten back something very important. Then instead she said, 'Lassair, because
of Derman I can't marry Haward.'

Whatever she had been about to say, it couldn't have
been worse that what she did say. Horrified, I protested,
'But he loves you! He really does, Zarina, and you're the
only woman who's ever really loved him back! You—'

She put up her hand and gently laid it across my lips.
'I know, Lassair. I love him too, with all my heart. But
Derman's—' Again she broke off. After a moment she
resumed. 'Derman is my responsibility. He is as he is,
and it's hard living with him. I ought to know,' she
added bitterly, instantly adding, 'It's not his fault, and
he's not bad, not really. There's no evil in him, that I'll
swear.'

'Then why—'

'I cannot inflict Derman on anybody else,' Zarina said
simply. 'Haward says it doesn't matter, that his – your –
family will accept him, but I can't see how it'd work. Your
parents live in that lovely little house that your mother keeps
so neat and tidy, and that's where Haward will take his
wife, at least till he can build a home of his own. Can you
see Derman there, Lassair?'

'Yes I can!' I said stoutly.

Zarina laughed. 'That's because you don't live there
yourself,' she said kindly and, I have to admit, accurately.
'The day Derman and I moved in would be the ruin of

your mother and the family,' she went on, her voice serious now. 'I really like your mother, and I won't do that to her. Besides, it's impossible anyway, as I said, because – well, it's not going to happen.'

I sat there holding her hand, listening to the echoes of her voice. Then I leaned over, kissed her and got up. As I went out, I turned and said, 'We'll see.'

Then I hurried off after Edild.

We searched for a long time. We covered the ground all the way from Lakehall to the lonely island where Granny lay in her grave. We criss-crossed here and there, venturing off the tracks and the paths, following the winding water-ways and creeping right up to the water's edge to stare down into the black mere. We found no sign of Derman. If he was really out there, looking in vain for his dead love, then he had hidden himself so well that we could not find him.

The long day was at last starting to come to a close when finally we gave up and turned for home. We walked without speaking. I had apologized to my aunt for not having told her I'd come across Derman the previous morning as I raced for help after making my discovery, and for omitting to repeat the discussion concerning him that I'd had with my mother. She had forgiven me, graciously agreeing that so much had happened recently that it was not surprising I had been so uncharacteristically forgetful.

I was so tired that I could hardly put one foot in front of the other. I was stumbling along with my head down, concentrating so hard on the simple act of walking that I did not realize Hrype was there until he spoke. Looking up, I saw him standing on the track in front of us. Sibert and Haward were with him.

'What are you doing out here?' Edild asked. Her tone was courteous, no more; she has a way of disguising her feelings for Hrype so skilfully that sometimes even I, who know better, doubt that the two of them are any more than colleagues and friends.

'Zarina told Haward that you and Lassair had gone to

look for Derman,' Hrype replied. 'We came to find you.'

'We have discovered no sign of him,' Edild said. 'We have searched the ground between the island and the hall, without success.'

'We t–too have been searching, out on the other side of the village, and we didn't find him either,' Haward said. I met his eyes and tried to smile. He must have seen my exhaustion on my face, for straight away he hurried to my side and put his arm round my waist. 'You should g–g–go home!' he said to me. 'You're w–worn out.'

'We must find him,' I said dully.

'We will search again in the morning,' Hrype announced. 'For now, it is too dark to pursue the hunt. Besides, you two should not be out here by yourselves.' He looked at Edild, a worried frown on his face.

She was tired too, but not so tired that she did not stiffen at his words. 'Why not?' she asked, and I detected a warning chill in her tone.

'Someone has just been murdered,' he said gently, 'not a mile from where we now stand. We have no idea why she was killed and no idea who killed her. It is not safe for you.'

'But it is all right for you men to risk the danger of being attacked?' Now Edild sounded plainly angry.

Hrype sighed. 'Edild, there are three of us, and we are armed.' He carried a long knife in a scabbard at his belt. Haward and Sibert held heavy clubs.

I glanced at Sibert. He raised his eyes to the darkening skies in a gesture of exasperation, and I very nearly laughed. He knows his uncle – his father – pretty well, although I don't think he's aware of the relationship between Hrype and my aunt.

I was sagging against Haward, and I guessed he was having quite a job to support me. 'I want to go home,' I said. 'I'll search for Derman all day tomorrow, but now I need to sleep.'

Edild brushed past Hrype and Sibert and, beckoning to Haward, said, 'Bring her back to my house, please, Haward.' She shot Hrype an icy look. 'We shall speak of this in the morning.'

We plodded the remaining mile or so to Aelf Fen in silence. When we reached the first of the houses, Edild stopped, for our way led off up to our right and the others would go straight on into the village. 'I will take her now,' she said regally to Haward, who relinquished his hold on me, kissed me briefly on the cheek and strode away.

'I can manage on my own!' I exclaimed, twisting away out of her reach as she went to take my arm. I'd had enough. Without a backward glance, I strode away up the track to Edild's house. I was aware of Hrype's and Edild's voices muttering in the darkness behind me, although I could not make out the words. I did not care. I wanted my bed.

I made a detour to the jakes and the water trough before I went inside. Even the chill of cold water on my hands, face and neck did not revive me; I was worn out. I stumbled back round the side of the house, and my hand was on the door latch when I heard it.

He was singing the same song. The same eerie sequence of notes filled the night air, eloquent of misery and loss. The hairs on the back of my neck stood up, and I shivered as some strong emotion evoked by the chant coursed through me. I wanted to weep for all the sorrows in the world.

Slowly, I turned my head. Where was he? I stared wide-eyed into the shadows, but I could make out no human shape. But he was close, he must be! Why couldn't I see him?

Dread filled me. Perhaps he wasn't human at all. Perhaps he was a spirit, a sad ghost trapped here on earth by his grief and impotently singing his pain to the stars . . .

All at once my nerve broke. Flinging open the door, I fell inside the house, slamming the solid wood behind me. I stood for some moments with my hands behind me, pressed against the door. It took a while for me to realize that I could no longer hear the singing.

I threw myself down on my bed and, just in case it started up again, covered my head with my pillow.

The singer watched as the young girl with the copper-coloured hair and the boyish figure wrested open the door of the little

house and disappeared inside. *You hear me, don't you, lass?*
he thought. *You listen to my song and you go rigid as you
perceive my pain. You have a good heart, and I am sorry
that I frighten you.*

He heard footsteps on the path: a quick, light step that
he recognized as belonging to the older woman who lived
in the little house. He slipped back into his hiding place
and watched as she hurried up to the door and let herself
in. She was a healer; his sense of smell was strong, and he
could detect her profession from the scent of her clothes,
as he could from those of the copper-haired girl. The house
itself smelt of clean, fresh things: of herbs and fresh-cut
grass. He liked the smell. He liked being close to the house.
It gave him comfort, of a sort.

But there was no real comfort, not any more. His world
had come to an end. He was alone, away from the place
he had known all his life. He felt the great surge of anguish
rise up in him, and a few notes of his song emerged from
his lips. As if the music lanced his pain, for a few moments
it eased.

Music. There was always the music.

His sense of hearing was even more finely developed than
his sense of smell. Ever since he had been a small boy he
had heard music in the natural world all around him: in birdsong, in the rustle of leaves in spring, in the rush of water
over a stream bed, in human activities such as hammering
and sawing. In the cool breeze of evening, and in the distant
stars that lit the heavens. He had a small harp that he liked
to play, although his preferred form of expression was his
own voice.

He used to sing with *her*. His love for her had begun
when she was quite young, and it had started with a song.
He had been singing at a village celebration, a well-known
song that everybody knew and, a little drunk as they were,
the people had bawled out the chorus. He didn't mind; in
fact he liked it when people joined in. It was good to sing.
It made you happy, made you forget the hardships of life.

He knew a lot about life's hardships. He had endured
many; one in particular, vicious and bitter, that had taken

all the joy from living. Until that day at the festival when he had suddenly realized that a sweet, high voice was not just singing the chorus but joining in with him for the verses.

She was harmonizing with him.

His heart had filled with happiness. He had turned to see who it was, feasted his eyes on the vision of her sweet face and fallen in love.

It had been as simple, as easy, as that.

And now she was dead.

His eyes filled with tears. He crept away, leaving the safe place from where he watched and sang and melting back into the darkness.

She was dead. And he knew what he must do.

First, he must write a song for her, for he would not allow her to be forgotten and it was up to him, who had loved her, to make sure that her sweet essence lived on.

There was another task too, a far less pure and gentle one.

Straightening his back, his jaw set in a hard line, he went hunting.

SEVEN

My brother is a habitually early riser, wide awake and padding quietly about so as not to wake anyone else long before the rest of the family stirs. I am not; Edild often has to shake me quite hard. The exception is when I have something serious on my mind, and that was the case the morning after we'd got back from our hopeless search for Derman and I'd heard the invisible singer for the second time.

I love my brother Haward dearly. I had so hoped he would find happiness with Zarina; she was so *good* for him, and I'd noticed that his love for her – and hers for him – had filled him with a new belief in himself so that now he barely stuttered at all. Last night, as he'd hurried to support me, the tongue-tying stammer had come right back.

He filled my mind as I lay awake in the thin light of dawn. I sensed he was calling out to me. Silently, I slipped out from under the bedcovers, pulled my gown over my shift, picked up my boots and let myself out of the house. The chill air struck me like a slap, and quickly I reached back inside for my shawl. I ran across the village, and just as I approached my parents' house, the door opened and Haward emerged.

We grinned at each other, both of us struck by the strange link between us that had brought us to this spot at precisely the same instant. He opened his arms and hugged me. He smelt of home. After a moment he said, 'We're going to search again as soon as it's light. If we make an early start there's a while before we have to start work.'

We. 'Who's going? I can come, for a while anyway.' It would not be long, for Edild had warned me we had a great deal to do that day and I dared not be absent when she wanted me.

Haward smiled. 'You'd be an asset, for sure. Hrype and Sibert will come, and Father said he'd spare us as much time as he can. He's going to bring Squeak.'

'That's good.' My little brother is one of the most observant people I know. 'I'll—'

Haward grasped my hands in his. 'There's something else I'd much r–rather you did,' he said. The stutter, combined with his sudden, deep frown, gave away his anxiety.

I said a silent goodbye to my happy little daydream of me being the one to find Derman – quite unharmed, of course – and bringing him safely home, cries of, *However did you find him, Lassair? Did you use your magic powers and dowse for him?* ringing in my ears. I looked at my brother and said, 'Whatever it is, I'll do it. You only have to ask.'

His face intent, he said, 'Watch Zarina for me.'

'I will!' I replied. 'Only, I've got to get back to Edild's quite soon, like I said, because—'

He shook his head. 'I don't mean right n–now. I meant, watch out to see how she copes with Derman's absence. Whether she goes on being as distressed as she is now, or whether—' He stopped, shaking his head.

I did not understand. 'But you'll probably find him this morning, or else he'll come home by himself!' Even as I said the words, I did not believe them. 'Or perhaps not,' I muttered.

Haward opened his mouth to speak, then, with a glance over his shoulder towards the house, took my arm and led me away along the path. Whatever he wanted to say, I knew it was very important. I waited, dread flooding through me.

'Lassair, Zarina will not m–m–m–marry me,' he said in a harsh tone, struggling so hard over *marry* that his face went dark red. 'I know she loves me, and I certainly l–love her, b–b–but she will not inflict D–D–Derman on our family.'

I stroked his arm, trying to soothe him. 'I know,' I murmured. 'She told me.'

I don't think my brother was listening. 'Sh–sh–she says he is not c–capable of killing anyone,' he went on, 'b–but he was missing on the m–morning the girl was found dead, and we all kn–kn–know he was sweet on her. If she rejected him, wh–who's to s–s–s–say how he'd react?'

Haward stopped speaking, his eyes intent on mine. Clearly, he did not want to put it into words, but I had no such compunction. 'You mean he might have been so angry and frustrated that he killed her. That's why I found him weeping, and that's why he's run away. Because he realized straight away what he'd done and could not face us?'

'Or because he knew he would be hanged for her murder,' Haward said harshly and with no trace of a stammer. I understood then the depths of his resentment and perhaps even hatred for Zarina's brother.

I took in the implications of what my brother had said. If Derman had murdered Ida – and my head told me it was quite possible – then once he was found, he would be tried, convicted and punished. Then he would be dead, and Zarina could marry Haward.

I stared into Haward's eyes. I could not believe that my beloved brother, gentle, peace-loving, kind-hearted, *good* Haward, would wish anyone to hang, even the impediment to his happiness that Derman was. Haward just wasn't that cold and selfish, that he would wish another's death so that he could get what he wanted. Even if that other person was a murderer . . .

I had to ask. 'Do you hope you find him?'

I thought he was going to say yes. For a moment, I really believed Haward was going to act so out of character that I'd hardly recognize him. But then the uncharacteristically hard expression left his eyes. His shoulders sagged and he said, 'No. Of course I don't. I hope he runs so far and so fast that we *never* catch him.'

I realized then why Haward wanted me to watch Zarina. He wanted to know how *she* would feel if her brother didn't come back. And I think he already had a very good idea . . .

I walked slowly back to Edild's house, so many thoughts and impressions warring inside my head that I was back there before I knew it.

'I've been to see Haward,' I said by way of explanation.

She nodded. There was no need to explain. 'The search resumes?' she asked.

'Yes.'

As if she fully understood Haward and Zarina's terrible dilemma – well, undoubtedly she did – she muttered, 'Poor, poor things.' Then she fixed me with a determined look and said, 'A messenger came from the hall. You are to go up there and tend Lady Claude.'

'*Me?*'

'You.

'But – it's the hall, and *you're* the healer!'

'You, too, are skilled, adequately so for what is required.' Her face softened a little and she added, 'They did in fact ask for me, but I cannot go. I have to tend a nervous new mother who needs urgent reassurance that her baby girl is not going to die, as well as a lad with a very painful boil that has to be lanced and a case that I suspect is quinsy, for the man can barely breathe.'

'What's the matter with Lady Claude?' I ran my eyes over the contents of my leather satchel, waiting for my aunt's reply before deciding what remedies and potions to add.

Edild said, 'She has a headache, and she cannot sleep.'

I reached for feverfew, wood betony and lavender, out of which I would make an infusion for the headache. I always carry lavender oil, which I would mix with almond oil as a massage for the brow and temples, if the lady would allow it. In our herb garden Edild and I had a patch of wild lettuce that had gone to seed; I would make a preparation that would have Claude sleeping like a baby tonight.

Edild watched as I came back inside, carefully wrapping the lettuce before stowing it in my satchel. She said, 'Remember that the body exhibits its inner state in external symptoms.'

I understood; it is one of her most frequently-repeated maxims. She believes that disturbances in the mind bring about aches, pains and sickness in the body. I don't understand how this can possibly happen, but she is my teacher and I deeply respect her wisdom and experience. 'I am to question her and see if anything is troubling her?' I asked.

Edild sighed. Sometimes I feel I have a tremendously long way to go before I am anything even approaching a healer. 'You know something troubles her, and you also know what it is,' she said patiently.

'Her seamstress is dead, and she feels bad because it was she who brought Ida here to the hands of her killer,' I said.

'Yes. And?'

'Her initial reaction, which she made the mistake of speaking aloud, was regret at the loss of a fine needlewoman, and she probably feels bad about that too.'

'Good,' said my aunt. 'Now, off you go. The lady is waiting.'

Lady Claude had taken to her bed. On announcing myself at Lakehall, I was ushered inside, across the wide hall and through a curtained doorway on the far side. A short stair led up to a bedchamber; Lord Gilbert was clearly advanced in his domestic arrangements and liked to offer his guests a room for the use of themselves and their personal servant, for there was but the one bed in the chamber, with a truckle bed tucked away beneath it where the servant slept.

The bed was high, the sheets were fresh, crisp linen. The occupant was dressed in a high-necked linen shift, beautifully sewn, and her head was bare. She was lying back on her pillows regarding me through half-closed eyes. She beckoned to me, and I approached, dropping a swift courtesy. Her short hair, I now saw, was of an indeterminate, light-brown shade, fine in texture, thin and lying flat on her head. I studied her face. She had been pale before, but now she looked grey, her eyes sunk deep in her head. I felt her pain coming off her in waves, and instinctively I summoned my defences. It was not that I wasn't sympathetic – far from it – but I would be no help to her if I, too, collapsed with a similar, agonizing pain.

Without asking, I put my hand to her brow, my open palm hovering a finger-joint's length over the skin. Left temple, left side of forehead, right side, above the eyebrows, up in the hairline, right temple. Yes. I had felt the heat of the pain as my hand hovered over Claude's left eyebrow but, as Edild had taught me, I covered the whole area before I began the treatment, in case the malaise was centred in more than one place.

I had asked the man who showed me in to bring hot water, and he had quietly slipped into the chamber and put a big, steaming jug on the floor, together with a mug. Now I selected the herbs from my bag, mixed them in a strong potion, tied them in a little cloth of fine linen and set the bag to steep in a mug of hot water. Then I poured almond oil into the small clay dish that I carry in my satchel, dropping in lavender oil and mixing it well. Returning to the bed, I said very quietly, 'My lady, have I your permission to soothe your poor head?'

Her eyes were closed. She nodded: a tiny movement, barely perceptible.

I leaned over her and began the massage. I paused after a while to give her the infusion, then went back to the massage.

After quite some time, her eyes fluttered open. She looked up at me, and I read two things: the pain had eased its iron grip, and its recession had allowed what was really troubling Lady Claude to push forward and dominate her.

I went on stroking her head. I did not know what to say. I was not Edild, who can ease a patient's extreme distress with the right words. It was quite possible that my attempts to help would do more harm than good. I kept quiet.

Presently, she gave me a rather tight-lipped smile and, taking hold of my wrist, removed my hand from her forehead. 'The pain has gone?' I asked. I knew it had, but it would be good to hear her say so.

'It has. I thank you.'

I studied her. The colour in her cheeks had improved slightly. 'You should perhaps stay in bed today,' I suggested. 'I have brought herbs to ensure that you will sleep. I will make an infusion for you.'

But even as I had spoken she had thrown back the bedclothes, and she now stood before me in her shift. 'Only the sick and the weak sleep in the daytime,' she declared. 'Hand me my gown.' She pointed an imperious finger. I did as she ordered, picking up the rich, black silk gown

and dropping it over her head, helping her with the side
lacings. Then she indicated her snowy-white headdress, and
I handed her that too. She nodded towards her leather belt
with the little velvet bag hanging from it – I noticed that
there was also a large iron key suspended on a chain – and
took it from me, fastening it around her thin waist. Beckoning
me to follow, she led the way to a small room along the
corridor, and as soon as she unlocked and opened the low
wooden door, I recognized it as her sewing room.

I stared around the chilly, narrow space. Ida, I observed,
had slept the nights of her guard duty on a tiny straw mattress
with one thin blanket.

'My linens.' Claude swept her hand around, and I took
in white sheets, linen cloths and personal undergarments,
all of the finest fabrics and beautifully sewn with tiny
stitches and delicate, subtle embroidery, much of it using
the form and colour of our local fenland wild flowers. If
this was Ida's handiwork, she had indeed been gifted.

'It's beautiful,' I said, and I wasn't just being polite.

She brushed aside the praise, leading me on towards the
end of the room, beneath the window, where a large wooden
frame stood. She looked down at what was stretched over
the frame, and for the first time I saw a smile on her face.
'This, now, this is my work,' she said. 'These panels will
hang around my marriage bed.'

I followed the direction of her eyes. The frame held a
large piece of coarse linen perhaps three yards deep and
a yard across; only a section of it was clamped in the frame,
the remainder hanging down either side. It was, I observed,
one of a series that she was working on. I leaned over the
work, studying the careful stitches and the pleasing colours.
It was only after looking at it for some time that I appreciated the subject matter.

For the intimate place that she would share with her new
husband, Lady Claude had chosen to depict the Seven
Deadly Sins. She was working on Gluttony, and a fat man
sat on a stool cramming food into his mouth even as the
cloth of his garment and his own flesh began to tear open,
spilling red guts out on to his yellow robe. I glanced around

to look more closely at the other panels, which were suspended from hooks along the walls. There was Pride, a pretty but vacuous-faced woman staring at herself in a mirror while her house burned down behind her with her agonized children inside. There was Lust, a scarlet-gowned woman lying with her eyes closed and her mouth wide open in sexual thrall, a man's dark outline over her while devils with pitchforks edged ever closer out of the shadows. Wrath was depicted as a well-muscled man, red-faced with fury, holding an axe above his head and in the very act of swinging it down on the head of his child – a little boy holding a catapult in one hand and a dead fowl in the other, eyes wide with terror as he pleaded for mercy. Avarice showed a miser sitting on a golden stool, his hands clutching at handfuls of gold coins that were stashed in a sack at his feet, his attention so thoroughly absorbed that he did not see the skeletal woman, child and tiny baby that lay drooping beside him, the woman's claw-like hand extended palm uppermost in the universal gesture of the beggar.

Sloth and Envy were, it seemed, still to be embroidered.

I was lost for words. The lady's skill with her needle was extraordinary, and her artistry was evident in the strong emotions that her designs provoked in me. The subject matter was worthy; our priest regularly regales us with the dangers of yielding to all sin, but the perils of the deadliest seven are a theme to which he returns again and again. In the right place, Claude's panels would have provided a timely reminder that we should watch our behaviour and not yield to temptation. But these vivid, startling, horrifying panels were to go around her bed . . .

I wondered if Sir Alain had any conception of what his future wife was working on. In a flash I knew that he had no idea; she would have coyly said it was to be a wonderful surprise that would be unveiled on their wedding night.

Poor man.

I cast around for some comment that I could make with sincerity. I said, 'My lady, what outstanding skill you have! These depictions seem almost to live and breathe.'

She nodded. 'We must ever be on our guard,' she muttered.
She was picking at one of the completed panels: Wrath.
'The Devil awaits all the time,' she went on in the same
soft, monotonous tone, her eyes burning with fervour. 'One
small slip in our vigilance and there he is, forcing our hand.
We—' Her mouth shut like a trap, and she turned away.
Perhaps it was that she had recalled who I was and that such
remarks were unsuitable from a lady to a village woman,
but I doubted it.

I thought it more likely that the thwarting of her life's
ambition to give herself to God had turned her mind a little
and that she might even be slightly mad.

I put out my hand to her, catching her sleeve. 'My lady,
why not do some sewing now?' I said gently. 'You are feeling
better, and it is peaceful here. If you stay here where it is
nice and quiet, you will not run the risk of the noise and
the clamour of the hall bringing your headache back.'

She must have seen the sense of that. Nodding – I had
noticed that, nunlike, she did not speak unless she had to
– she drew up her stool and sat down before the frame. In
a gesture that appeared automatic, she reached down for
the black velvet bag, putting it on her lap and opening the
drawstrings that held it closed. She extracted a thimble, a
small pair of sewing scissors, several hanks of different
coloured wool and a pincushion in which four or five needles
were stuck.

I recalled how I had wondered what was in the velvet
bag, that she should clutch at it like a talisman on the dreadful
day when Edild and I had come to lay out Ida's body. Now
I had the answer.

Calm now, she threaded her needle and, gazing fiercely
at her panel, stabbed it down through the thick canvas.
Her other hand was behind the fabric, waiting to receive
the needle, and, her fingers moving so swiftly that I could
barely follow her movements, she thrust it back up again
and started another stitch. I watched her for some moments,
listening to the soft grunts of exertion that accompanied her
actions; embroidery of this sort was, I observed, quite
hard work.

There was, I decided, something of the fanatic about Lady Claude. Uneasy suddenly, I wanted to be gone. I backed away towards the door, murmuring, 'I will take my leave now, my lady. I have left a potion to help you sleep, but please call me if you need me.'

I very much doubt she even heard.

I needed to be back with Edild, back with my own kind. I hurried away from Lakehall, trying to rid my mind of the image of Lady Claude, hunched over her frame, sewing an image out of hell.

I might have finished with the hall, but the hall had not finished with me. I heard the sound of running feet and a voice called out my name. I turned to see Sir Alain de Villequier hurrying after me. I had no choice but to wait for him.

'Lassair, Lady Emma says you came to treat Claude,' he said, panting. 'How is she? Is she feeling better?'

I wondered that he consulted me instead of going up to ask the lady herself. 'She is, I believe, sir,' I replied. Edild stresses that we must not discuss a patient's symptoms and sickness with anyone else, so I didn't tell him what had troubled her. 'I left her in her sewing room.'

'Her sewing room,' he echoed tonelessly. 'Ah. Er, good.' He flashed a smile at me, and I thought again what an attractive man he was. It wasn't his looks, which were pleasant but unexceptional; it was the impression he gave of irrepressible good humour and a determination to enjoy life. You just knew he'd be fun to be with and that, I find, is more of a draw in a man than the most perfect features on someone devoid of personality.

He stood there, still smiling, and I said delicately, 'If that is all, sir, I ought to be on my way. My aunt has work in plenty for me today.'

'Of course, of course!' he exclaimed. But instead of turning back to the hall, he nodded towards the village and said, 'We'll walk together, shall we?'

I could scarcely have said no.

We paced along in an amiable silence for a while. He

might have been a justiciar and a man of wealth and influence, but I felt at ease with him. Drawn to him, in a way, for all that my heart was firmly lodged with another. Perhaps he felt it too; perhaps – far more likely – he just couldn't resist the appeal of a young woman beside him. Presently, he took my arm, and it felt like the most natural thing in the world.

He said, giving my arm a squeeze, 'What of this missing man, then, Lassair? This Derman, who may or may not have attacked Ida?'

'We went out looking for him last night,' I gabbled, 'and they set off again at first light this morning. We're doing our best to find him, sir!'

'Are you?' He looked down at me, quirking an eyebrow. 'Or are you planning to let him slip off into the wilderness and so leave your Haward free to marry the lovely Zarina without her shambling brother coming too?'

How did he know? *Who had told him?* I tried frantically to work it out, then realized that nobody had told him. He had been appointed to his new position because he was an astute, observant man who didn't need to be told things because he worked them out for himself.

There seemed little point in lying to a man such as he. 'It is true that Derman presents an obstacle to my brother marrying Zarina,' I said quietly. 'She is unwilling to impose the care of him on anyone else.'

'A noble sentiment,' Sir Alain remarked. 'Although, of course, disappearing into the wilds is not the only way in which the obstacle that is Derman might be removed.'

I believed I knew what he was thinking and, in the same instant, I knew it was up to me to stop him. Praying I was doing the right thing, I said, '*If* Derman did this terrible thing and is caught and hanged, then yes, the way would be clear for Haward and Zarina to marry.' I turned to stare up at him, putting my soul into my eyes. 'I have known my brother all my life,' I said, 'and I give you my word that he would rather forsake his chances of happiness with Zarina than watch as she suffers the pain of seeing Derman apprehended, tried, found guilty and put to death.' Haward's words of that morning flew into my mind: *I hope he runs so far and so fast that we never catch him.*

Sir Alain regarded me for some moments. Then he said, 'I believe you.'

I could have cheered.

'What will happen now, sir?' I asked.

'We'll have to find Derman,' he replied. 'I, too, have sent a search party to look for him.'

My heart filled with dread. We in the village had managed only a handful of people with a limited amount of time. The resources that surely must be at Sir Alain's disposal would be far, far greater. I doubted if Derman stood a chance.

Sir Alain must have read my expression. 'Don't you want Derman caught?'

Before I could think about it I blurted out, 'I don't want *your* men to catch him.'

I thought I had gone too far. But, when at length he spoke, his voice was gentle. 'He may be a ruthless killer, Lassair. Ida was—' He cleared his throat. 'Ida had done him no harm. If she rejected him, as is speculated, she would have done so kindly and gently.'

'Yes, I know,' I said wearily. 'But what if he didn't kill her? What if he's just a convenient, defenceless fool who was silly enough to fall for her and just happened to be in the vicinity when she was killed?'

He looked at me for some moments. Then a faint smile twitched at the corners of his mouth and he said, 'Do you imagine I haven't thought of that?'

EIGHT

I was ravenous when I finally got back to Edild's house. I'd been far too tense that morning to think of food, and my ministrations up at the hall had taken me long past the hour of the midday meal. My aunt had thoughtfully left bread and cheese ready for me, and I crammed the food into my mouth as if I hadn't eaten for a week. She waited while I took the edge off my hunger, then asked how I had found Lady Claude. I told her, thinking hard to make sure I relayed all my impressions as well as what Claude had actually said and done.

'Hmm,' Edild said when I had finished. 'Her grief eats at her, it seems. And I would guess there is some battle going on in her head between what she sees as her vocation – to answer God's call and enter a convent – and her duty to her family.' She frowned. 'I am disturbed at these embroideries you describe. They speak of a mind in torment.'

'And she's going to hang them round her *bed*!' I added.

Edild smiled grimly. 'Hardly the best images to induce a mood of love and romance, for either a man or a woman.'

I pictured the panel depicting Lust. 'No.'

Edild fell quiet, and I knew from her expression that she was thinking. Then she said, 'Lassair, who do you think fathered Ida's child? And did her mistress know of her condition?'

I could not answer either question and shook my head. 'She was pregnant before she came to Lakehall,' I said. 'Remember? I asked Sir Alain when she arrived in the area, and he said under a month ago, so that would be towards the end of May. She'd already have been three months gone then, if you're right about her being four months pregnant when she died.'

'I believe I am right,' Edild murmured.

'Lady Claude's family home is in the Thetford Forest,'

I said. 'Hrype told us it was near the place where the ancestors mined the flint.'

Edild nodded. 'They call it Grim's Graves,' she said. 'Our forefathers believed the gods quarried there. It is long abandoned now. Morcar and the other flint knappers acquire their raw material from other sources.'

Morcar is my cousin, who lives with his mother – Edild's twin sister – in the area known as the Breckland. But I was not thinking about him then. I had just felt a deep-seated shiver, as if a cold finger out of the past had run down my back. 'Lady Claude's family live near such a place?' I asked. I would not have cared to have my dwelling close to such a site of power.

'Their estate is called Heathlands,' my aunt replied. 'Hrype says it is close to the little hamlet of Brandon.' I opened my mouth to speak, but Edild said, 'I know exactly what you're thinking, but listen to me, Lassair. You would need permission to leave Aelf Fen, and you can't go and ask Lord Gilbert, because this matter concerns him closely and he will not allow you to interfere. Also, there is a killer walking the lonely places out there and you would be putting yourself in grave danger.'

There was that word again. *Grave*. I shook off an instinctive shudder of fear and commanded myself not to be so silly. 'But the only way we'll find out more about Ida and her lover is if I go and ask,' I protested.

'Why must we know more?' Edild demanded. 'Can we not just let the poor girl rest in peace?'

'Everyone thinks Derman killed her and Zarina's terribly distressed and Haward loves her!' I blurted out. It didn't make a lot of sense, but Edild seemed to understand. 'I don't think he did, and I believe Sir Alain has his doubts too, but all the time Derman's missing and there's suspicion all around him, nobody's going to get any peace. *Are* they?' I almost shouted the question, my anxiety transforming into anger.

'No,' my aunt agreed.

Suddenly, I knew how to persuade her to let me go. 'I bet some married man got her pregnant, and then when she threatened to reveal his identity, he killed her!' I exclaimed. 'Oh, Edild, that *has* to be what happened! If Ida comes from this tiny little village, then probably everyone there knows everybody else's business and this married lover would have had his nice, peaceful existence broken apart if Ida had named him as her child's father.'

'But Ida had left her home village,' Edild pointed out. 'She came here with Lady Claude.'

'Yes, but she'd be going back again once Claude and Sir Alain were married and there was no more wedding sewing to do,' I said. 'Wouldn't she?' Surely that was right, unless Claude had been planning to keep Ida in her household after the wedding. Suddenly, I wasn't so certain.

Edild shrugged. 'You tell me, Lassair. You seem to have worked it all out.'

I thought hard. Then I said, 'This is how it must have been. Ida had a lover, a married man in the village. She went to work for Claude, and one day Claude told her she was going to stay at Lakehall with her cousin Lord Gilbert and Ida had to go too because Claude was going to be working on her trousseau. Claude came here because Sir Alain is based in the area at the moment –' I was speaking faster now as it all came together – 'and Claude wanted a chance to meet him, spend time with him and get to know him before the marriage.'

Edild nodded. 'Yes, that sounds credible.'

'Ida probably didn't know she was pregnant when she left Brandon,' I plunged on, 'and when she found out, somehow she sent word to the man, and he panicked because he thought she was going to ruin him. So, before anyone else could discover the secret – especially his wife – he came here, asked Ida to meet him in the middle of the night and then strangled her.'

Edild looked at me for a long moment. 'It is possible, I suppose,' she said grudgingly. Then a faint smile touched the corner of her mouth. 'Take Sibert,' she said. 'He's looked after you before when you've hared off on such wild missions.'

'You mean you're allowing me to go?' I could hardly believe it.

Edild's smile was wider now, but she also looked

exasperated. 'We'll get no work out of you till you've
followed this particular trail all the way to the end,' she
remarked. 'Go tomorrow, at first light. You can be there
and back by sunset.'

Excitement bubbled up in me. 'Can I go and tell Sibert?'

'You may go and *ask* Sibert,' she corrected. 'You're
inviting him to wriggle out of a day's work and set out
on a journey without permission, and, considering the
trouble he'd be in if anyone found out, he has every right
to say no.'

He did, yes. But I knew he wouldn't.

Sibert and I had a really lovely day for our walk. We had
some eight or ten miles to go, and in the warm sunshine,
with the birds singing all around us and the scents of summer
filling the air, I'd gladly have gone twice as far. The weather
had been dry of late, and the ground was firm. Our way
took us up out of the fens towards the higher ridge that
cups them to the east, and for the first few miles we climbed
gently but steadily.

There were many questions I wanted to ask Sibert. The
revelation that Hrype was not his uncle but his father had
hit him very hard; he had attacked Hrype when he'd first
found out. He was still living with Hrype and Froya, his
perpetually pale and anxious-looking mother, and I would
have sworn that neither Hrype nor Sibert had told Froya
that her son now knew the truth about his parentage. It was,
of course, none of my business, but that did not stop me
burning to ask Sibert about the mood between the three of
them.

'I saw Hrype the other day,' I said as we trudged along.
'He—'

Sibert sighed. 'Lassair, I know what you're working up
to asking. Don't waste your time. I'm not going to tell you
anything.'

Oh. 'But are you all right?' I persisted. 'Have you and
Hrype—'

'*Enough.*'

I had rarely heard my friend speak so harshly. An angry

flush had spread up his neck and over his face. I realized
he meant what he said.

We walked on in a hurt silence – well, *I* felt hurt – for
a while. Then Sibert spoke, and his voice sounded so normal
that you'd never have thought he'd been so furiously vehe-
ment only a short while ago. 'We're on the Icknield Way,'
he said. 'They say it's one of the oldest tracks in the land.'

'Oh.' I did my best to make the short syllable sound
disinterested.

Sibert chuckled. Reaching for my hand, he gave it a swing.
'Don't get huffy, Lassair,' he said. 'I agreed to come on this
ridiculous search with you to keep you out of mischief, and
you ought to be grateful.'

'You didn't need much persuading,' I observed.

'Maybe not, but neither of us will enjoy the day if you're
sulking.'

'I'm not sulking!'

'Yes, you are.'

'I'm not!'

'Are.'

We carried on like that for a while. Then he nudged me,
I nudged him back harder and we both started laughing.

Brandon was a very small village of about ten or a dozen
little dwellings. The wide acres of Thetford Forest stretched
away on the horizon, and I thought that somewhere out there
was the grand baronial home of Claude's kin, where sooner
or later she would no doubt be returning with her new husband.

Our business was not with the great men and women of
power who lived in vast castles and manor houses, however.
We were there to ask about a little seamstress who someone
had impregnated and someone had killed. In my own mind,
I was quite sure that the two men were one and the same.

The door to one of the cottages was open, and a man
stood there looking at us. He wore a heavy leather apron,
and there were shards and chips of flint on the ground at
his feet, radiating in an arc from the wooden stool where
he must sit to work. He said, not unpleasantly, 'What do
you want?'

There was no point in prevaricating. 'We come from a village near a place called Lakehall, on the fen edge,' I said.

If he had heard of it he gave no sign. 'And?'

'Lady Claude is at present staying there. Her family home is at Heathlands, I understand?'

'What's it to you?' Now he was frowning slightly, but in puzzlement, I thought, not suspicion.

'She took a young girl with her, by the name of Ida, and—'

The man's face fell. 'Ida's dead,' he said baldly. 'They sent word. We were all truly sad to hear it. She was a grand lass.'

'Has she family here?' I asked. I had in mind, I think, to seek them out and perhaps say a few consoling words, although what those words might be, considering how she had died, I did not know.

'She was an orphan,' the man said. 'Used to live with her old father, just the two of them, but he took sick and died, two years back. Ida did her best, poor love, and she had a neat hand with a needle, but we're poor people hereabouts, we can't afford new clothes and our women folk do their own mending. We all tried to help her a bit but, like I say, we're poor.' There was no need for further explanations. Ida had indeed been much liked, as I'd always thought, and it must have been hard for her neighbours not to have been able to do more for her.

'Then she came to the notice of them up at Heathlands,' the man continued, jerking his head in the direction of the surrounding forest, 'and before we knew what was happening she'd packed up her few belongings, the Lord's man had come and closed up her little house and she'd gone to live at the manor.'

'Was she happy there?' I asked.

'Happy? Who worries about happy, as long as you've a roof over your head and food in your belly?' the man demanded.

He was right. King William's rule had not eased the hardships faced daily by most of his more lowly subjects. 'I'm sorry,' I said humbly. 'It's just that I saw her body, you

see, and I felt I'd have liked her. She had a face that looked
as if it smiled a lot.'

The man relented. 'You're right there,' he said. 'I reckon
you'd have warmed to her, lass. Everyone else did, and not
a few loved her.'

My attention came into sharp focus. What was he saying?

While I was still framing a tactful question, Sibert spoke
up. 'Pretty girls always attract followers,' he remarked,
giving our new acquaintance a man-to-man glance.

'Aye, so they do, and Ida was no exception,' he agreed.
'Not that she was easy, I'm not suggesting that,' he added
quickly, frowning at us as if we'd questioned Ida's morals.
'No, no, she kept herself pure and decent. She was always
kindly, don't mistake me, but when a young lad had his
head turned because she smiled at him and started making
a bit of a nuisance of himself, she had a sweet way of gently
letting him know he was sniffing round the wrong bitch.'
Instantly, his face coloured and he said, 'Sorry, I'm sorry.
Shouldn't have said that. There's no need to be crude,
especially about a girl like Ida.' We waited while he remembered what he'd been saying. 'No, like I said, she never
encouraged any of them. Treated them more like brothers
than potential lovers, I'd have said. It was no fault of hers
if they loved her.' He dropped his head, eyes on the ground.
'If *he* loved her,' he said in a whisper.

I could have corrected him and told him he was wrong
about Ida keeping herself pure. But there was no point; let
the poor girl keep her good name. I was far more interested
in this *he* that the man spoke of.

'There was someone in particular who had fallen for her?'
I asked. I wanted to know so badly, but I was afraid that if I
pushed too hard he would get suspicious, clam up and shut
the door on us.

By good fortune, however, Sibert and I seemed to have
encountered the village gossip, which was probably why
he'd been working outside his house in the first place: so
that he could catch the attention of anyone who passed by
and exchange a word or two with them. Several more than
two, in our case.

The man leaned towards us, elbow resting on the top rail of the simple fence that ran round his yard. 'It's a sad tale,' he said, 'but if you knew Ida and have taken the trouble to seek out those who used to be her neighbours, then I reckon you've a right to hear it.' I hadn't known Ida, and Sibert and I had had no intention of seeking out her former neighbours except to find out the identity of the man who had been her lover, but this was no time to be pedantic.

'Please tell us,' I said.

The man gazed out along the narrow, rutted track that wound between the houses. 'We are few who live here,' he began, 'and we work hard. Flint knapping's a special skill. Most of us learned it from our fathers, and they learned from *their* fathers.' I knew a little about the life of a knapper because of my cousin Morcar, and I nodded. 'There's not much other work hereabouts, and that's a fact,' the man added lugubriously, 'and, like I say, most of us have a struggle supporting ourselves and our families. Still, us in Brandon have a rare bit of good fortune because we've got our own minstrel. Well, of course he's not really, he's a knapper like the rest of us, only he plays that little harp of his like one of the Lord God's angels, and whenever we have the least excuse for a bit of fun, out he comes with a tune and a song. Sometimes it's something he's written himself, and sometimes he'll smile and agree to play one of the old tunes so we can all join in.' A reminiscent smile spread across his face, revealing three crooked teeth and a lot of gaps.

'You are indeed fortunate,' Sibert said. 'It raises a man's spirits at the end of a hard day to down a mug of ale and sing a good song.'

'Alberic didn't often get the mug of ale, not while that sour faced bitch of a wife of his was watching,' the man said forcefully. 'And it's a tribute to his music that it could make him smile with all he had to put up with. And it did make him smile – he used to look like he was in heaven, on God's right hand, when he was singing.' He shot us a sly glance. 'Especially when Ida sang along with him.'

I knew it! I thought. *Ida* did *have a lover, and he* was *married!* I felt my heart beat speed up.

'This Alberic,' Sibert was saying, 'has a shrew for a wife, then?'

'Shrew's putting it mildly,' the man replied. 'We were all amazed when Alberic agreed to wed her, for she was a few years older than him, and whatever bloom she'd once had had long worn off. We warned him, but he said he'd given his word and that was that. Soon as she'd got the ring on her finger she started on at him, and I don't reckon she as much as paused to draw breath even once after that. She was named for a martyr, was Thecla, and she made poor Alberic's life one long martyrdom too. He didn't work hard enough, he spent his money in the tavern and not on her, the snug little house he built for her was no better than a pigsty – that's the sort of thing she hurled at him. Then there was his music, and you can guess what she had to say about him wasting his time with something as frivolous as *that*.' Leaning close again, he confided spitefully, 'Tone deaf, old Thecla. Couldn't carry a tune if it had handles.'

'No wonder Alberic fell for Ida,' I put in softly. 'It sounds as if she was everything Thecla wasn't.'

'That she was,' the man agreed, 'and her sweet young face looking up at him while he played fair touched Alberic's heart, and she was only a girl back then. Not that there was anything improper going on,' he added. 'In those days – and I'm talking a few years back now – Alberic loved her like a daughter. It was only later that he started to see her like a man sees a woman, if you take my meaning.'

We did.

'Well, nothing could come of it,' he went on with a deep sigh. 'Alberic was a married man, and nothing was going to change that. He loved Ida far too dearly to make advances to her when he knew he could not do the right thing and offer marriage.' *That*, I said to myself, *is what you think*. 'So he loved her from afar, and he had to watch helplessly as she nursed her dying father and grieved for him after he'd gone. She was all alone then.' He paused, and I noticed his eyes were wet. 'Of course,' he said after a moment, 'Alberic knew he couldn't offer to help her because it would soon get back to Thecla and she'd have her revenge on him. She tried to burn his harp once,' he added matter-of-factly. 'Just because she thought she'd seen him smile at a pretty woman in a red dress at the Lammas fair.'

'He must have been relieved, in a way, when Ida went to work at the big house,' I suggested. 'At least he no longer had to see her every day.'

'You'd have thought so, wouldn't you?' he agreed. He shook his head. 'Wasn't like that. Soon as she'd gone, Alberic began to fade away, almost before our eyes. We thought he was ill, but if so it was a strange sickness that didn't progress or get better. We began to think old Alberic was on his way to meet the Maker. Then we heard Ida had gone off with Lady Claude to stay with some cousin of the lady, where she – Lady Claude, I mean – was going to get to know the man she's to marry and work away on her marriage chest. Which was why Ida went with her too, her being a seamstress.'

His brow creased in concentration. Then, as if he had been working out the dates, he said, 'That were back in May. Next thing we know, a miracle happens and Thecla died.'

I was framing the question, but Sibert got in first. 'What happened to her?'

Our informant chuckled. 'Alberic didn't kill her, if that's what you're thinking, although there's not a man here that wouldn't say she'd deserved it if he had done. No. Thecla had grown very fat over the years –' so much for Alberic not providing sufficiently for her, I reflected – 'and she tripped over her own slippers and fell down the step leading to her door. Cracked her head on the hard stone and burst her skull like a walnut. Alberic found her brains all over the path.' He recounted the details with great relish.

'So Alberic was free to court Ida?' Sibert said.

'Aye, so he was, and he barely waited till Thecla was in the ground before setting off to find her,' the man agreed.

'When was this?' I demanded suddenly. An awful thought had struck me.

The man's eyes flew to meet mine, and I knew from the

compassion in them that I was right. 'Not four days ago,' he replied.

I worked it out.

Oh, no.

Alberic had hurried to find the love of his life to tell her he was now free to marry her on the very day somebody killed her. I was aching for him, aching for both of them. My brilliant solution to the mystery of Ida's death – that her married lover had slain her to stop her revealing that she carried his child – seemed to have flown right out of my head.

I couldn't stop thinking about her; about both of them . . .

Sibert and I thanked our friend and set off on the road back to Aelf Fen. It was not long past midday, and the sun was hot, so quite soon we found a shady spot a few paces off the track under some trees and sat down to eat the supplies we had brought with us.

I took a long drink from my flask and handed it to Sibert. 'That's better,' he remarked as he set it down. He stretched out on his back while I prepared the food. 'Did you believe that man when he said Alberic hadn't seduced Ida?'

'No,' I replied, busy slicing dense dried meat. 'She was pregnant, Sibert. Of course he'd seduced her. Perhaps,' I added, 'she seduced him. She probably felt sorry for him. Everyone else did, apparently.'

'Poor man,' Sibert muttered. He sat up, and I handed him his food. 'He thought he'd found happiness at last after a lifetime of misery, only to have it snatched away from him.'

Poor man indeed.

I chewed my bread and dried meat, idly wondering where Alberic was now. Had he gone straight back to Brandon after learning Ida was dead, or had he decided to wait to see her buried? He might have—

Then I knew where he was, or at least where he had been the night before last. It had taken me a long time to realize it, but then, in my own defence, the man described by our informant sounded very different from the one I had heard.

Two nights ago, when I had dragged my exhausted body back to Edild's house after our hopeless search for Derman,

I had encountered an invisible singer. I had heard him the night before that, too, at the end of that long and dreadful day when I found Ida's body. Somehow Alberic had learned that she was dead, and he stayed in Aelf Fen, pouring out his grief for his dead love the only way he knew how. In my mind I could hear the echo of his lament, so tragic and so ethereal that I had thought him not human but a spirit: longing to fly away, but bound by grief to the indifferent earth.

I was no longer hungry. Surreptitiously, I slid my share of the food over beside Sibert's. Then, saying that I was sleepy and would have a brief nap before we went on, I lay down, turned my back to Sibert and quietly mourned for a man, a girl and a love that had had to die.

NINE

Sibert and I slipped quietly back into Aelf Fen in the early evening. We took great care to make sure nobody spotted us, although in fact there wasn't a soul watching out because almost all the village had gone to the churchyard to witness the burial of Ida's body.

We hurried along after the last stragglers, panted up the slight rise to the church and found a place on the edge of the silent crowd. The priest was just finishing his prayers for the dead girl's soul, and at his feet the linen-shrouded corpse lay in the freshly-dug grave. It was a beautiful evening, and the westering sun was casting long shadows from the stumpy trees around the graveyard, illuminating the watchful faces with a soft, golden light. Somewhere nearby a chaffinch was singing, the fluting notes ending in a repetitive little phrase that seemed to say, *too young to die!*

Immediately behind the priest, on the highest ground, stood Lord Gilbert and Lady Emma, their heads bent. Lady Emma's lips moved as she added her own pleas to those of the priest. Lady Claude stood beside her, very pale, her mouth compressed as if to hold back the tears. There were dark circles under her eyes, and her eyelids were puffy. I felt a stab of compassion for her; it did not look as if my sleeping draughts were helping very much. On the far side of Lord Gilbert and a little behind him, Sir Alain de Villequier stared out over the assembled villagers. I noticed that Lady Claude kept shooting him anxious little glances, and I was touched that she seemed to be trying to draw strength from him. Perhaps, despite those terrible embroidered panels and her tight features that spoke eloquently of rigid self-control, there was a chance that their marriage would be happy . . .

I thought back to Brandon, going over everything that Sibert and I had learned. Was Alberic here, watching as the body of the girl he loved was buried miles from her home? Suddenly filled with the conviction that he was, I copied Sir Alain and began scanning the crowd for an unfamiliar face, only to realize pretty quickly that it was an impossible task, for there were dozens of strangers present. I guessed everyone who had a friend or relative in Aelf Fen had heard of the mysterious death of a young seamstress and come hurrying over to witness the burial. Part of me wanted to shout at them, tell them to get back where they belonged and not be so ghoulish. Then, reflecting on how rarely anything at all exciting happened in most people's dull and monotonous lives, I relented. After all, they weren't doing any harm. Villagers and outsiders alike were standing listening respectfully to the priest's endless prayers, and one or two even had tears on their faces. As for Ida, if any part of what had made up the living girl was present and watching the proceedings, then she would surely be gratified that so many had come to see her off.

Still, the presence of so many strangers meant that Alberic could very well be here among us and no one would know.

I wondered if Sir Alain was also searching the faces for the stranger that might be Alberic and feeling similarly frustrated. Then I realized that, unless he, too, had heard the invisible singer, followed the trail of Ida's life back to her village and found out about her lover – which was unlikely because if he had, our informant would have told us – he didn't know of Alberic's existence. Just as I was wondering if I ought to tell him, something else occurred to me. If Sir Alain wasn't looking out for Alberic, who *was* he hoping to see in the crowd?

The answer came quickly: Derman.

Oh, *oh*, but it was just what poor, simple Derman *would* do! He must surely be in torment, hiding away from his sister, his home and everything that made up security for him in a cruel world. If somehow he had managed to find out that they were burying the girl he had loved this evening, then he would undoubtedly have been drawn back to say his farewell to her, no matter the danger to himself if he were to be spotted and apprehended. Did he even understand that there *was* danger to him? He must have done, I reasoned, for why else had he run away?

I let my eyes wander along the rows of silent people. Derman is big and bulky – I suspect he is very strong – and quite hard to overlook. I saw my parents, standing with Edild on the edge of the crowd. Squeak and Haward were with them, standing either side of Zarina. I thought suddenly that the two of them looked defensive; Haward had his arm round her waist. But there was no sign of Derman.

The priest had finished at last, and the gravediggers were starting to heap earth down on top of the shrouded body. I did not want to watch. I grabbed Sibert's hand, said, 'Come on!' and, hurrying through the villagers and the strangers as they milled about on the track and began to think about turning for home, caught up with my family. I reached out to grab Haward's arm – he was nearest – and he spun round, his face angry and his hand clenched in a fist.

Then he saw it was me. 'Oh. Hello, Lassair.' He called out to my father and asked him to take his place at Zarina's side. Then, his hands on Sibert's and my shoulders drawing us close, he jerked his head in the direction of the slowly-dispersing crowd of villagers and said quietly, 'They've t–taken against Zarina. They say her brother's a k–k–killer and ought to be hanged for what he did.'

'But they don't know yet that he did anything!' I protested.

'Hush!' Haward glanced around hastily to see if anyone had heard, but the people closest to us were muttering avidly about the priest, his prayers and likely span of the dead girl's sojourn in purgatory. 'You know what they're l-like,' he said bitterly. 'Derman was seen near the island –' I thought it very restrained of him not to add that it was I who had seen him there – 'and now he's run away. As well as that he's simple, and he and Zarina are strangers, and it all adds up to his guilt.'

'They've been here since Lammas last year!' I said. 'They're not strangers any more.'

Haward sighed. 'Yes, they are. And they're *different*.' He did not need to elaborate; I knew what he meant. Dropping his voice, he muttered, 'We've got to find Derman and warn him. If he returns to the village they'll very likely take him out and st–st–string him up.'

I imagined the scene. A group of strong village men, stirred to violence by gossip and righteousness, setting out to avenge a girl they hadn't even known, when their real motive was to hound the outsider, the man who was *different*, and be rid of him once and for all. Poor Derman. Poor Zarina – she must be terrified.

'Still no sign of him?' Sibert was asking.

Haward shook his head. 'No. Sir Alain has organized search p–parties – most of the village men and b–boys were summoned – and they've been out most of the d–day. Nobody's reported anything that might lead to Derman.'

With the image of a local gang bent on murder still vivid in my mind, I wondered if somebody *had* seen something but, preferring village justice to Sir Alain's kind, had kept quiet. Would this man, whoever he was, even now be spreading the word to the others? *Wait for darkness, then we'll creep out of the village and I'll lead you to him. We'll show him how we deal with murderers!*

It was horrible. It was also all too easy to imagine. I looked ahead to where Zarina walked between Squeak and my father, her head up, her back straight, her eyes fixed on some object in the distance. I thought I heard the sound of angry bees buzzing and, as I looked around, I could see the villagers getting their heads together, murmuring and shooting furtive glances at the woman they would shun because she was the sister of a simpleton who they had decided was a murderer.

It just wasn't fair.

'I'll go and sit with her for a while,' I said, overcome with the urge to give her my support. 'She won't want to be alone with just old Berta for company.' The washer-woman Zarina lodged with was highly likely to be first in the line of those denouncing Derman, for all that he'd lived under her roof and uncomplainingly done far more than his share of the rough and heavy work.

'Zarina won't be alone,' Haward said, giving me a quick smile. 'She's coming home with us.'

Yes, it was typical of my parents to have asked her. It might be unseemly for a single girl to sleep in the same room as the man who wanted to marry her, but then there would be three other people present. 'But I'd be really pleased if you'd t–talk to her,' Haward added. 'You remember what I asked you to do?'

He'd asked if I'd try to judge how Zarina would feel if Derman didn't come back, and all I'd done so far was have one brief conversation with her. 'Yes, of course,' I said. I thought quickly. 'I'll go to her now and offer to go back to her house with her to help her collect what she needs for the night.'

Sibert suppressed a snort of laughter and said, 'Very subtle, Lassair. I'm sure she'll never guess you're trying to get her on her own.'

Haward glanced at him and said coolly, 'Lassair's doing her b–best and I'm grateful.' My brother doesn't really understand my relationship with Sibert.

'It's all right,' I whispered to my brother. Then I hurried on to catch up with Zarina.

Berta was still out somewhere muttering with her cronies, so Zarina and I had the little house to ourselves. I watched as she made a desultory attempt to gather a few belongings together, then she slumped down on her cot and put her hands over her face. I went to sit beside her, unsure whether or nor to put my arms round her. I wanted to, but there's something a little distant about Zarina.

I said after a while, 'It must be a good sign that they haven't managed to find him yet.'

She murmured something that might have been an assent.

'There have been heaps of people searching,' I plunged on, 'and if Derman has avoided them, then he must have found a good place to hide. Perhaps he'll—'

She uncovered her face and spun round, halting my well-intentioned words. 'And just what do you think he'll be doing out there in this hiding place?' she demanded.

'Er – well, he'll have built a shelter,' I improvised, 'and maybe he thought to take food and drink with him, and perhaps even a blanket, and—'

'Lassair, Derman hasn't the first idea how to take care of himself,' Zarina said heavily. 'He ran away with only the clothes he stood up in. I checked, and his spare shirt and hose are still in the lean-to, with his blanket and his cloak. As for food and drink, if I don't put it before him he doesn't eat.'

'Couldn't he forage?' I suggested hopelessly.

She laughed harshly. 'What do *you* think?'

No. He couldn't.

Derman had been gone for at least two days. If the search party or the village gang didn't find him soon, it would be too late.

Zarina must be thinking the same thing. Surely it would not shock her if I put it into words? Very tentatively I said, 'How long could he survive?'

She shrugged. 'Six days, a week, maybe. Thirst would drive him to find water, although whether he'd know to make sure it was clean enough to drink, I couldn't say.'

I nodded. I knew very well what I wanted to ask her, but I could not find the words. To me – probably to everyone else – Derman just seemed a burden, a big, shambling adult with the body, the strength and the natural urges of a man but the intelligence of a child, and a pretty odd and dim-witted child at that. I viewed the prospect of his dying out there in the wild as something very regrettable, but if it happened – through nobody's fault but his own, he being the one who had chosen to run away – it would remove the obstacle to her wedding with my brother that Zarina saw as insurmountable. What I was overlooking was the possibility that she might love him.

I said carefully, 'If he doesn't return, it may of course mean he's got right away from the area – which is why the search parties can't find him – and perhaps someone has taken him in.'

She looked at me, her golden-green eyes unreadable. 'Why would anyone do that?'

'There are good people out there,' I replied, then, warming to my theme, I plunged on. 'There are monasteries and convents full of holy men and women whose duty it is to look after the needy and the helpless. There are lots of hard-working people who would be pleased of an extra pair of hands to help them on the land, or even in the home, and Derman's very strong, isn't he?'

She sighed, a faint smile on her face. As if she found my speculations about charitable nuns and monks and farmers desperate for hearty workmen too foolish to comment on, she said dreamily, 'He was in a strongman act. When we were with the travelling entertainers, that's what Derman's job was.'

It was the first time she had ever spoken to me about her past. I said encouragingly, 'What exactly did he do?'

Her smile broadened. 'Not very much. He was always hard to teach, and he found it virtually impossible to remember anything very detailed. He'd stand with his legs apart and his arms out straight by his sides, then these other men would climb up his body and stand on him, and then more would stand on *them* till they'd made a mountain of men. Finally, one by one, starting from the top, they'd all leap off again, turning and twisting as they fell and landing in a circle all round him.'

I remembered. I'd seen the act at the fair when Zarina and her brother had first blown into our lives. It had been most impressive. The seven men who had just jumped down started turning tumbles and flips, then after a while seven girls had run out to join them. The girls had been dressed in extraordinary garments: tight little velvet bodices and layers of floaty fabric that formed their skirts, with their legs and feet bare. Their long hair had been loose, bound only with strands of ribbon plaited into it. They had tumbled and turned with the men, running round in a circle in the opposite direction, then they had formed into pairs – seven men dancing with seven girls – and their move-ments had speeded up till they'd been a brightly-coloured blur. I still couldn't believe some of the things those men and girls had done. I'd never known the human body could bend like that.

Zarina had been one of the dancing girls. They had all been pretty, but she was the prettiest. I don't know what life with a troupe of travelling entertainers had been like, but Zarina had given it up because she'd fallen in love with my brother.

Where had she and Derman come from? Who were their parents, and what had happened to them? Had they also been entertainers, and the rest of the troupe had taken in the orphaned brother and sister when they died?

Now might be my chance to find out.

'Were your parents entertainers too?' I asked, trying to keep my tone casual.

'Dear Lord, no,' she said. I thought she shuddered, but she might just have been chilly. It was decidedly cool, now that the sun had set. 'No. My father was a nobleman.'

'A – *nobleman*?' And she was contemplating marrying my brother!

As if she had read my thoughts, she said, 'He was neither very rich nor very important, but the title was an old one.'

'Was he – is your family Norman?'

She burst out laughing. 'No, Lassair. Neither are we Saxon.' She regarded me, and there was still lively amusement in her eyes. 'I was born a long way from here,' she said. 'In a country where a woman's position is even lowlier than it is here. Where a man can give his daughter to a villain, a dullard or an octogenarian, even if it is so much against her will that she would rather die.'

A man can do that here, I thought, but I did not speak. I did not want to interrupt her.

'My father wanted me to marry his oldest friend,' she said, so quietly that I strained to hear. 'If you can call it a friendship, when one man makes a loan to another and then demands it must be settled, and the only thing the debtor possesses that his creditor wants is his own daughter.'

'So . . . your father used you to pay his debt?'

'He tried to,' Zarina said with spirit. 'I would not have it. In a barbarous, lawless region, my father's *friend* was famous for his cruelty. He liked to arrange spectacles in which men he'd had arrested on imaginary charges were given the chance of fighting for their freedom. He'd have them let out into animal cages, two prisoners to a cage, then they'd be armed with swords, knives, clubs, anything, and at the end the one on his feet over the dead body of the other would be set free. Only, one of Haglar's men would be sent to fetch him back and he'd be quietly beheaded. Haglar liked beheading people,' she added. 'They say he beheaded his first wife because she bore him two daughters.'

I realized I was sitting there with my mouth open, and quickly shut it. 'And this Haglar hoped you would bear him a son?'

Zarina made an impatient sound. 'There was little chance of that, for his other two wives had no more luck. Mind you, Haglar had an illegitimate son by one of the hundreds of women he'd seduced or raped, and this son did not want his father to have a son born in wedlock, so it's very likely the baby born to the third wife was suffocated. It wasn't even a boy,' she said in a whisper. 'He didn't stop to make sure.'

In her dreadful tale, that seemed the worst atrocity of all. 'So you ran away,' I said.

She nodded. 'I did. I'd seen the entertainers in the town square, and I knew they never stayed anywhere very long. I thought that if I could hide in one of their wagons until we were far away, then I might be able to convince them I could be useful to them and they'd let me stay. They seemed like friendly people, and I'd always been a good dancer.'

'And there was Derman,' I said.

'Derman?'

'Yes! They must have seen the potential in your brother. Being so big and strong, he'd have been very useful to them, and I bet they quickly realized it.'

'Yes, yes,' she said. 'They did.'

'Did he understand that you could never go back?' I asked. 'Did he appreciate why you had to leave?'

'I'm not sure,' she said slowly. 'All I can tell you is that from the time I joined the troupe, Derman looked after me. We had hard times, and we faced danger. Not just things like fierce storms, flooding, desperate hunger and extremes of heat and cold, all of which you learn to take in your stride when you're on the road.'

'What other danger do you mean?' I had an idea I already knew.

'Haglar sent men after me,' she said tonelessly. 'He had one of my maids tortured till she told him what I'd been planning. Fortunately for me, although not for her, I didn't tell her the truth. But they burst into my father's house and searched my rooms, and when they found I'd taken only my jewels and none of my rich and costly garments, one of the men guessed where I was. He came alone. I guess he thought I'd be no trouble and he could claim all the glory from having brought me back. Haglar would have been very generous, I'm sure. But he never got the chance to discover how generous because Derman killed him and hid his body where it would never be found.' She was staring at me, eyes wide with the drama of her tale. 'He put it in a—'

She stopped. Just like that, in the middle of a sentence.

My mind was reeling. She had escaped from a ghastly future, and her brother had gone with her. He had protected her, to the extent of killing for her. He had hidden the body in a . . . In a grave? Was that what Zarina had been about to say? And, having come up with such an unexpectedly good idea – for who would think to look for a body in someone else's grave? – had Derman then employed it again when he had killed Ida?

It sounded horribly likely.

In the same moment that I accepted Derman might very well be guilty, I understood why his sister could not abandon him. He had give up so much for her, even if he did not realize it. Whether or not she loved him – and I still wasn't sure – she owed him so much. She owed him her life.

I no longer cared if she would shy away from me. I reached out and took both her hands in mine, moving so close to her that our hips touched. 'Zarina, we must find Derman and bring him back,' I said urgently. 'He must stand trial, but if he is innocent –' oh, I hoped I was wrong and that he wasn't a killer – 'he'll be freed, and then when you marry Haward –' she made as if to speak, but I wouldn't let her – 'you and Derman will *both* go to live in my parents' house till Haward builds you one of your own.'

She snatched her hands away and turned on me, all the soft gold gone from her eyes, leaving them glittering green and hard as emeralds. 'I cannot marry Haward!' she cried.

'But he loves you! You love him!'

She emitted a great sound of fierce anger and frustration. '*Love!*' she echoed. 'You think it is all that matters!'

I didn't understand. 'I know you are bound to Derman and cannot forsake him, but my mother and my father will not try to make you! It won't be easy, naturally, especially at first while everyone's getting used to—'

Zarina had had enough. She leapt up from her cot and began flinging her few possessions into an old leather bag. 'I cannot marry Haward,' she repeated.

I, too, had reached the end of my rope. 'I want to see my brother happy!' I shouted. '*You* can make him happy, Zarina, I know you can because I—' I almost said *because I've seen it in the runes*, but I remembered just in time that such things were secret. 'I appreciate that you care for Derman,' I went on more calmly, 'but he's not the only person to consider. *I* care for Haward, and I refuse to see his chance of happiness with you taken away from him because you are—'

'*I am?*' She rounded on me. 'I am what?' She screamed at the top of her voice, a great *aaaaagh* that tore out of her. 'You do not know what I am!' she cried. Then, pausing to draw breath: '*You know nothing about me!*'

It was very late.

The man lurking on the edge of the village watched as the last lights were extinguished. He waited a little longer and then, keeping to the shadows, crept along the track and up the path that sloped up to the church. The melody of his song ran through his head as he walked. He would sing it soon.

He went straight to the new grave. He knew exactly where it was. He had not dared go too close earlier, while they were burying her, instead keeping to the back of the crowd, his hood drawn up around his face.

He had heard the prayers. He had listened to the villagers as they muttered together. They spoke of *him*, that shambling, drooling simpleton. There were search parties out hunting for him, and many of the villagers believed they should take matters into their own hands. The singer agreed with them, although he would be the one meting out the richly-deserved punishment. *You killed her*, he thought. *You put her body in the grave on the island. I know you did, for I saw you do it. I saw you there, although I did not know until later what you were doing. You left her there, my beautiful Ida, then you ran away and sobbed because you knew you had done wrong and would be made to pay the price.*

Now, standing over her as she lay dead in the ground, his love, his loss and his grief welled up uncontrollably. He closed his eyes, opened his mouth and softly, sweetly, heartbreakingly, he began to sing.

TEN

n the morning Edild said as she stirred the breakfast porridge that I ought to go up to Lakehall and see how my patients were faring.

'Patients?' I echoed. I could only think of one. Claude.

Edild went on stirring. 'You told me that you tended Lady Emma when she fainted,' she reminded me.

'I didn't do much,' I protested. 'She sort of fell against me, and I bathed her face with cold water when she'd recovered from her faint. Anyone else there could have done the same,' I added, modestly lowering my eyes.

'Naturally, since what you did was common sense rather than healing skill,' Edild said crushingly. I know she loves me dearly – I have good reason to – but sometimes she is all stern teacher, reminding me how far I have to go before I can call myself a healer. 'However, it does no harm for an apprentice like you to make their mark with the lady of the manor,' she continued, 'and if, as it appears, Lady Emma is inclined to trust you, it would be wise to do what you can to develop her dependency.'

'But you're the village healer,' I said. 'It ought to be you looking after the lady of the manor.'

Edild gave me a small smile. 'I am not really at home in the halls of lords and ladies,' she murmured.

That was a surprise. I'd have said that my aunt, with her dignity, her grace and her slight air of aloofness, was happy anywhere the sick and injured needed her, be it a peasant hovel or a castle. As she ladled out porridge into a wooden bowl, stirring in a generous spoonful of honey from her own bees, I thought about what she had said. I realized quite soon that she was right. With the poor and lowly, the full force of her personality emerged. When she and I had gone to Lakehall to lay out Ida's body, Edild, although perfectly polite, had sort of withdrawn into herself. I must have noted the difference in her without really thinking about it, and it was only now, when pointed in the right direction, that I understood.

As if she knew what I was thinking, she said gently, 'The rich can buy the assistance of whomever they choose, Lassair. The poor have to make do with what they can get, and in many villages that amounts to some ignorant old woman who probably does more harm than good.'

Yes. One of my sister Goda's friends had almost lost her baby – and her own life – because a village midwife hadn't known what she was doing. Goda had had the good sense to send for Edild, who had saved both mother and child. We learned later that the woman had afterwards spent a lot of time on her knees in church praying to the Virgin Mary, most honoured of all mothers, to look favourably on Edild and take special care of her. Edild, when she'd heard of this, had smiled gently. I think that the Great Mother to whom Edild prays is far, far more ancient than the Mother of Christ, but no doubt she appreciated the sentiment. Maybe, in some strange and unfathomable way, the two are one and the same . . .

Edild was instructing me on how to conduct myself up at the hall; I made myself pay attention. Then, when I had washed and put away our mugs and bowls, tidied our beds and swept the floor ready for the day's work, I straightened my headdress, put on a clean apron, packed my satchel and set out for the hall.

As I passed the track that led up to the church, I looked over in the direction of Ida's grave. I decided I would go and spend a few moments there with her on my way home. Preoccupied with working out who had killed her, I had forgotten the sheer sadness of her death. She was young, cheerful, pretty, and people had liked her. *Loved* her. She should have grown up to be cherished and adored by a husband and a whole clutch of children, in addition to the one who had died with her. Instead she had been brutally strangled, and now she lay in the cold ground.

I walked on, deliberately putting those thoughts to the

back of my mind. You have to approach all healing work
with the right mental attitude, and I knew I would do Lady
Emma and Lady Claude no good at all if I was brooding
about Ida. I began planning the questions I would ask and
the remedies I would prescribe, and soon the healer had
taken over from the emotional girl and the threatening tears
had been firmly put in abeyance.

Bermund showed me into the hall with only the smallest
hint of disapproval. I would not go as far as to say he was
growing to like me, but then I don't think he likes anyone,
really. It was, I felt, a major achievement that he hadn't kept
me waiting at the bottom of the steps while he went inside
to see if it was all right to admit me.

He held out a hand to stop me and walked on towards
where Lady Emma sat on a dais at the end of the hall. She,
however, had looked up at the sound of our footsteps and
was already beckoning to me to approach.

'Thank you, Bermund, that will be all,' she said softly
to him. Then, addressing me: 'Good morning, Lassair. You
have no doubt come to see Lady Claude.'

It would have been easy to bow and mumble meekly,
Yes, my lady. Recalling Edild's words, I walked right up to
her, dipped my head and instead said very quietly, 'I have
also come to attend you, Lady Emma. You are quite recovered from your faint, I hope?'

She looked up at me and smiled. I could see just by
looking at her that she was fully well again, for her face
had a good colour, her eyes shone and her hair, neatly
smoothed back under a thin gold circlet holding in place a
fine silk veil, was glossy with health. 'How very kind,' she
said. 'I am indeed, although there is a small matter I would
discuss with you.'

'Of course, my lady.' I swung my satchel down off my
shoulder and was about to put it on the floor when she stood
up and said, 'My own little concern is not grave, Lassair; I
would prefer it if first you tended to Lady Claude.' Moving
gracefully, accompanied by the swish of silk from the full
skirt of her beautiful green gown and whatever she wore
beneath, she walked regally across the hall, and I followed.

We went through the curtained doorway and up the short flight of stairs, and once again I stood outside Lady Claude's chamber. Lady Emma tapped gently on the door and called, 'Claude? Are you there?'

I was not surprised when there was no reply. Lady Claude had made it very clear what she thought of people who lay in bed all morning. I had a very good idea where she would be. Lady Emma walked on up the passage and rapped on the closed door of the sewing room, so sure, it seemed, of an immediate response of *Come in* that her hand was already on the latch.

I did not want to go back into that narrow chamber with its lurid depictions of sin. I did not want to sit closeted with Lady Claude and breathing the close, fusty air while I asked about her headaches and her insomnia. To be frank, she smelt. Her breath had the faint odour of dead meat, and I suspected that lack of fresh air and exercise had resulted in a sluggish digestion. I had herbs that would swiftly relieve her constipation, but I hesitated to offer them unless she mentioned her complaint, and I did not think she would. Besides, she troubled me, and my instinct was to get away from her. That, I told myself very firmly, was no attitude for a healer. I recalled how she had been yesterday in the churchyard, standing by the grave of her dead seamstress, rigidly controlling her distress except for those tell-tale glances at Sir Alain. She wasn't so bad after all, I realized. She might appear chilly and distant, but that little moment of weakness had proved that she was human after all.

A smile on my face, I waited to confront my patient.

Having received no answer, Lady Emma knocked again. This time when Lady Claude did not reply, she gave me a puzzled glance and opened the door.

The completed panels still hung on the walls, and I noticed that Lady Claude had stretched a new piece of canvas over the wooden embroidery frame. On it there was an outline of figures. I thought this one must be Envy; a skeletal, mean-faced woman with cruel, narrow eyes was depicted crouched at a doorway, one long, thin arm stretched out towards a plump baby in a crib. The woman's fingers were curved into hooks, her hand poised over the baby's round little head. One nail had already made contact, and there was the suggestion of a drop of blood. The image was shocking, its message plain: childless, eaten away by envy of another woman's child, the woman was about to grab what she so desperately desired.

I turned away from it, sickened.

Ida's narrow bed had been taken away. Perhaps it was too eloquent a reminder. Lady Claude's stool stood to one side of the room, around it neat piles of linen and skeins of different-coloured wools. Of the lady herself there was no sign.

'That's strange,' Lady Emma said. 'Wherever can she be?'

'Perhaps she is resting in her chamber and did not hear your knock,' I suggested. It did not seem very likely, but Lady Emma nodded, strode back along the passage and opened the door to Claude's room. The chamber was as clean and tidy as the sewing room and as empty of inhabitants.

Lady Emma seemed unreasonably disturbed by her guest's absence. Pregnant women should avoid distress, so I took her arm, gently steered her back down the steps and into the hall and helped her sit down on her grand chair. She was frowning, a deep crease cutting the smooth skin of her forehead. Her hands clutched at each other, and I noticed she was biting the inside of her lip.

'Lady Claude has probably gone outside to take the air,' I said calmly. 'It's a lovely morning, and I dare say sitting too long over her sewing was threatening to bring back her headache. I expect she's—'

Lady Emma interrupted me. With considerable force, she said, 'Claude *never* goes out! She appears for meals promptly whenever she is summoned, although she eats very little and scurries back upstairs to her sewing as soon as good manners permit. Lord Gilbert and I have repeatedly invited her to join us after supper – we do not wish her to feel unwelcome – but again she excuses herself and insists she must get on with her work. We have suggested that she goes out for a ride, or accompanies me when I take

my daily walk, but Claude will have none of it!' There was
a flush on Lady Emma's face now, and I had the impression she was heartily sick of her uncongenial house guest.
I felt very sorry for her. I know enough about the habits of
her kind to realize that, if her husband's second cousin had
come for an extended visit, she had no choice but to put
on a smile and say, *How lovely, please stay for as long as
you like!* Among the titled rich, hospitality was an almost
sacred requirement.

'Well, she's gone out now,' I pointed out, 'unless she's
hiding in some other chamber of the house!' I made my
tone light, trying to encourage Lady Emma to relax. Her
tension was making me anxious for her.

She managed a grudging smile. 'Not very likely,' she
murmured.

'Would you like me to go and look for her?' I offered.

Lady Emma's mouth opened, and I was almost sure she
had been about to protest. In a flash of understanding, I
realized it must actually be a relief to have Claude's awkward
presence out of the house for a while. Then she thought
better of it and said, 'Perhaps you should. You have come
to minister to her, Lassair, and I would not have it that you
had made a wasted journey.'

'I also came to see you, my lady,' I reminded her gently.

She turned to me, and I could see from her expression
that she was still worrying about Claude. 'So you did,' she
said absently. 'So you did . . .'

I had been about to ask her if she would like to tell me
about the small matter she had mentioned earlier, but I
sensed she was too distracted. Well, if she wanted to talk
about Claude, why not encourage her?

'You are plainly disturbed by Lady Claude's inexplicable
absence, my lady,' I said. 'Do you fear for her safety?'

As soon as the words were out of my mouth, I regretted
them. Somebody had strangled Ida; that somebody was still
out there somewhere. Was that why Lady Emma was so
worried? Because she feared that Lady Claude might also
fall victim to the unknown killer?

Lady Emma took my hand impulsively, gave it a squeeze

and released it. 'No,' she said softly. 'It's broad daylight out
there, and people are working on the water, along the shore
and in the pastures on the higher ground. Wherever Claude
is, I'm sure nobody's about to set on her.'

'What is it, then?' I prompted.

Lady Emma gave a small, embarrassed laugh. 'I suppose,
Lassair, I am a little aggrieved,' she said. 'My husband and
I have done our very best to make Claude feel welcome,
yet she has insisted on shutting herself away in that stuffy
little room and working on her linens and her embroidery.
Her industry is commendable, and I am sure Sir Alain will
greatly appreciate her efforts once they are wed, but—' I
waited. 'I am *very* surprised to discover that she has slipped
out without a word!' Lady Emma burst out. 'Why, this very
morning I suggested that the two of us take our sewing and
go out to a pleasant, shady spot that I know of down by the
water. I thought we could take the children and, if the weather
remained clement, our midday meal could be brought out
to us. Claude said – quite brusquely – that she preferred to
work in her sewing room because the bright sunshine might
fade the colours of the wools.' Her incredulous eyes met
mine. I had to agree, as an excuse it was feeble to the extent
of being almost an insult.

I did not know what to say. Since speaking about Claude
was clearly distressing her – or rather, I realized suddenly,
it was the effort of not giving in to temptation and saying
what she really thought of her guest's rudeness – it seemed
prudent to distract her. 'You could move outside now if you
wish, my lady,' I said. 'I would be happy to assist.'

Her chin went up. 'Yes, why not?' she said. Then, turning
to me, 'But there is no need for you to help, Lassair; you
will no doubt have more important calls on your time. The
servants will make the arrangements.'

I bowed my head. 'Very well, my lady.'

Shortly afterwards, I was on my way back to the village.
I had promised to make up a remedy for Lady Emma's
mild indigestion – the *small matter* – and run back with it
later. I was puzzling over where Claude might be, and why

she hadn't told her hostess she was going out, when, drawing level with the church, I saw a sudden movement.

Recalling my resolve to visit Ida's grave, my first thought was that someone else had had the same idea. Then I thought: *it might be Lady Claude.* If it was, I decided to suggest gently that Lady Emma was worried about her, hoping she would then go back to the hall and make a polite apology.

My imagination got busy with the scene back at the hall. I'd got as far as thinking Lady Emma might be grateful to me for sending her house guest home to her, when I recalled that she actually didn't seem to like Claude very much. I was so preoccupied that it took me a moment or two to realize that whoever it was by Ida's grave, it wasn't Lady Claude.

It was a man, and I had never seen him before.

He was crouched on the grass beside the grave. His eyes were closed, and he was muttering to himself, although his words were inaudible. He was probably praying. I wondered if I ought to tiptoe away; it did not seem right to disturb him. I studied him. He was, I guessed, in early middle age; maybe seven or eight years younger than my parents. He was slight, not very tall and rather hunched, as if he habitually crouched over his work. His hair was long, its colour brown streaked with grey. He wore a soft leather belt fastened over a tunic that was too big for him, as if he had lost weight and had not bothered to have the garment taken in. His hose were of good wool but much darned, although there was a fresh hole in one knee. He carried a knife in a scabbard hanging from his belt.

Then I noticed his hands. They were quite large, the fingers long and strong-looking.

I had an idea that I knew who he was. Why not ask him? If I was right, then perhaps he would take comfort in speaking to the person who had found Ida's body. I could tell him I'd found her in a sacred spot – well, it was sacred to my family, although possibly an outsider would prefer to have her lie where she now lay buried – and say that death would have been swift.

My instinct to give comfort overcame my diffidence. I

moved forward and lightly touched him on the shoulder.

He spun round, his eyes wide with surprise and fear. Instantly, I said, 'It's all right! I mean you no harm – you're Alberic, aren't you?'

His face had been pale already, but now it went ashen. He tried to speak – then, when no words emerged, he wet his thin lips and said in a horrified whisper, *'How did you know?'*

I knelt down beside him. 'We went to Brandon,' I said, careful to keep my tone even and soothing. 'My friend Sibert and I, that is. We knew that's where Ida came from, and we wanted to find out more about her.'

His eyes narrowed with suspicion. 'Why?'

'Because she died here, and we did not wish her to be buried like a stranger,' I improvised. I certainly wasn't about to say, *Because she was pregnant and we wanted to find out whose child she carried*; not when the likely father was right beside me. He might not know she'd been pregnant, and if I told him it would double his grief.

He had returned his gaze to the hump of earth over the grave. He stretched out his hand and stroked it as if he were trying to touch the dead girl beneath. 'She was so lovely,' he said, his voice breaking. 'I've loved her since she was a lass. I wanted to marry her, you know,' he added conversationally. 'But I couldn't, for I was already wed. I kept my love to myself, for Ida meant far too much to me for me to dishonour her by forcing my attentions on her when I was bound to another.' I studied him. I had just caught him telling a lie, yet there was no sign of that in his demeanour. I am usually quite good at detecting when people are lying. Squeak, for example, looks me straight in the eyes and widens his own alarmingly, and my sister Goda always sounds even gruffer than usual. I've noticed other symptoms too, such as hesitation and overemphasis of whatever falsehood people would have you believe.

This man, this Alberic, had simply stated the fact, and my initial reaction was that maybe it wasn't a lie after all . . .

'She worked for the Lady Claude,' I said. 'Lady Claude is sewing for her wedding.'

'Ida sewed beautifully,' he responded eagerly. 'That Lady Claude was lucky to have her.'

I was inclined to agree. 'Everyone seems to have liked her,' I went on. 'They speak well of her up at the hall where she and Lady Claude were lodging.'

He nodded. 'She made friends wherever she went. She had that gift – people seemed to smile more when she was around. And she was so good – her mother died when Ida was young, and she cared for her old father with such love and devotion that the priest said she was an example to all of us of how a daughter ought to be.'

I risked a smile. 'And people *still* liked her?' It is my experience that it's actually quite hard to be fond of a person who is held up as an example, especially when the one doing the holding up is a priest.

Alberic understood what I meant. Smiling too, he said, 'That they did.' He shrugged, still smiling. 'There was just something about her.'

'You weren't here by the grave when she was buried, were you?' It was a guess, for he could have been standing at the back with his head down and his hood up and I wouldn't have known.

He shot me a quick look. 'I keep to the shadows.' It was an enigmatic remark, but he did not explain. 'I shouldn't be out here now,' he added in a whisper, 'only I wanted to see the place where she lies. See it *properly*.'

Again, I didn't understand. 'There were a lot of people here,' I offered. 'Most of the village turned up, or so it seemed, and there were plenty of outsiders as well.' No need to tell him they'd undoubtedly come out of morbid curiosity because Ida was the victim of violent death. 'Lady Claude came, and Sir Alain de Villequier, who she's going to marry. *And* Lord Gilbert and Lady Emma, from Lakehall.' I pointed. 'They stood just there.'

He nodded, taking it all in. 'She'll be in heaven, won't she?'

I hesitated. We are told that few people go straight to

heaven, the majority having to spend several ages in purgatory while their sins are cleansed so that they are fit to go
before God. I am not at all sure I believe it. In any case,
it was scarcely what this grieving man wanted to hear. 'She
was good,' I said gently. 'I don't think she had any mortal
sins staining her soul.'

Strictly speaking, Ida had been guilty of fornication, for
she was pregnant and not married. I studied Alberic closely.
If it had been he who'd fathered her child then he'd know
all about the fornication and he would surely not have been
sufficiently naive to suggest she'd already be in heaven.

I reckoned I had nothing to lose by a direct question. I
said, 'Alberic, were you her lover?'

His head shot up, and he fixed me with such a piercing
stare that I flinched. I saw several emotions flash across
his face, fury and raw grief the main ones. He seemed about
to speak – I could imagine the torrent of heated words that
would probably have emerged – but then he shook his head
and turned away. After a moment he turned back to face
me and said calmly, 'No, I was not. As I told you, I loved
and respected Ida far too much to dishonour her by initi-
ating intimacy when I could not be united with her in the
eyes of God and his church. In addition –' for the first time
there was the hint of a smile, albeit a rather grim one –
'you didn't know my wife.' In a flash of memory I recalled
the man in Brandon, who'd told Sibert and me how this
same wife had tried to burn Alberic's harp just because she
thought he'd looked at a pretty girl.

'I assure you,' Alberic went on, 'if I'd as much as taken
Ida's hand, Thecla would have known. She knew I was
sweet on my lovely girl – I couldn't help that. A man can't
always be watching his expression, and I only had to look
at Ida and I'd feel myself smile. Thecla informed me in
no uncertain terms that if ever I did more than look, she'd
– well, I'm not going to tell you.' I noticed that he was
stroking his fingers along a deep scar that ran across the
back of his right wrist. It looked as if someone had tried
to cut his hand off.

And he was a harpist.

Horrified, I said, 'She threatened she'd cut your hands off. Didn't she? And at least once she did more than threaten.'

Slowly, he nodded. 'I'd just got back from the fair. There had been music, and I'd been playing and singing. Ida joined in a duet with me on one of the old songs. Although I say it myself, we sounded good together. Thecla must have seen how I looked at her. When I came indoors, she was waiting with the axe. She swung it at me before I knew what was happening.' He glanced down at his scarred hand. 'Couldn't play for two months,' he added, his tone devoid of emotion.

I was so full of pity for him that I dared not speak. I watched him. He was stroking the earth again, his large hand tender in its touch. 'My little Ida,' he murmured. 'She used to sing like a nightingale.' Then he crossed his arms on the grave, bowed his head and began to weep.

Tears filling my own eyes, I crept away.

ELEVEN

I said to my aunt as we ate our midday meal, 'I do not believe Alberic fathered Ida's baby,' and I told her about Thecla and the axe.

Edild nodded, chewing thoughtfully. I had been all ready to back up my belief, but I wasn't required to. Feeling a little warm glow inside that she should trust my judgement in something so important, I waited to see what she would say.

'*Could* it have been Derman?' she mused.

'Shall I go and ask Zarina?' I was crouched ready to spring up immediately if Edild said yes, but, with a soft laugh, she pushed me down again.

'Oh, Lassair, don't be so impatient!' She smiled affectionately at me. 'It's not really your fault,' she added, 'too much of quicksilver Mercury in your stars. What would you do? Rush round to Zarina's house and blurt out, *Hello, Zarina, I've come to ask if your brother is capable of sexual intercourse and if he might have made Ida pregnant?*'

Since I'd thought no further than that, I hung my head in embarrassment. Edild took pity on me and, reaching for my hand, she took it in hers and said, 'It is something that we do need to find out, although we must be very tactful, as I am sure you very well know.'

She had given me time to think, and now I said, 'The difficulty is that nobody except us seems to have known that Ida was pregnant, so we'll have to raise the matter with Zarina without making her suspicious.' An idea was taking shape in my mind; Edild waited patiently. Then, thinking as I spoke, I said, 'I could say that I realized Derman had taken a fancy to Ida. Then I could say that maybe he'd imagined marrying her, and that grief because she's dead, and his dream will never come true, is the reason he's run away.' I met my aunt's eyes. 'Do you think that might do?

It would be sort of like asking if Derman could be a proper husband, if he can—' I stopped, embarrassed all over again.

'Lassair, you are a healer, and you must accustom yourself to speaking of sexual intimacy between man and woman without this silly awkwardness,' she said briskly. 'However, I think your suggestion is sound.'

I leapt up. 'I'll go straight away!'

'Be careful,' she warned. 'Zarina is in turmoil.'

Turmoil. Poor Zarina.

I found her down at the little pool where she and her washerwoman widow spend much of their day. She was alone. Looking up, she saw me approaching and smiled, her eyes bright. Then, apparently reading my expression, her face fell and she said, 'No news.'

She'd thought I'd come to tell her they'd found Derman. I sank down beside her and took her hand. 'No. I'm sorry, that's not why I'm here.'

She had slumped against me but now, with a detectable effort, she straightened her back. 'Why, then?'

I sensed her slight hostility. 'Not to harangue you again about marrying Haward,' I said, and was rewarded with a fleeting grin. 'It *is* about Derman. I just wondered, Zarina –' I paused, choosing my words – 'd'you think he hoped to make Ida his wife, and that his grief because he never had the chance to do so is why he's run away?'

She looked up into the clear sky for a moment, her face working as she strove for control. Then she said, 'It is a moving thought, Lassair, and it is indeed true that he loved her very dearly. But –' now it was her turn to search for the right words – 'he is not as other men, as indeed you are aware, and he does not begin to comprehend the true nature of how a man and wife live in physical intimacy together. He—' She paused, frowning. Then she said, 'Think of him as if he were still a child, who observes a cat with her kittens or a hound with her pups and is filled with joy at the pretty young creatures, yet has no more idea of how they came to be there than if they'd appeared by magic.'

'So he—'

'He adored her from afar, Lassair,' Zarina said gently. 'He saw a lovely smile, long, shining hair, dimpled cheeks. He probably sensed a kindly heart and ready laughter. That was what he loved. I can assure you, the idea of touching her, of any sort of physical closeness between them, is just not possible.'

I studied her. Was she right, or was she telling me what she fervently hoped was the truth? Derman might still have been overcome with longing – he had the body of a man, that was clear to see – and he could have attacked Ida, raped her, impregnated her. Oh, but she'd conceived back in February or March, weeks before she'd come to Aelf Fen. It was, I supposed, possible that Derman had come across her when she had lived in Brandon – he did sometimes go off wandering, although it was a long walk to Brandon – but if he'd assaulted her then, surely she'd have accused him at the time? For sure, once she'd arrived at Lakehall and seen him, she'd have cried out against him and fled from his presence. She certainly wouldn't have been *kind* to him.

It was still possible, if unlikely, that Derman had killed Ida, perhaps because she had stopped being kind. But it appeared that neither Derman nor Alberic had fathered her baby.

Then who had?

I sat with Zarina a little longer, then old Berta came hobbling down the path from her cottage, and I could hear the vulgar abuse she was hurling at Zarina when she was still fifty paces away.

'*Go!*' hissed Zarina.

'I'll explain to her!' I cried, leaping up, filled with guilt because I'd got Zarina into trouble.

'No you won't, you'll only make it worse,' Zarina flashed back. Still I didn't move. This was the woman I fervently hoped would be my sister-in-law, and I felt I ought to defend her. 'I know how to deal with Berta,' Zarina said firmly. She, too, had risen to her feet, and I noticed how much taller she was than the crude, fat old woman for whom she worked. 'Go on!' she repeated, and this time she was smiling.

I went.

*　　*　　*

Edild and I worked hard all afternoon. Midsummer is a busy time for us. Although the warm, dry weather means less serious sickness – for we believe that the all-penetrating damp of the fens is the cause of many of the illnesses that crop up again and again – nevertheless, late June is the time when many plants are at their best, and we dare not waste the opportunity to harvest what we will need for the remainder of the year. The struggle to remember the hundreds of facts with which my aunt daily bombards me often wakes me in the night, when I lie there in the dark telling myself silently *hemp nettle for open wounds, use the flowering stems,* and *woodruff flowers for ulcers, rashes and heart palpitations.* I was heavy with fatigue by the time we stopped work, more than ready to eat, drink and, above all, rest. However, when the long day finally ended, we had a visitor: Hrype.

I had the usual dilemma over whether I ought to leave the two of them on their own but, reading my thoughts as easily as if I'd spoken them aloud, Hrype said kindly, 'Stay, Lassair. The three of us must talk together.' *About what?* I wondered, starting to feel anxious, but he read that too and added, 'I saw Edild while you were with Zarina. We all are puzzled by the same question, and the time has come to share our thoughts with each other.'

Ida's baby, I thought. I did as he bade and sat down beside the hearth, my aunt beside me and Hrype opposite to us. He said, 'We do not know who killed Ida and, even if we are not convinced by those in the village who lay the crime at the feet of poor Derman, still it remains true that little progress can be made until either he is found or returns to Aelf Fen of his own accord. You found him close to the island, Lassair –' he turned his strange eyes to me – 'and it seems logical that his distress could well have been caused by having seen something pertaining to the girl's death, even if we do not go so far as to say he had a hand in it.' He paused. 'However, Ida's death is not the only tragedy: there is also the matter of the young life that was within her when she died. Ida may in some way have brought about her own death; we cannot say until we know more of the circumstances.' I was about to protest – whatever could a girl of my age have done to deserve being strangled and stuffed in someone else's grave? – but my aunt caught my eye and silently shook her head, so I stayed quiet.

'The child, however,' Hrype continued, 'was innocent. No sin of its mother could be its fault. It was blameless. The same, though, cannot necessarily be said of the man who fathered it. There are many reasons why a man will not, or cannot, admit to paternity.'

There was a short silence. We were all thinking the same thing, I was quite sure, for Hrype himself had not told his own son of their true relationship until last year, and his reasons for keeping the secret from Sibert had been sound, even if Sibert found that hard to accept.

None of us referred to Hrype's own history. None of us needed to.

'It is this perplexing question, of who fathered Ida's child,' Hrype went on after a moment, 'to which we must now address ourselves. You are convinced that neither Derman nor this man, Alberic, was the girl's lover?' He looked at Edild, then at me. Both of us nodded our heads. 'Very well. Ida came to Lakehall about a month ago, in the employ of Lady Claude de Seés, and the reason for *her* visit was to allow her to spend some time getting to know her future husband, Sir Alain de Villequier, who, as our justiciar, was already resident in this area. As Lady Claude's treasured seamstress, it was natural for her to accompany her mistress, who was to be working on her trousseau whilst under Lord Gilbert's roof.' He paused. 'You judge, Edild, that the child was conceived at the end of February?'

Edild nodded. 'Thereabouts, yes.'

'Then her lover was someone she knew at home, either in the village where she lived or at Lady Claude's family estate of Heathlands,' Hrype said.

'The man whom Sibert and I talked to in Brandon said she didn't have any followers among the village lads,' I put in. 'He said she had a nice way of putting them off and that she treated them like brothers.'

'I wonder why that was?' Edild mused. 'Was she, do you

think, aware of Alberic's devotion and quietly, unobtrusively, returning it?'

'It would explain why no handsome village boy ever took her fancy,' Hrype agreed.

But I shook my head. 'Alberic would not agree,' I said firmly. 'According to him, he never let her know he loved her.'

'Perhaps he did not need to,' Edild said shrewdly. 'Perhaps she loved him in total ignorance of his feelings for her and never dared let him know because of this gorgon of a wife you speak of, Lassair.'

'Mm, I suppose it's possible,' I agreed, although reluctantly. 'If Ida knew Thecla had tried to cut off Alberic's hand because he'd sung with her, she'd make even more certain no one ever found out what she felt for him. *If* she felt it,' I added firmly.

'You do not believe she did?' Hrype asked. His eyes on mine were as disconcerting as ever.

But I made myself stare right back. 'I do not,' I said.

'Why?' he persisted.

'Because she was young, pretty, lively, she laughed readily, she was kind to people and much beloved,' I said in a rush. 'He was married to a dragon, he was much older than her, and she could have done so much better.'

The last observation had flowed out without my intending it. Alberic couldn't help being almost old enough to be Ida's father, and it was unkind to diminish his undoubted love for her and say she could have done better. I'd said it now, however. I waited for my aunt or Hrype to comment.

For a while neither of them did. Then Hrype said, more generously that I felt I deserved, 'For myself, I am prepared to accept what Lassair feels so strongly. Of the three of us, it is she who is closest to Ida in age. Let us propose, then, that Ida met her lover after she had gone to work up at Heathlands. Let us say that he was perhaps a stable boy, a young groom, a household servant—'

'That's more reasonable,' Edild observed. 'After all, Ida was a seamstress so she would have been more likely to fall for someone else working inside the house.'

I was thinking. 'You said that Lady Claude's family needs a grand title and Sir Alain de Villequier needs money, and that's why they're marrying,' I said.

Hrype smiled faintly. 'In essence, that is so.'

'Then the manor – Heathlands – is luxurious?'

'They say so.'

'A huge staff of indoor servants?'

'Probably.'

I grinned. 'Then we shall just have to narrow down the likely boys and young men till we find the one that was Ida's lover.'

Edild smiled too, but hers was slightly pitying. 'You intend to march up to Heathlands, demand admittance and start asking highly personal and embarrassing questions of all the male servants?'

'Oh.' She was right. Whatever had I been thinking?

Hrype reached out and took Edild's hand. He muttered something – it might have been, *Don't crush her enthusiasm* – and turned to me.

'You reason well,' he said. 'Yet, as Edild implies, you have not thought your idea to its conclusion.'

'I—' I began.

He held up his hand. 'I have a suggestion.'

I looked at him, feeling both excited and apprehensive. 'Yes?' I prompted.

'You recall, no doubt, that it was I who told you both about Lady Claude and Sir Alain's background?' Edild and I nodded. 'And you will also recall the source of my information.' It wasn't a question; he knew we'd remember.

'Your wizard friend Gurdyman,' I said.

'Quite right,' Hrype agreed. 'He is, as I told you, an authority on the history of the great Norman families. It is, as he is wont to say, a wise man who strives to comprehend his enemy. His knowledge of the de Caudebecs, the de Seés and the de Villequiers is, as I told you, extensive, although whether it extends to the number and nature of the male indoor servants at Heathlands, I cannot say.'

I smiled. I thought he was making a joke.

'We will,' he said, rising to his feet, 'just have to go and ask him.'

He was looking straight at me, an enquiring look on his face.

'You're asking *me*?' *Me* came out as a squeak.

His smile broadened. 'Yes, Lassair. Will you come to Cambridge with me and speak to my wizard?'

There was only one answer. 'Yes.'

There was plenty of time during the night for me to regret my impetuosity. Cambridge was half a day's walk away; perhaps a little less now, when the weather was good and the roads and tracks correspondingly dry and firm. Hrype and I might well have to stay overnight with this wizard friend of his, which was quite alarming enough a prospect, but in addition we'd be travelling away from our village without Lord Gilbert's knowledge or permission. For the same reason that Sibert and I couldn't reveal that we were going to Brandon or why, Hrype would have to keep our mission to Cambridge a secret. Still, I comforted myself as I tried to make myself relax into sleep, it wouldn't be the first time I'd left the village without permission, and it probably wouldn't be the last.

No. What really alarmed me about the morning's mission was the prospect of a day or more with Hrype. I'd done that before too – travelled on my own with him, I mean – but I'd been quite a lot younger. I'd been scared of him then. Now, when I knew quite a lot more about him, that fear had not receded. If anything, it had increased. I couldn't say tomorrow, *Sorry, Hrype, I've changed my mind, and I'm not coming*. You just didn't say things like that to Hrype. Besides, it hadn't escaped my notice that he could perfectly well have gone to consult this Gurdyman by himself. He didn't need me there with him to ask the right questions.

There had to be something else. Was there some element in this mission that presented a chance for Hrype to further my studies into his own particular type of magic? It was perfectly possible, considering we were going to visit a

wizard. What would the new lesson be? I could barely dare
to think . . .

That was the real reason why I couldn't sleep.

Edild woke me as the dawn was lightening the sky, to a
chorus of birdsong so loud that I was amazed I'd slept
through it. She must have known how nervous I was, but
she made me eat and drink, reminding me I had a long
walk ahead. While I washed and dressed, she packed up
food and a flask of water and set them ready by the door.
I checked in my leather satchel to make sure I had my basic
kit of remedies – you never know when someone's going
to call on a healer – and I also packed my wash cloth and
my shawl. The nights could be chilly, and I had no idea
whether or not I'd be back in my own bed that night.

There came a soft tap on the door. Edild opened it, and
Hrype looked in. Seeing that I was ready, he nodded and said,
'We'd best be on our way before curious eyes look out to
see us.'

I slipped out of the house and, side by side, we set off
for Cambridge.

We reached the town shortly before midday. I had no idea
what to expect. I'd been to Ely, and I'd seen the port of
Dunwich from a distance, but Ely had struck me as a random
collection of buildings round an abbey and, as I said, I
hadn't had the chance to see Dunwich at close quarters.

Cambridge was a revelation.

As we'd walked along, Hrype had told me that the town
had been occupied before the Romans had come. For ages
now the town had held a market that was famous in the
area and a great attraction to local tradesmen and their
customers. The Vikings had sacked, burned and destroyed
the town, only to have the irrepressible residents build it
up again even better than before. It had burned again only
three years ago, when holding out for the Duke of Normandy
against King William. The first King William – our present
king's iron-fisted father – had built a castle on the north of
the town's river, up on a specially constructed earth motte,

and on the south bank of the river there were extensive wharfs for the barges bringing goods to Cambridge from far and near. A sturdy bridge spanned the water, busy with a variety of traffic, from heavy carts to fleet-footed lads weaving in and out of the throng. There was a definite air of purpose and general busyness. Many of today's towns-folk were, according to Hrype, very prosperous.

We crossed the bridge, and as we entered the maze of narrow, crooked streets, my eyes were wide open in wonder. There were so many houses – most of them timber-framed, although some of the smaller ones were mud-brick – and all had thatched roofs. The evidence of the fire three years ago was still visible, although it looked as if the towns-people had been as swift to rebuild as they had been in Viking times, and many of the dwellings were clearly new. There were even one or two big houses made of stone, most certainly the dwellings of the very rich, for everyone knew stone had to be imported into the fens, where we have none of our own. The buildings huddled together shoulder to shoulder, all but blocking out the daylight. The only open space appeared to be where there was a church. We passed one that had a tower reaching up into the wide sky, and Hrype said it was dedicated to St Benedict and had been built by the Saxons.

Hrype led the way down a dark little alley that dived off between an imposing stone building and a smaller, clay-walled house. The entrance to the alley was concealed by a wood-roofed stall that jutted out from the smaller house. A very large woman stood behind a trestle table inside the stall, from which she was selling pies and loaves of bread. Busy yelling out mouth-watering descriptions of the food on offer, she barely glanced at Hrype and me as we slipped past her.

The alley went dead-straight for about five or six paces, then turned abruptly to the right. We were now in an even narrower passage, with the rear wall of the clay house on our right and another, similar dwelling on our left. We twisted and turned down several more alleys and, although I tried to memorize the turnings this way and that, I soon realized that I was lost. Presently, we came to a set of steps leading up to a stout, iron-studded wooden door set in a graceful stone arch. Hrype sprang up the steps and tapped on the door. Nothing happened for what seemed like a long time. Then the door opened just a crack and a pair of keen eyes peered out.

'Hrype!' cried the owner of the eyes. The opening widened enough to admit us, and swiftly we were ushered inside.

The passageways had been quite dark, shaded as they were by the buildings on either side. The light out there, however, had been bright in comparison to the interior of this house, and for some time, as my eyes adjusted, I could barely make out anything except vague shapes. We were led down a corridor and, lacking my sight, my other senses seemed to sharpen as if to compensate. I could hear two distinct sounds, one of which was a sort of fizzing, as if something were sizzling in hot fat over a fire. The other was the steady breathing of the person leading the way down the passage.

The air smelt strange: incense mixed with other elements, one of which I thought could be cinnamon. There was also an animal smell, like goats. I sniffed cautiously. In my work with Edild I have learned not to sniff hard at an untried substance as the effect can be disturbing. I detected rosemary, which I know is used to increase the potency of a mixture, and also something that I thought might be bay laurel, although it seemed strangely sweet, as if the leaves were being steeped in honey. In addition, there was a metallic tang that I was rather afraid might be blood.

We turned to the right, went down some steps, left along another passage, and then left again, down more steps that led through a low archway. The room into which we emerged was lit by a single candle and seemed to be vast, as if a cellar had been hollowed out beneath this house and perhaps the one next to it. Very quickly, however, I realized that this had been an illusion; I was probably still disorientated by the twists and turns of the walk through the dark corridors. Recovering, I stared around me and saw a small, square room, its vaulted roof supported by several thick pillars.

A workbench ran along the wall to the right of the steps, there were shelves of bottles and jars on the wall opposite and, to the left, a low cot on which there was a pillow and a stack of neatly-folded blankets. Beside it there was a little table covered with rolls and sheets of vellum and a quill pen beside a small flask of ink. Beyond the cot, the wall was covered with a large, heavy hanging. If there was a design or pattern on the hanging, the light was too dim for me to make it out.

My eyes were drawn to that single candle flame burning on the workbench. Now that I was able to detect more detail, I saw that there was a bulbous glass container suspended over the candle, resting on a three-legged iron stand. Some dark liquid was bubbling away in the container, and it was, I realized, the source of both the loud fizzing noise and the curious smell.

What on earth was going on? What terrible, secret potion was being created down here in this hidden, underground room? Did those jumbled pages of vellum contain the formula that all men sought, the one that bestowed eternal youth? I felt a shiver of dread slide down my back, and I took an involuntary step closer to Hrype. Hrype was weird, and at times very frightening, but at least he was familiar . . .

The person who had admitted us was bending over the candle and lighting others from its flame. He – or it could have been she, for I couldn't yet tell – had his back to us, and I was able to study him in the waxing light. He was short – almost a head shorter than me – and gave the impression of a certain rotundity, unless this was because he was bulked out by the voluminous garments he wore. It was chilly in the room, and he appeared to be wearing several layers, topped off by a generously-sized and gloriously-coloured shawl with a long fringe, which covered his head and shoulders and almost touched the floor at the back.

There were now seven candles burning brightly on the workbench. The person turned round, flung back his shawl and looked right at me. He was a man of late middle age, his hair styled like that of a monk, with a bald crown surrounded

by a fluff of hair. His eyes were bright blue and full of
laughter, set in a face with regular features and a wide mouth.
There was something odd about him, and I soon saw what it
was: although he was quite old and his hair was white, his
face appeared to be almost completely unlined.

He stepped towards me, studying me intently. I felt a
strange sensation – it was as if someone were running a
feather all over my skin – and I knew this man was looking
inside my mind. I wanted to drop my eyes, for the sensation that he was somehow creeping into my head was
disconcerting, but his gaze held me and I could not look
away. Something in me began a timid protest at the intru-
sion and, almost without my volition, I made a feeble attempt
to raise my defences. After a few moments, the feeling
altered subtly, and in place of the stern inquisition I felt
approbation and welcome.

Hrype was standing behind me. He said, addressing the
man, 'May I present Lassair?' Pushing me forward, he
added, 'Lassair, this is Gurdyman.'

TWELVE

Hrype watched as the man who was his mentor and friend studied the girl. Hrype had been looking out for an opportunity to bring the two together for some time now, and the need to discover more about the household of Ida's former mistress had presented the perfect excuse to bring Lassair here.

Hrype was almost certain now that Lassair had a quite extraordinary gift. He knew that Edild felt the same, although she was hesitant to say so because she feared that her love for the girl was making her see things that were not truly there. Bringing Lassair to meet Gurdyman was the test: the sage had schooled and trained many young men and women, and he always recognized talent if it was there. Hrype might still be wrong about her, but he did not think so.

He studied her, reaching out with his senses and testing her mood. She was afraid – well, that was only natural, since even someone with a fraction of her gift would sense what Gurdyman was and fear it – but she was also excited and extremely curious. He looked at Gurdyman, and just for a heartbeat Gurdyman looked at him and one eyelid closed in a swift wink.

She had, it appeared, passed the first test.

Gurdyman was speaking to her. Hrype relaxed and began to listen.

'I have almost finished down here,' the sage was saying, 'and indeed I had hoped to have concluded my work before you arrived, in which case I could have been upstairs ready to greet you.'

'But—' Lassair began, only to blush and cut off whatever remark she had been about to say.

Gurdyman looked kindly at her. 'But?'

'I thought – well, I saw the cot over there –' she nodded

towards the little bed – 'and I assumed you *lived* down here. All the time, I mean.'

Gurdyman chuckled. 'It was a reasonable assumption, but wrong,' he said, still smiling. 'However, very often my work demands that I spend many hours here in my little crypt, and then I am grateful to be able to restore myself with short periods of sleep. Now –' he turned away from Lassair and went back to his workbench – 'let me just see how this is progressing . . .'

Nothing happened for quite some time. Hrype, used to Gurdyman's ability to forget everything and everyone when his attention was focused on an experiment, stood still, enjoying the moment of restorative calm. He was aware of Lassair beside him trying, not very successfully, to quiet her breathing and restrain her impatience.

Presently, Gurdyman nodded, muttered something and blew out the candle beneath the glass container. He spun round, rubbing his hands together, and, catching sight of his guests, gave a start. Recovering quickly, he said, 'Dear me, I do apologize. I had momentarily forgotten you were there.' Then he blew out all but one of the other candles and, picking up this last one, led them out of his cellar, along the passage and back up the steps. He turned away from the door that opened on to the alley and went towards the back of the house, passing a door on the left before opening one immediately in front of him. He flung it open and, standing back, ushered his guests into the space beyond.

Hrype heard Lassair give the same surprised exclam-ation that he had given the first time Gurdyman had brought him here. In a bustling, rapidly growing town where the dwellings fought for space and people lived on top of each other, the sage had contrived a secret, leafy space within the walls of his house that was open to the sky. He had once revealed to Hrype that the concept originated in the far south, where the sun beat fiercely down and there was no rest without shade, and where people who had the means constructed little courtyards in the middle of their houses where they could sit and enjoy the air whilst remaining cool and comfortable under the specially-planted trees. 'In the

south it is palm trees and the like,' he had added. 'Here in
the cooler north, I have had to adapt.'

In Gurdyman's courtyard a vine covered one wall, a wild
rose another, and in a large earthenware pot grew a very
healthy-looking bay tree with fragrant, glossy leaves. There
was a wooden table in the centre of the paved floor and,
beside it, a sturdy oak chair with a high, carved back and
arms ending in dragon claws. A smaller table stood to the
right of the chair; on it lay a rolled manuscript, a horn of
ink and a quill. There was also a bench, which Gurdyman
now pulled forward so that it was on the opposite side of
the table from his chair.

'Sit down,' he urged his guests. 'I will bring refresh-
ments. Enjoy the sunshine and the sweet air,' he exhorted
them, 'for it is good to be outside again after the fug in my
crypt.'

He spun round and dipped back inside, humming to
himself. Hrype, sensing Lassair's tension, waited. When she
could contain herself no longer, she burst out in a hissing
whisper, 'What was he making down there?'

Hrype smiled to himself. 'Why don't you ask him?'

'I daren't!'

'He frightens you?'

'He—' She paused. 'Yes.'

Hrype did not reply. There was no need for her, of all
people, to fear the sage, but it was up to her to find that
out for herself. She would not believe him, Hrype decided,
if he told her.

They waited. After some time Gurdyman returned, bringing
mugs of beer, lightly flavoured with honey and rosemary,
and roughly-sliced chunks of gingerbread. He urged both
food and drink on his guests, and only when they had
consumed all they wanted did he sit back, fold his hands
across the curve of his stomach and say, 'Now, then. Hrype
sent word that you had something to ask me.' He looked
enquiringly at Lassair.

She in turn spun round to Hrype, who almost laughed at
her terrified expression. 'Go on,' he murmured, 'he won't turn
you into a goblin.'

She gave a sort of snort, which might have been hyster-
ical laughter. Then she gathered her courage and said, with
admiral brevity, 'A young woman has been killed. She was
from Brandon, but came to Aelf Fen with her mistress, Lady
Claude de Seés, being her seamstress. Ida – that's the dead
girl – was pregnant, and the child must have been fathered
by someone she knew before she came to our area. She
had no followers among the young men of the village – an
older man who loved her did no more than admire her from
afar – so her lover must have been someone she knew when
she worked for Lady Claude at Heathlands. We – er, Hrype
says you know quite a lot about Lady Claude's kin, so I
hoped you might be able to tell us of the household at
Heathlands, so we could perhaps make a guess as to which
of the servants fathered the child.'

She had done well, Hrype thought, silently applauding
her. She had kept out all unnecessary detail, which suggested
she had already realized that Gurdyman's exceptional intelligence and astute mind needed nothing but the bones of a
tale. He waited to see how the sage would respond.

With a question, as it turned out, and a not altogether
unexpected one: 'Why do you concern yourself with this
matter?' he asked Lassair.

'Because people think a simple-minded man called Derman
killed Ida, and I'm sure he didn't,' she replied promptly.
'Ida was not married, and my suspicion is that her lover
discovered she bore his child and killed her so that her condition did not become known. Perhaps he did not wish to marry
her, or was already wed, and such a revelation would have
ruined him.'

'You know of this child she carried,' Gurdyman observed.

'Yes, my aunt Edild and I realized she was pregnant as
soon as we saw her – my aunt's a healer – but since it was
us who laid her out, nobody else found out, and we have told
nobody but Hrype, and now you.'

'You, too, are a healer,' Gurdyman murmured.

Lassair looked momentarily disconcerted and even
slightly annoyed, as if she were wondering why Gurdyman
had ignored all that she had said about Ida and was speaking

of her. Hrype, who knew him well, did not doubt that the sage had heard, digested and decided upon every word. The truth was, Hrype decided, that Gurdyman was far more interested in Lassair than in the mission that had brought her to him.

'I'm *learning* to be a healer,' Lassair said shortly.

Gurdyman sat forward in his chair, his compact and beautifully-shaped hands grasping the dragon claws that formed its arms. 'I have visited Heathlands,' he said. 'I knew Ralf de Caudebec, who fought with the Conqueror, for although we did not agree on the subject of kings, there were other matters on which we were happy to share our thoughts. Through him I met his cousin Claritia, mother of your Lady Claude, and I have been a guest at Heathlands on several occasions, the last one at the time when a husband had been selected for the elder daughter of the house.'

'The one who fell sick,' Lassair put in.

Gurdyman nodded. 'Indeed she did.'

Hrype waited to see if Lassair felt sufficiently comfortable now with the sage to ask the question that he sensed burning in her. She did. 'What was the matter with her?'

Gurdyman did not speak for a few moments, and it seemed to Hrype that he withdrew into himself as if searching for whatever thoughts and impressions he had had at the time. 'I believe,' he said after a while, 'that Geneviève de Seés suffered a severe shock, and that the fear engendered in her by this experience turned her mind.'

Hrype listened attentively, for he had not heard this theory of Gurdyman's. *I did not ask the right question*, he thought ruefully.

'What sort of experience?' Lassair was saying.

Gurdyman weighed his words. 'Geneviève is a shy young woman, very modest, sheltered and innocent. Her mother was, I believe, wrong to push the proposed marriage. It was her desire to unite the de Seés with the de Villequiers that drove her, but she ought to have had more thought for her elder daughter's suitability for the match.'

'Sir Alain's quite a nice man,' Lassair said. 'He seems sympathetic and kindly, and he's—'

Gurdyman put up a hand. 'I do not speak of his nature, but of Geneviève's,' he said. 'She was, as I said, an innocent. She had been told by her mother what a wife is to expect on her wedding night – knowing Claritia, who is a somewhat coarse and insensitive woman, I do not imagine she spoke gently or cautiously – and Geneviève was said to be fearful and apprehensive. Then, as negotiations proceeded, she was found one morning wandering outside in the cold dressed in nothing but a thin shift. She had seen something that had terrified her, or so it was deduced, but she was unable to say what it was. The result, however, was that her quite understandable nervousness concerning the proposed marriage turned to abject horror. Then, when her mother attempted in her robust way to bring Geneviève to her senses, the girl fainted dead away and could not be revived for two days. Since then she has been a slight, silent shadow who flits on the periphery of her family's life and, in the main, is left alone.'

Hrype watched Lassair digest this. Her face revealed her emotions very clearly. Then she said, 'So Lady Claude had to be betrothed to Sir Alain instead, even though it meant giving up her desire to be a nun.'

'She did.' Gurdyman sighed. 'Claritia must have seen all her hopes of allying her insignificant family with the de Villequiers, and thereby regaining the position in society that she believes is her rightful one, rapidly disappearing. Claude did not stand up to her mother's determination for very long.'

'Hrype said she shaved her head and started wearing a nun's habit,' Lassair said. Hrype was gratified that she had remembered.

Gurdyman smiled sadly. 'She did, although it did her no good. The maltreatment was what finally wore away her resolve.' He drew a hand over his face. 'For a mother to beat and starve a daughter is cruel, but Claritia is a determined woman.'

Nobody spoke for some moments. It was as if, Hrype reflected, all three of them were quietly sympathizing with

Claude; mourning with her for the life she had wanted so desperately and been so ruthlessly forced to give up.

It was Lassair who broke the silence. 'Please, sir,' she said, eyes fixed on Gurdyman, 'will you tell us if you can think of any boy or young man in the service of Lady Claude's family who could have fathered Ida's child?'

Hrype watched the sage and the young healer, each focused so thoroughly on the other that he might not have been there. He sensed Gurdyman's interest in the girl; his fascination, even, for Hrype could feel how the sage was sending out subtle probes into Lassair's mind, testing, assessing, exploring. She was holding her own. Amused, Hrype saw her shake her head violently as if ridding herself of a persistent wasp, at which Gurdyman, with a wide grin, withdrew.

'I will tell you what you wish to know as well as I am able,' he said. 'Heathlands is a very well-run, efficient household, as anyone would expect who was acquainted with Lady Claritia, for she is a hard mistress and tolerates no laziness, slackness or mistakes. There is no need to look beyond the indoor servants for your girl's lover, for in truth I can think of no circumstances in which she would have been free to form the necessary liaison with any of the outdoor workers. She would barely have had the opportunity to meet any of them, never mind take one as her lover.' He paused, frowning thoughtfully.

'And the indoor servants?' Lassair asked eagerly.

'It is possible that some handsome lad caught her eye, but, again, there is the question of opportunity,' Gurdyman said slowly. 'Ida would have slept in Lady Claude's quarters, the lady being fanatical about the needlework she was producing for her marriage and insisting that Ida guard the finished objects and the costly materials at all times.'

'Yes, she did the same when they were at Lakehall,' Lassair put in. 'That's her cousin Lord Gilbert's manor, on the edge of our village.'

'Yes, I know of Lord Gilbert,' Gurdyman murmured.

Once more, silence fell. Hrype sensed the frustration build up in Lassair until it spilled over and she cried, '*Somebody*

fathered Ida's child! It can't be anyone she met since she
went to Lakehall, because she was already pregnant when
she arrived there. She didn't have lovers among the village
lads and the man who wanted so badly to marry her once
he was free to do so never *touched* her!' She paused for
breath. 'Now you say she wouldn't have had the chance to
meet a lover while she was at Heathlands, so what are we
to conclude?' She looked round at Hrype, and he saw that
her grey-green eyes were alight with the strength of her
passion. The crescent moon scar on her left cheek stood
out white against her flushed skin.

Pitying her, he said, 'If the suggestion is that it was this
unknown lover who killed her, his reason being that he had
cause to fear the revelation of her secret, then should we
not ask whether any of the other servants accompanied Lady
Claude from Heathlands to Lakehall?'

Lassair flashed him a beaming smile. 'Yes!' she breathed.
'Yes, of course, he loved her, and he'd have wanted to be
with her, so he'd have—' But then her face fell. 'Lady
Claude wouldn't take a male servant,' she said dully. 'Would
she? I mean, what would he do for her that Lord Gilbert's
staff couldn't do? She only took Ida because she was such
a good seamstress. She didn't even take a personal maid,
or if she did, nobody's told me, and I tended her when she
was unwell so I'd have probably met or heard about any
maid then.'

Hrype watched as she shouldered her disappointment.
He understood why this mattered so much to her, and he
wondered if she would confess her interest to Gurdyman.
It would depend, he mused, what impressions she was
forming of the sage . . .

Favourable ones, it appeared. 'My brother is in love with
Derman's sister, Zarina,' she said suddenly, addressing
Gurdyman. 'Derman's the—'

'The simpleton accused of murdering Ida,' Gurdyman
supplied. 'You said.'

'Derman's run away,' Lassair went on, undeterred by the
mild irony, 'which might be a good thing, since Zarina says
she can't marry Haward – my brother – because she doesn't

want to impose Derman on my family, but the problem with
that is that she really cares about him and she won't be
happy all the time he's missing and she's so worried about
him. So you see—'

'You must discover who really killed Ida, so that Derman
may be exonerated and return home and Zarina's fears for
him will cease,' Gurdyman finished smoothly. 'Whereupon
she will realize she was wrong in permitting the existence
of her brother to come between her and Haward, and they
will marry and be as happy as you have seen them to be.'

Lassair's mouth dropped open. 'You – *how did you
know?*'

Gurdyman laughed delightedly. 'I did not know, I guessed,'
he corrected her. 'You have a set of runes in your satchel,
unless I am much mistaken, and they resonate with your
power. You have just revealed what is uppermost in your
mind: over and above your determination to find out who
killed the young woman and her unborn child, you want
your brother to be happy because you love him dearly.
Therefore, I concluded that what drove you to consult the
runes was your overwhelming desire to know if all will end
aright for him.'

'The runes showed them together,' Lassair whispered.
'They were laughing, and they were devoted to each other.'
Gurdyman nodded. 'Was that true? Did I read it right?' she
asked him.

Gurdyman said gently, 'The runes are enigmatic, Lassair.
It is very often the case that we consult them and end up
less than satisfied, for reading is in itself a complicated
business and one which takes many, many years to learn.'
He glanced at Hrype, his bright eyes crinkled in a smile.
'Hrype here is a rune master,' he said, 'and if he is prepared
to teach you, you are fortunate indeed.'

'She shows some promise,' Hrype allowed.

'In this case, however,' Gurdyman went on, 'I believe
that a simple question received a simple answer.'

Lassair went on staring at him. 'You mean—' she began.

But he shook his head. 'Do not ask me,' he said with sudden
firmness. 'It is between you and the spirits who guide you;

I will say no more.' Hrype watched as she slumped down on her seat, a small frown of perplexity on her face. Then Gurdyman got to his feet, took Hrype's arm and drew him over to the small table beside his chair. Unrolling the manuscript, he spread it on the larger table, and Hrype, staring down at it, recognized what it was.

'You have done it!' he exclaimed.

'No, no, for I cannot claim to have produced anything other than the vaguest of outlines,' Gurdyman said. 'It is here in my head –' he tapped the bald dome of his skull – 'but I am unable to find a satisfactory way of expressing what I see in my mind in a visible form.'

Lassair's interest was piqued. Hrype saw her quietly get up and lean over to look at the manuscript. 'What are you trying to do?' she asked.

Gurdyman spun round to her. 'You travelled here to Cambridge from Aelf Fen this morning, did you not?'

'Yes.'

'Then think, if you will, of the line made by your feet as you journeyed. Think of the land over which you passed, the streams and rivers that you crossed, the hamlets, villages and towns you passed.'

'Ye–es.'

'Now, imagine I asked you how to get from here to Aelf Fen. What instructions would you give me?'

She closed her eyes and said, 'Leave your house, turn right, then left, then right again, then – oh, several more lefts and rights until you emerge into the street. Go on past the big stone houses, past the quays and over the bridge, then go right, and on through the outskirts of the town till you—'

'Yes, that will do,' Gurdyman interrupted smoothly. 'Now, Lassair, instead of telling me, draw it for me.' He smoothed out another piece of manuscript – it had clearly been a practise piece and was fluffy from erasures – and held out his quill.

Hrype could see in her face that she was at a loss. Nevertheless, she tried, and, quickly becoming absorbed in the challenge, soon had drawn a wiggling line that made abrupt turns here and there, passed swiftly-sketched trees and buildings, and finally ran off the edge of the parchment. 'Aelf Fen is sort of there,' she said, pointing to a place halfway across the table.'

Gurdyman smiled. 'A good attempt,' he observed, 'although I fear your drawing would not help me find your village if I did not already know where it was.'

'Oh.' She looked downcast.

'Do not be distressed,' Gurdyman said brightly. 'Many wise men are working on this problem, and not a few do worse than you, my girl.'

'What is the destination that you are trying to illustrate?' she asked, leaning against Hrype as she studied the manuscript, peering as she tried to make out the tiny writing and the details of the colourful little pictures.

'Can you read?' Gurdyman asked.

'A little. My aunt is teaching me, as well as instructing me in the use of written letters.'

'A sensible skill for a healer,' the sage remarked. 'You cannot, however, read that word?' He pointed.

'No.'

Hrype could: the word was *Rus*, and it was written over an area on the right hand side of the parchment. But then Hrype had the advantage of knowing what Gurdyman was trying to do.

Like Hrype's own ancestors, Gurdyman's forefathers had come from Sweden. Explorers and traders, they had manoeuvred their long ships south and east down the great rivers of the mighty, endless land mass that stretched apparently into infinity, encountering people who spoke different tongues, worshipped different gods, wore different dress, ate different food. They had sold the goods that their own lands produced in such abundance – chiefly furs – and brought back extraordinary objects unheard of in the homelands. Hrype's own ancestor had brought the jade from which Hrype's runes were made; Gurdyman's uncle had brought the glorious, heavy silk shawl that he habitually wore. Gurdyman, with his quick, enquiring mind that ranged far and wide and recognized no boundaries, was attempting to translate the ancestral voyages into a form that could be read like writing on a page.

Hrype became aware that Lassair was trying to attract his attention. Turning with some effort from his fascinated study of Gurdyman's work, he raised his eyebrows in impatient enquiry. 'If we go now we can be back by dark,' she whispered.

He studied her for a moment, and he understood. She was upset because she had failed to find the answer she had gone looking for, and the talk of the journey to Aelf Fen had prompted the strong desire for home. 'Very well,' he said.

Gurdyman led them back along the passage to the door on to the alley. He, too, seemed to recognize Lassair's dejection. Stopping beside the open door, he said, 'I am sorry that I could not help you.'

'It doesn't matter,' she said, managing a smile. 'It was good to meet you anyway.'

He bowed. 'Thank you. We shall meet again.'

Lassair, apparently unable to think how to answer, merely nodded.

Hrype had followed her down the steps and was about to turn to take his leave when Gurdyman said thoughtfully, 'What has Sir Alain to say on the matter?'

Hrype looked at Lassair, then said, 'What matter?'

Gurdyman tutted. 'The lad at Heathlands who made Ida pregnant.'

Hrype saw his own incomprehension mirrored in Lassair's expression. 'What would he know of the household there?' he asked. 'He didn't know Lady Claude personally before she came to Lakehall. The idea, or so we understand, was for her to stay with her cousin Lord Gilbert while she met and became acquainted with her future husband, who had recently been appointed justiciar and was living close by.' He shook his head. 'Sir Alain de Villequier would not know any more about the servants at Lady Claude's home than she chose to tell him, and I can't imagine the two of them are so desperate for conversation that they have to discuss the staff.'

Lassair gave a little gasp. Gurdyman turned to her, his eyes twinkling. 'And what has Lassair to say?' he enquired.

'We have made a false assumption,' she whispered. 'We all thought that Lady Claude went to Lakehall to meet her future husband. We believed that the marriage designed to unite the two families – first between Sir Alain and Lady Geneviève and, when that failed, Lady Claude – was arranged before the bridegroom had met either bride. That is not so, is it?' She looked up at Gurdyman standing on the steps, her eyes wide.

'No, it was not,' he said. 'Sir Alain was a frequent visitor at Heathlands. Before he was awarded his new appointment and went to live at Alderhall, his home was close to Thetford. He used to ride over regularly to play chess with Claritia, and usually he let her win.'

Hrype found himself saying their goodbyes by himself. Lassair, lost in her own thoughts, barely said a word until they were almost home.

THIRTEEN

One good thing about Hrype as a companion is that he's content in his own thoughts and is about as loquacious as a door post. On the long walk home from Cambridge, he seemed to accept that I didn't want to talk and so left me to the whirl of conjecture and suspicion that filled my head.

Sir Alain de Villequier had visited Lady Claude at Heathlands! To begin with, I was totally preoccupied with trying to decide how, and when, I had become so certain that the two had not met until she was staying with Lord Gilbert. Moreover, it was not only I who had been convinced. Hrype had been too, for he had just told Gurdyman that Lady Claude had gone to Lakehall to meet Sir Alain. Had Lady Claude said something that had allowed me to receive this wrong idea? I cast my mind back over the two occasions that I had met her, and I realized swiftly that she had not even mentioned her future husband except indirectly, when she had showed me the beautiful but sinister embroidered panels that would decorate the marriage bed. What about Lord Gilbert and Lady Emma? Again, I pieced together all that I could recall of their exchanges with me and came up with nothing.

But there had to be *something*. I knew it, and I could not cease worrying at the problem until I found it.

In the end the memory surfaced while I was thinking about a different matter. Breaking the long silence as we trudged along, nearing the end of our journey, Hrype asked me if, having seen Gurdyman's attempt to represent a journey as a diagram on a piece of parchment, I now felt better able to do the same for the road from Cambridge to Aelf Fen. I had been fascinated by what Gurdyman had shown me, and for some moments Hrype and I discussed the extraordinary potential in what the sage was trying to do.

Then we came to a place where the road forded a shallow stream and, once we were safely across and had replaced our boots to walk on, once again we lapsed into silence.

And out of nowhere I heard Sir Alain's voice: *When she knew she was to marry me it was arranged that she should come here to meet me and stay for these weeks before our wedding with her cousin, Lord Gilbert.*

It was the day that Edild and I had laid out Ida's body. Sir Alain had walked with us back to the village, and I'd thought it was because he'd wanted to repair the damage that Lady Claude had done by her apparently callous remarks about Ida, to the effect that she mourned her only as a skilled seamstress and not as a likeable human being. Now, thinking back, I realized the extent of my mistake. For one thing, the opinions of lowly folk such as my aunt and me mattered not a dried bean to the likes of Sir Alain de Villequiers. It would make no difference to him and his future wife *what* we thought of her. We were totally unimportant.

I also realized – far more significantly – how very clever he had been. Subtly, skilfully, he had slipped in that innocent little comment and thereby removed himself from the list of men who had known Ida at the time she became pregnant and, horrified at the news that she bore a child, might have had reason to dispose of her.

I thought the possible sequence of events through again, right from the start, this time without the erroneous conclusion concerning when Sir Alain and Ida had first met . . .

Lady Claude was informed by her formidable mother that, with her elder sister sick and unfit for marriage, it would be Claude, the younger sibling, who would marry into the powerful and influential de Villequier family, in the shape of Sir Alain. Lady Claude did her best to protest, but her mother was adamant. Lady Claude conceded and set about sewing her trousseau, engaging the help of the skilled and personable Ida. With Sir Alain now resident at Alderhall, close to the home of Claude's cousin Lord Gilbert, what was more natural and compassionate for a reluctant bride than to suggest she went to stay at Lakehall, where she and her bridegroom could get to know each other before the wedding?

The purpose of the visit was not, however, for the pair to meet each other, for they had already done so. According to Gurdyman, Sir Alain had been a frequent visitor at Heathlands. He used to play chess with Lady Claude's mother.

Now I wove another thread into my tapestry. I made an image in my mind of Sir Alain arriving at Heathlands for the first time and being escorted into a great hall, richly furnished and with an extravagant fire burning in the hearth. Well-trained and expensively-clad servants were hovering in the background, ready and waiting for the subtlest signal that would make them spring into action to obey the least whim of their mistress. There she was, Lady Claritia – I pictured her as a fleshed-out version of her daughter Claude, with the same stiff, mirthless face and the same small, carefully expressionless eyes – dressed in a gorgeous gown of heavy silk, the cuffs lined with fur, with heavy gold jewellery encrusted with precious stones at her throat, ears and wrists. *Here is my daughter*, she would say to Sir Alain, and Lady Claude would step forward, pale, skinny, unlovely, unloved, unlovable, the black habit-like gown as effective as a smack in the face proclaiming fiercely *I don't want to be your wife, for it is my vocation to be a nun.*

They would have negotiated, that rich and determined woman and the man who knew his duty and would do it to the best of his ability. Power he had, for he belonged to the de Villequier family; money he needed, and money his wife would bring. How much did he demand as her dowry? Did he add on a sum for each of her drawbacks? I did not know, could not know, how these matters were arranged. Sir Alain had impressed me as a pleasant, even kind, man. He was certainly attractive, and I had no doubt that any woman whose hand he sought would readily give it. Yet he had agreed to marry Lady Claude. Perhaps it had even been he who had initiated the proceedings, for his new appointment must surely offer the possibility of advancement if he performed well, and advancement needs money if it is to be sustained.

I sent my mind back to that day, the first meeting between Lady Claude and Sir Alain in her mother's great hall. I saw Sir Alain as at last he took his leave. I saw him mount his beautiful horse – I recalled the bay mare with the star on her brow – and ride away, his emotions a mix of triumph because he had secured a wealthy heiress as his wife and dejection because of who and what that wife was. I saw him turn a corner in the track and come across a young woman with a bunch of wild flowers in her hand. I sensed the instant attraction that flared between the man and the young woman, shooting out like a visible, tangible thing. A thread, fine but unbelievably strong, that drew them to each other and then bound them together.

I do not know if that was how it was; the circumstances might have been different – they probably were – but the result was the same. Sir Alain and Ida fell in love, they became lovers – the most secretive lovers there have ever been – and then Ida conceived a child. Sir Alain's child.

How did she react? Was she apprehensive, nervous, delighted, exuberant? She was happy, of that I had no doubt, for both Lord Gilbert and Lady Emma had spoken of her as cheerful and smiling. She must have known what difficulties the future would hold. There would be many, of that there could be no doubt, for her lover was to be married soon, and Ida would always have to remain hidden in the background of his life. If she had appreciated this – and surely she must have done? – then it had not dented her delight. Perhaps she had trusted him to make provision for her and the child. Perhaps he had suggested some workable arrangement whereby she would be set up in a little house, not too far away, where he would be able to visit regularly. There would, after all, be plenty of money once he was married to Lady Claude. Would he see anything immoral in using his wife's money to support his lover and her child? Would his conscience be pricked as he lay in the luxury of his marriage bed with the chilling depiction of Lust staring down on him?

I was temped to condemn him for his immorality and his dishonesty. Then I remembered that he was going to have to share the remainder of his life with Lady Claude, and I began to have a little sympathy. My impressions of her were singularly unfavourable. It might not be her fault, but she would, I was quite sure, be a reluctant wife and do her uxorial duty with clenched teeth and tightly-closed eyes, her bony body rigid and unreceptive. I tried to feel sorry for her, too. She wanted to be a nun, not a wife, and perhaps, having set her feet on that difficult path, she had already eschewed any thoughts of physical love. Chastity, charity, obedience; those were the vows of a nun, as I knew from my sister Elfritha.

Unbidden, into my mind came a memory of Elfritha and her nuns at Chatteris, faces alight with laughter and eyes full of joy. It was very hard work being a nun – you could not help being aware of that if someone you loved entered a convent – but it had become clear to my parents, my siblings and me that the life had its compensations, and that these were rich and sometimes unexpected. I tried to imagine Lady Claude in the company of the Chatteris nuns, and I failed. Before I could prevent it, I had the unkind thought that the Lord Jesus would have accepted poor Claude, but even he might have been a little reluctant.

The poor woman would have—

Suddenly, I was struck by a thought so dreadful that I stopped dead. Hrype turned to stare at me and, not ready to share my suspicion, I forced a smile and started walking again. We were close to home now, but all thoughts of something to eat and drink and the wonderful expectation of taking off my boots and soaking my sore feet in cool water flew out of my mind.

But I like Sir Alain! I wailed silently. *He's a man who loves life, and who is naturally cheerful and affectionate!* Reluctantly, I admitted to myself that I found him attractive, as indeed I suspected most women would.

I ought not to like him. He was not – could not be – what he seemed. For his own and his family's sound reasons, he was betrothed to a stern and unforgivingly righteous woman whose idea of suitable decoration for her marriage bed was a harsh depiction of the Seven Deadly Sins. He had impregnated his future wife's seamstress – and if Claude ever found out, he could swiftly wave farewell to the life he envisaged with her, the life that her money would buy him. He would lose his grand new appointment – Lady Claude's mother would make sure of that – and the name of Alain de Villequier would fade inexorably from the consciousness of everyone who mattered in King William's realm, the king himself included.

I ought to *hate* him. He had seduced poor Ida and made her pregnant. Unable to risk the possibility that she would reveal her secret and run to her mistress to tell her who had fathered the child in her belly, Alain had killed her.

Trying not to let emotion overwhelm me, I thought about that. How had he managed to get her out on the artificial island? Had they had a regular trysting place where they went under the kind cover of darkness, and had he, knowing what must happen as they met for the final time, suggested crossing to the island? They would, he might have said, be even less likely there to attract unwelcome attention, even as he planned to use the lonely location for his own violent purpose.

How had he appeared, that day I led him out to where I had found Ida's body? I had attributed the emotion in his face and the gruff break in his voice to his sorrow at a young life choked out; I had been wrong. He had been horrified because his careful hiding place had been so swiftly discovered.

What a clever, efficient dissembler the man was . . .

Something in me that had warmed to him, trusted him, liked him, cracked and broke.

Hrype felt the sorrow flow out of his silent companion. He was aware of the trend of her thoughts; indeed, his own had worked to the same conclusion. If Sir Alain had fathered Ida's child – and the possibility could not be discounted – then it was highly likely he had killed her to prevent her condition, and his responsibility for it, becoming known to Lady Claude.

Hrype was aware of the machinations of the men of power in the world, although he did not comprehend their

motivation. There were things to which he gladly dedicated, and would probably give, his own life, but political
power and position were not among them. He knew he
would never have agreed to marry a woman like Lady
Claude de Seés. He might not have met her, but he did not
need to. He had lain with two women in his life; he felt
sympathy and deep responsibility for one of them, and he
loved the other wholeheartedly. She was so very different
from Claude that the two might have belonged to separate
species.

He sighed. There was half a mile to go before they were
back in the village, and he knew he must hurry on to the
house he shared with Froya and Sibert, for it was late and
Froya had probably decided he would not be home that
night. She would be alarmed by his unexpected return, and
it would take some time to settle her again. The sooner he
began, the sooner they could all go to sleep.

He did not want to go home. He wanted to go on with
Lassair to Edild's house. He and Edild kept their secret, as
Ida and Alain had kept theirs; Edild would never conceive
Hrype's child all the time their love had to be hidden – she
was far too well versed in the power of herbs to permit an
unwanted pregnancy – but, despite the fact that he could
never say so out loud, it was with her that his heart lay.
His instinct was to sympathize with Alain de Villequiers.
Steadily, carefully, he inspected this instinct, for he had
learned to trust such an awareness that came to him
unbidden.

Had Alain killed Ida? He had the motive, and it would
not have been difficult for him to persuade her to slip out
of Lakehall by night to meet him in some lonely place, for
she'd loved him and must have longed for the chance to be
with him. Coolly, Hrype tried to imagine Alain winding a
length of tough braid around the neck of the woman who
bore his child. Drawing it tight, pulling on the ends until
the life was choked out of her. Looking down at the dead
face. Slipping the inert body into the grave so conveniently
at hand.

Hrype thought about it for some time.

He could not convince himself that Alain de Villequier had killed Ida but, on the other hand, he could not have sworn that he hadn't.

They were in the village now, approaching the track that led up to Edild's house. Hrype stopped, and Lassair turned to face him. Studying her expression, he knew he had read her thoughts correctly. She looked utterly desolate.

He reached out and laid a swift touch on her arm. 'We have work to do,' he murmured.

Her eyes widened. 'But he is the justiciar!' she said in a loud whisper. 'Who do we go to if there is a crime to lay at *his* door?'

'Shhh!' He put a warning finger to his lips. 'We cannot yet swear that he has committed any crime.'

'But—'

Again he hushed her. 'We can make no accusation until we know more,' he said soothingly.

'And where will we go to find out what we need to know?' she asked scathingly.

He smiled to himself. He had always admired her spirit, even if it was still too wild. Once she had learned to control her fire, what a woman she would be.

'We *will* find out,' he assured her. 'I will come to your aunt's house tomorrow, and we shall talk together, the three of us.' She looked slightly mollified. He suspected, however, that her anger and her bitter disappointment in the man she had taken at his own value would not allow her much sleep. To distract her, he said, 'You made quite an impression on Gurdyman.'

Her expression changed, and he saw both pleasure and apprehension in her face. 'How do you know?' she demanded. 'You had no chance to speak to him privately, and I did not hear you discussing me.'

He smiled. 'We did not need to.'

She nodded, and he knew she understood. Her cheeks flushed slightly – he knew she was modest and did not yet appreciate her undoubted gift – and, gathering her courage with a visible effort, she said, 'I thought you'd taken me there for some special purpose. I thought that asking him

what he knew about Lady Claude's household at Heathlands
was just an excuse and the real reason for the visit was so
that he – Gurdyman – could teach me something.' She gave
a rueful grin. 'I was very scared.'

'I know,' Hrype said gently. 'And you are right, there was
a purpose in my taking you there.'

'What was it?' She frowned as she thought back. 'There
was the potion he was making when we got there – was it
something with incredible power and I was meant to guess
what it was from the ingredients?' Her face fell. 'Oh, but
I *did* know what was in it – some of the elements at least
– but I've no idea what it was for. Is he – can he make the
elixir of life?' The last words were barely audible, breathed
rather than spoken aloud.

'He was making a remedy for gallstones,' Hrype said expres-
sionlessly. 'A very painful condition, I am told, and among
Gurdyman's elite company of magicians, not a few suffer and
go to him for a remedy.'

'Gallstones!' she murmured. He watched as the apprentice healer took over and she said softly, 'Of course – I
thought I smelt billy goats, and saxifrage has that aroma
and is commonly used to break up internal stones.' Then
her face fell and she said, 'But I know about gallstones
already, or at least Edild is beginning to teach me.' She
frowned in thought. 'Was it the chart of his ancestors' jour-
neys, then? Was I supposed to learn something from that?'

He guessed she believed she had failed somehow, and he
could not allow that. For one thing it was untrue, and for
another, it would prevent her sleeping almost as effectively
as her distress over Sir Alain.

'No, Lassair,' he said. 'Gurdyman showed you his chart
because he had already made up his mind about you. I
suspect,' he added, 'that he shows it to very few people.'
While she digested that he went on, 'Gurdyman has heard
about you from me. He has long wished to meet you and
see for himself if what I have told him is accurate. Today
he put you to the test.'

Her eyes lit up. 'I sensed him!' she exclaimed. 'I felt him
trying to get into my mind. It felt very odd, but I thought I'd

better let him get on with it, but then I realized I'd had enough and so I tried to lock him out.'

He studied her. 'With some success,' he observed wryly.

'*What?*' Her mouth dropped. 'You mean I prevented him doing it?'

'You did.' He remembered how Gurdyman had caught his eye and winked. 'I cannot think of many other people who can prevent Gurdyman penetrating their thoughts, especially ones as young as you. It came as quite a surprise to him.'

He watched as she digested this. After a moment she said quietly, 'He said he would see me again.'

Hrype detected both fear and excitement in her at the prospect. 'As indeed you will,' he said.

She looked up and met his eyes. Hers were frank, their expression open. 'Thank you, Hrype,' she said.

'For what?' He felt he already knew.

'For giving me something else to think about,' she replied. 'Instead of turning to and fro in my bed and keeping my aunt awake while I lament my failure over Sir Alain de Villequier, I shall instead lie there wondering what marvels Gurdyman will reveal next time we meet. I hardly know,' she added in a soft voice as she turned to go, 'which is the more likely to rob me of my sleep.'

He stared after her as she hurried away. She had done well today, very well. Silently, he sent his love with her, using her as his intermediary for soon she would be with Edild. As he watched Lassair open the door a crack and slide her slim body through the gap, he thought that he would not mind if she kept a little of that love for herself.

FOURTEEN

I slept the deep sleep of physical exhaustion and awoke, with no memory of even having dreamed, feeling heavy and lethargic. I told Edild the stark facts – that Sir Alain and Lady Claude had been introduced while she still lived at Heathlands, and that he had been a frequent visitor to the house – but, when she quite naturally wanted to discuss the implications of this, I shook my head in denial.

'Hrype will come to see us this evening,' I said. 'Let us wait till then.'

She accepted this, but I noticed she was eyeing me with curiosity. I thought I'd be able to ignore it, but in the end I weakened. 'What is it? Why are you staring at me like that?'

She smiled. 'Yesterday you were taken to see a wizard,' she replied. 'I was hoping you might tell me what he was like.'

I laughed, and for a moment the heaviness lifted. 'I'm sorry,' I said, reaching for her hand. 'Gurdyman is extraordinary. He has such a sense of power about him, yet he's careful to keep it veiled. He looks like the most genial, cheery, everyday sort of man till you happen to find him staring at you, then you feel as if someone's pushing tiny filaments into your body and trying to find the core of you.'

'It sounds alarming,' Edild observed.

'It is,' I agreed. 'But he realized I was disturbed by his scrutiny, and immediately he stopped. I wouldn't wish to be his enemy.' I shuddered. 'I should think he could be ruthless.'

I pictured Gurdyman's round, smiling, strangely unlined face. Then the image was superimposed by another. The sage's face grew stern and seemed to alter shape, so that the bones under the plump cheeks and the smooth brow became prominent, the flesh melted away and the kindly eyes turned harsh and penetrating. I gave a small gasp, and instantly the familiar, friendly face returned.

Was it my imagination? Had the image of the frightening wizard been conjured up by my own mind because I had been wondering what it would be like to be his enemy? Or had Gurdyman himself planted it, as if to say, *You saw my genial face. Do not be fooled into believing that is all there is to me*.

I did not know.

Edild had cleared away our breakfast bowls and cups, and now I hastened to my feet to tidy our cots, folding the bedding and stuffing it and the pillows out of sight beneath the bed frames. The daylight was waxing fast, and soon our first patients would be coming to call.

I tried to concentrate on my work, but I kept being distracted. I thought of Sir Alain and Ida. I imagined them together, those two people who seemed made for happiness and laughter, and who, if the world were arranged differently, would undoubtedly have wed, raised a family and lived as happily as it is possible for humans to live. I dare say I was romanticizing them, believing what I wanted to believe, and I was undoubtedly making too much of what scant evidence I had so far. I had been told that Sir Alain had visited Heathlands, and I kept telling myself that was all I knew. To leap from that one simple fact to proposing that Alain and Ida were so well suited that they would have married if they could was pure invention.

Yet, as the morning wore on and my battle to fix my mind on my work became more and more challenging, the quiet little voice at the back of my head insisting that I was right refused to be silenced. And just how, I wondered in silent frustration, could that rose-tinted vision of the pair of them accord with my new certainty that it was at Sir Alain's hands that poor little Ida had died?

In the end Edild lost patience with me. In our work, inattentiveness is potentially very dangerous. I muddled someone's symptoms, reporting to my aunt that the man had bellyache when in fact, as he was quick to correct me, he was severely costive. Then, later, I handed her a jar containing dried wormwood stems instead of the pot of willowherb leaves she had asked for. She noticed instantly – of course she did, the two are quite dissimilar – and quietly but forcefully thrust the wormwood back into my hand. 'Go and wait for me outside!' she hissed.

I went. I do not often make my aunt angry, and I hate it when I do. I waited until her patient emerged, clutching the infusion Edild had just prepared that would swiftly ease his headache, and after a moment she followed.

She studied me for a while. Then, instead of the castigation I had expected and richly deserved, she said, 'You are no use to me today indoors. Go and gather some sweet flag root. We're getting low.'

I dipped my head meekly in acknowledgement. I fetched my collecting basket from the outhouse and hurried away before she could change her mind.

The yellow flag – which we also call gladden – serves mainly as a purgative, using the fresh roots. It likes wet, marshy ground, so I went down the path from Edild's house, crossed the track leading towards the hall and set off towards the soggy ground where land gives way to water. I worked steadily, taking a little from several plants rather than filling my basket from one single place. Edild says we must respect that plants have a right to life too, and that taking too much of one plant's root would probably kill it. Each time I cut some root I chanted the little song of thanks that my aunt had taught me.

I found that I had wandered almost as far as the fen edge. Stopping, I put down my basket, which was getting heavy, and put my hands to the small of my back. I had been bending down for too long and short, sharp stabs of pain were my reward. I was quite close to the place where the little causeway goes across to the island. I decided to pay a quick visit to Granny, guilty suddenly because I had been neglecting her since the discovery of Ida's body.

I left my basket where it was to collect on my return and hurried off. The ground was reasonably firm now, so soon after midsummer, for the weather had been fair and we had not had much rain. It would be a different matter in autumn, when the equinox gales sweep in and the rain lashes the land. We would by then have taken away the planks and supports of our temporary bridge, the way to the island would become impassable and Granny Cordeilla would be left all by herself with the ancestors.

I did not think she would mind. They were her own kin, she had known and loved several of them in life, and she had no doubt communed with those who had died before her birth long before she went to join them.

I crossed over the narrow planks and jumped down on to the island. I went to stand over the big slab that marked Granny's grave, opening my mind and my heart to her. I was just closing my eyes when I noticed something: a tiny wreath made of grass wound into a circle and laced with wild flowers, the whole thing about the size of my palm.

I bent down to study it. It lay half under the stone slab, so that it had been hidden as I approached. It looked as if someone had wanted to put it as close as possible to the tomb, but without going so far as to move the slab and put it inside.

I don't know why, but I felt sure it had been left for Ida and not for Granny. Perhaps it was the furtiveness of the placement. If any of us had brought a little offering for our dead relative, we would have left it where all could see it. I looked at the craftsmanship of the little wreath, noticing that it was crude, the grass stems already beginning to unravel. It looked like the work of a child.

I heard a voice in my head. It was Sir Alain's. *He used to make little posies for her, clumsy things of grass stems woven together with a couple of flowers stuck in.*

Then I knew who had left it.

It made sense, too, because he probably thought she was still here . . .

I was filled with pity for him, poor Derman, mourning the girl he had loved from afar, driven to some furtive, night-time visit to the place where he believed her body was interred and leaving his pathetic little offering. I wondered where he was hiding, almost certain that he had not strayed far from this spot. He must have missed them when they came to take her off to Lakehall – he'd probably still been back at home with Zarina, where I had left him that terrible morning – and he could not have seen the sad procession when her body was taken to be reburied close by the church. Perhaps, exhausted by his grief, he had been sleeping somewhere, curled up in whatever nest he had made for himself. Perhaps he had been off looking for something to eat, for there was little to sustain a grown man in the immediate vicinity.

'Where are you, Derman?' I said aloud. 'I know you are afraid and do not understand, but you should go home. Zarina is very worried about you.'

Was that good advice, though? Even if Derman could hear me, should he obey? I was not at all sure. I was convinced he hadn't killed Ida – I did not allow myself to think about who might have done – but the rest of the village certainly didn't share that view. There was still too much talk of going out to hunt for Derman, and not with anything charitable in mind like wrapping him in a warm blanket and bringing him home.

The little wreath did, however, tell me something very encouraging that I could report to an anxious sister: the wild flowers were still fresh, which meant the wreath had only recently been made. Derman was still alive, and he was still close by.

I said a hurried farewell to Granny – I know she would have understood – and, leaping back across the planks, ran back to fetch my basket. Then, moving more slowly once I was encumbered by its weight, I went back to the village. I left the basket of roots beside the outhouse; I could hear the murmur of voices from within the house and knew better than to disturb my aunt and her patient. Then I ran down the path again and raced along the track until I reached the widow Berta's house.

Zarina was, as I had expected, down by the water, wringing out a long piece of sheeting with strong, red-knuckled hands. It looked as if it was of good quality, perhaps belonging to some grand servant up at the hall. She looked up as she heard me approach, her face anxious. 'What's the matter? Have you any news?' she demanded.

I waited while I caught my breath and then said, 'I've just been out to the island. Someone's left a little wreath, and I'm sure it must have been Derman, making an offering for Ida.'

Slowly, she let the sheet drop on to the ground. 'He's still alive, then.'

I could read nothing in her tone. If she was relieved at my news, she didn't show it.

'He must be hiding somewhere nearby,' I said encouragingly. 'He obviously thinks she's still in my Granny's grave, so that's where he left the wreath. Oh, Zarina, perhaps he goes there regularly to be with her! We might be able to lie in wait for him and persuade him to come home! If you like I'll help you. I could—'

'No.' She cut my offer dead. Then, managing a smile, she said, 'It's kind of you, Lassair, and I know you mean well.' I *hate* it when people say that because it usually means that you're so far from achieving your aim that you might as well not have bothered. 'But I think it'd be better if I went alone,' she went on. 'He'll be in a very bad state. He'll be frightened, hungry, thirsty and tired. He doesn't manage very well on his own.' Briefly, she turned her face away, and I guessed she was hiding sudden tears.

'Very well,' I said. 'You know best, I'm sure.'

She must have detected from my voice that I felt snubbed. Turning back, she said, 'You're very kind, like all your family. I really don't—'

She did not finish whatever she had been about to say. Without another word, she picked up the sheet, brushed off a few pieces of grass and went back to her wringing.

'When will you go?' I asked.

She shot me a quick glance, and then the golden-green eyes were covered again as she lowered her gaze. 'Soon.'

I had the strong sense that was all she was going to say. There seemed little point in staying, so I left.

Hrype came, as he had promised, soon after Edild and I had tidied up after supper. As before, we were sitting out under the trees, and he knew where to find us.

I had already told Edild what I had found out on the island, and now I repeated it to Hrype. We all agreed that the wreath must have been left by Derman. I had called in at my parents' house on my way back to Edild's after seeing Zarina, and my mother had said that, as far as she knew, nobody in the family had left any such offering for Granny.

'Zarina's going to go out to the island to see if she can find him,' I said now. 'I offered to go with her, but she said she was better on her own.'

I watched Hrype and my aunt exchange a glance. 'I wonder,' Edild said softly.

'You wonder what?' I demanded.

But she shook her head. 'Nothing.'

It wasn't nothing; of course it wasn't. What she meant was that, whatever it was, she wasn't going to share it with me. *They* weren't going to share it, because clearly Hrype knew what she meant. 'It would be a solution,' he murmured.

I was about to demand that they tell me but Hrype, as if he realized, turned to me and said, 'Now, you have told Edild what we learned concerning Sir Alain's familiarity with the household at Heathlands?'

'Yes,' I said shortly. I was cross with them.

'Don't sulk, Lassair,' my aunt said. 'So –' she was addressing Hrype – 'you are suggesting that Sir Alain and Ida were lovers before Ida accompanied Lady Claude here to Lakehall?'

'Possibly,' Hrype said guardedly. 'It seems likely that the two of them met. At the least, they could have done.'

'Let us assume he fathered a child on the girl yet was betrothed to Lady Claude,' Edild mused. Then, cutting straight to the point: 'Lady Claude is very devout and intolerant of sinners. If she discovered the man she was to wed had bedded another woman, moreover one to whom he was not married, and had made her pregnant, she would have nothing more to do with him.'

'Motive enough for him to kill Ida?' Hrype asked softly.

'Oh, I can't believe he killed her!' I burst out, earning urgent *Shhh!* sounds from my aunt and Hrype. 'I just can't,' I repeated in a whisper.

'Why?' Hrype asked.

It was a good question. I had been asking it of myself all day and still had no answer. My sensible, logical head said that of course he'd strangled Ida; who else could have? My heart, however, just would not accept it. 'Because he's nice,' I muttered under my breath. Fortunately, neither of them appeared to hear. 'I don't know,' I said lamely.

We talked long into the night, for there was no obvious way to test our tentative theory of Sir Alain's involvement with poor, dead Ida. The household at Heathlands would have been able to give us some answers, but the likes of us could hardly go marching up to the door and begin asking questions about Lady Claritia's future son-in-law and his possible dalliance with Lady Claude's seamstress. Hrype proposed trying to talk to some of the servants, but you could never tell how loyal a man or woman was going to be to his lord and lady and, if word got back to our Lord Gilbert that Hrype had been asking questions at Heathlands, it would undoubtedly lead to trouble.

I said, 'I could go and see Lady Claude again. She wasn't there when I went a couple of days ago, so it'd look odd if I didn't try again.'

Two pairs of clever eyes turned to me. 'What have you in mind to say to her?' Hrype asked. 'Other than asking how she feels, of course.'

I hesitated. 'I could try to draw her out about Ida,' I said. 'I could even tell her that her symptoms – the headaches and the sleeplessness – are often an accompaniment of grief, and that talking about the dead person sometimes helps. All of that is true,' I assured him. 'Isn't it, Edild?'

'Yes, it is,' she said slowly, 'although I do not like the idea of making use of your profession to extract information that is not strictly to do with healing.'

There was a pause. Then Hrype said, 'I am sure that Lassair would not permit her curiosity to interfere in any way with the correct treatment of her patient.'

It was very generous of him, and I hoped it was true.

Edild made up her mind. 'Very well,' she said eventually. She fixed me with a hard stare; she knows me better than

Hrype does, and she is never taken in by my dissembling. 'But remember you are there to heal,' she said forcefully. 'Anything else – anything at all, even if it does pertain to a young woman's death – is secondary. Is that understood?'

I made myself hold her eyes. 'Yes, Edild.'

Once Hrype had gone and my aunt and I were settling for sleep, I found that my mind was too hectic with thoughts and conjectures to allow me to relax. After what seemed ages, but was probably not all that long, I slipped out of bed, picked up Elfritha's shawl against the night chill and went outside.

I walked slowly down the path, looking out over the marshy ground to the fen edge and the island. I thought of Derman. Was he out there now? I wondered. Had his sister found him and was she even now reassuring him, encouraging him to come home? If so, we would all have to watch him, perhaps taking turns, because it would be best if he did not venture out until Ida's killer had been found. The people of Aelf Fen were not bad, I knew that well enough, but they had got it into their heads that Derman's hopeless love for Ida had led to murder when she'd turned him down – and, it seemed, they weren't going to change their minds.

I thought about Sir Alain. Had he killed her? If he had, and we could somehow prove it, what were we to do? We would have to approach Lord Gilbert, and that wouldn't be easy, and he would probably—

The singing began. From somewhere quite close by, I heard that eerie voice. For all that I had now met its owner, it sounded no less strange rising softly into the night air. I was tempted to seek him out, speak to him, try to comfort him, but if, as I guessed, he did not know I was there, then it might dismay and distress him further to know he had a witness to his pain and his grief.

I edged into the soft darkness beneath a group of alders and listened. I noticed then that, where before there had been no more than a hummed chant, a succession of heartbreakingly sad sounds, now there were words. I strained my ears, and eventually I made them out.

Alberic was singing his lament for Ida.

The singer of a thousand songs was I,
Yet now but one remains, the saddest of them all.
For now that in the fenland soil you lie,
I have no longer any hopes on which to call.

At first I was not free my love to show,
And then, by fate, another took your heart from me,
My dearest hopes were shattered by this blow
So cruel, and yet I knew I had to set you free.

Oh Ida, can you hear this sad refrain?
Can notes of music pierce your damp and peaty frame?
And would you hold me close if I were lain
Beside you? Could we sing the happy songs again?

He had stopped. I stood there alone in the silence for some time, tears on my face. Then I wrapped my shawl tightly around me and went back to my bed.

We were woken at first light by someone's fists hammering on the door. 'Open up, oh, for the Lord's sake, open up!' cried a voice.

Struggling out of sleep, I realized with horror that I recognized the voice. It was my brother's.

Edild was already on her feet, fumbling with the door latch. I elbowed her out of the way, wresting the door open. 'It's Haward!' I cried. 'Something's wrong – someone's been taken ill or is hurt!'

He fell into the little room. His face was wet with sweat, and his eyes were wide with horror. 'Is it our parents?' I demanded, my hands on his shoulders shaking him roughly in my terrible anxiety. 'Squeak? Oh, not Leir, lovely little Leir?'

Haward shoved my hands away, and I fell over my own feet and sat down hard on the earth floor. He rushed to help me up again, hugging me tightly. 'No, n–n–none of them. They are all unharmed.' He brushed a quick kiss against my cheek.

With my immediate fears allayed, there was time to think of others. 'Then who—?' I began.

My aunt took charge. In a quiet voice that was nevertheless full of calm authority, she said, 'What has happened, Haward? Tell us what we must do.'

He turned to her gratefully. 'Yesterday Lassair told Zarina that she'd found a wreath by Granny's grave, and we all guessed it had been left there by Derman, thinking Ida was still in the tomb. Zarina went out some time last night to see if she could find him.' Such was the power of Edild's effect on him that his stammer had temporarily vanished.

'She went *in the night*?' I protested. 'By herself? How could you let her?'

'I d–d–didn't!' He rounded on me as swiftly as when we were children and I had accused him unfairly. 'I thought we were going to go together, early in the morning, but she must have waited till I had g–gone home and was asleep, and then slipped away by herself.'

'I see,' I muttered. I ought to have known him better than that. 'Sorry.'

'Then what happened?' Edild asked, glaring at me as if to say, *Don't you dare interrupt him again!*

'I went j–just before dawn to see if she was ready to go. You know I always wake early, and it seemed a good time to try to c–c–catch him – Derman – unawares.' He stopped, swallowed and, his expression anguished, began again. 'She – she wasn't there. I s–s–set out for the island.' Again, a pause. His face was working, and I knew how hard it must be to try to force the words out past the gagging stutter. 'I m–m–m–met her c–c–coming back. Sh–sh–she was crying. I p–put my arms r–round her and for just an instant she h–h–hugged me. I knew then she hadn't found h–h–him s–s–so I t–told her to go on home and I'd h–h–have a look round.' He stopped, drew breath and said, 'I w–went out on to the island. I c–c–couldn't see any s–s–sign of him. Then I turned to c–c–come back and th–th–there was a sh–sh–shadow under the water. Sh–sh–sh–she w–w–wouldn't have s–s–s–seen it, there was only j–j–j–just enough light f–f–for me.' He shuddered to a halt, exhausted by the huge effort of stuttering out his tale.

'What was this shadow, Haward?' Edild's voice was gentle, soothing, hypnotic almost, and, responding to her again, for a few moments Haward calmed down.

He fixed his eyes on a spot on the wall above her head, breathed deeply and said, 'It was a body. A big body, face down in the water, the head and shoulders caught under the planks of the causeway on to the island.'

Nobody spoke. Haward dropped his head. Then Edild took his hand, bent down so that she could see into his face and said, 'Who was it?'

Haward's expression was dreadful to behold. Shock had taken hold, and he was shuddering, his teeth rattling. Although he was still sweating, he was deathly pale. His eyes on Edild's he said, 'It's Derman. The back of his head isn't there any more.'

FIFTEEN

In that first shocked moment as the three of us stood there wide-eyed with horror, I believe we all had the same unspoken thought: did *Zarina kill him?*

She had had the opportunity, for she had gone alone during the night to the island to seek him out. Did she find him? Perhaps she tried to reason with him, imploring him to come back to the village and speak to Sir Alain, to face those who believed he had slain Ida. Did he refuse? Did he – oh, it was horrible! – did he tell his sister that the reason he couldn't turn himself in was that he *had* killed poor Ida? If so, what would Zarina have done? Would she have hurled herself at him in such fierce anguish that he slipped from the causeway and hit his head as he fell?

Oh, I prayed to the silent, watchful spirits, oh please, *please* let it have happened that way! I could not bear the thought that the woman my brother loved and wanted so much to marry might be a murderer . . .

Through the wild panic of my thoughts I heard my aunt's quiet voice. She was addressing me: 'Lassair, go and fetch Hrype and Sibert. Tell them I require their assistance, but don't say why.' She studied me. 'Calm yourself,' she commanded. 'Breathe deeply and quietly.'

I did as she bade me. After a while I was in control, and I arranged my face into what I hoped was an everyday, pleasant expression. Edild was right; it would do no good to race across the village to Hrype's house with a face eloquent of horror. It might be early yet, but enough people would be up and about for somebody to spot me and spread the word that something was afoot. My aunt was watching me closely, and she gave a curt nod. 'Off you go,' she said.

I hesitated. 'Er—'

She gave an impatient *tut*. 'What is it?'

'Why do we need Hrype and Sibert?'

She looked at me pityingly. 'Derman was a large man,' she said, speaking slowly as if explaining to a child. 'How do you think we are going to bear him back here unless we have help?'

I hurried off. Part of me was full of admiration for Edild's courage, for surely what we ought to do was report the death to Sir Alain de Villequier and wait for him to give the orders concerning what was to be done with the body. Part of me, aware that I was equally involved in this surely risky piece of independent action, was just plain scared.

I tapped gently on the door of the house where Hrype, Froya and Sibert live. As the latch was lifted, I made sure I was smiling cheerfully. The door opened to reveal Sibert.

'Good morning,' I said, still smiling. 'I'm sorry to trouble you so early, but Edild has sent me to ask if you and Hrype could come and help her with something.'

I heard quick movement from within, and instantly Hrype appeared beside Sibert. 'What is it?' he demanded, just as Sibert, with a puzzled grin on his face, was asking, 'Why are you smiling like a village idiot, Lassair?'

Fortunately, Hrype didn't appear to hear. Addressing myself to him, I said, with what I hoped was a convincing shrug, 'I don't know.' As I spoke I fixed my eyes on his and tried to put my thought – *Derman's dead, and Haward found the body* – into his mind.

I don't suppose for a moment that he received my silent message, but he read enough in my expression to realize something bad had happened and Edild wanted to keep it secret for the time being. 'Of course we'll come,' he said easily. He turned back into the little house – I could see Froya behind him, crouched beside the hearth and stirring something in a pot, the usual anxious frown creasing her brow – and said, 'Eat, Froya. Sibert and I may be some time, so don't wait for us.'

'But—' she began, the nervous frown deepening. With Froya, I suspect there is always an anxious *but*.

'It's all right,' Hrype said soothingly. 'Don't worry.'

I thought that saying *don't worry* to a woman like Froya was a bit like telling the wind not to blow.

As soon as we were out of earshot of the house and its neighbours, Hrype said in a low voice, 'How did he die?'

I all but stopped dead in my tracks. He'd heard! But now was not the time to stand and wonder at my growing powers of thought transference. In any case, the credit should surely go to Hrype for picking up my wordless message rather than to me for sending it.

'How did who die?' Sibert was demanding in a fierce whisper. 'What are you talking about?'

I put out my hands to each of them and drew them closer. 'Haward went out to the island where my Granny is buried,' I hissed. I paused to explain to Sibert. 'We know Derman has been going there because I found a little garland he left for Ida, thinking she was still there.' I went on to tell both of them what Haward had just told Edild and me, finishing with the frightful discovery of Derman's dead body.

'We must bring the corpse back to Edild's house and determine how he died,' Hrype said as soon as I was done.

'That's what she thought,' I replied. 'That's why she sent me to fetch you two, because Derman's such a big man and we need help.'

'How is your brother?' Hrype asked.

Thinking it was compassionate of him to be concerned, I said, 'He's in a bad way. He's had an awful shock and—'

But it seemed that efficiency and not compassion had motivated the remark: 'It would be better if he did not come with us,' Hrype said. 'In addition, I would prefer to view the body without—' He stopped.

I could not think at first what he meant. Then, as a very frightening possibility dawned, I whispered, 'Without Haward present, do you mean? Oh, Hrype, surely you don't think *Haward* was involved in Derman's death?'

To my surprise Hrype took hold of my hand and gave it a hard squeeze. 'I am trying to *help*, Lassair! I know you love your brother and cannot imagine him guilty of anything so terrible, but the facts are these: Haward loves Zarina dearly and wishes to marry her, but she refuses because she will not inflict the heavy burden of caring for her simpleton brother on Haward and his family. We who know Haward are perfectly well aware that he would not even contemplate getting rid of Derman and removing the obstacle to his and Zarina's happiness, but others, I assure you, will not be so charitable.'

I waited until my outrage receded a little. 'So why do you want to view the place where Derman died without Haward there?'

'Because,' Sibert put in impatiently, 'when Hrype and the rest of us are asked about it, we can say what our impressions were, and everyone will know they weren't influenced by anything Haward said or did.'

I had to admit that it made good sense.

Edild had given Haward a mild sedative by the time we got back, and he was lying on my bed half-asleep.

'He should not be forced to return to the place where the body lies,' she said softly to Hrype. 'He has had a very bad shock and needs to recover his wits.'

Hrype nodded. 'The four of us will go. Between us we ought to be able to carry the body.'

I could see the sense of that. I went over to Haward and, crouching in front of him, softly called his name. He raised his head and stared at me. 'Don't stay here,' I urged him. 'Go home. Tell our parents what has happened, and they'll look after you.' I thought of something else. 'Fetch Zarina, and take her with you. She'll have to be told that he's dead –' despite the dreadful suspicions, she had still lost her brother, her only kin, and would undoubtedly need comfort no matter how he had died – 'and the best place to tell her is among loving people.'

If, indeed, she needed telling . . .

The people of my family were loving, that was certain. Whether or not they would live to regret having accepted Zarina so open-heartedly remained to be seen.

Edild rolled up a blanket and tucked it under her arm. I paused to bend over my brother and kiss his forehead – at first he barely seemed to notice, but then he met my eyes and gave a quick nod, presumably acquiescing to my suggestion – and then I hurried after the others.

We did not speak as we crossed the marshy ground to the fen edge. Too soon the upright posts set in the water to mark the crossing place to the island came into view. I tried to suppress my dread. *The back of his head isn't there any more*, my brother had said. What awful sight were we going to have to see? I shuddered, all the way from my shoulders to my feet.

Silently, Sibert took my hand. I could have kissed him.

Hrype went first on to the planks between the uprights. He moved slowly, looking over the side to the right and the left, searching the black water for what we knew was there. Very soon he gave a soft exclamation, pointing down to the left. 'There he is.'

We hurried to join him.

Derman was floating just below the surface, face down, his sturdy, powerful arms outstretched as if he were trying to fly. The coarse fabric of his patched and darned shirt was full of air, rising like a huge bubble up to the surface. His legs bobbed gently up and down in a horrible parody of walking.

Realizing that I was looking at every part of him save the crucial area, I turned my eyes to his head.

The back of his skull had received a series of blows. Whoever had attacked him had hit him so hard that the bone had smashed. We could see the leathery white matter beneath, and that, too, had ruptured, revealing a mass of bloody pulp in which there were fragments of the skull.

All hopes of a terrible accident flew away. Had it happened as I had so hoped, had he slipped, cracked his head on the planks of the causeway and fallen, unconscious, into the water to drown, there would have been only the one blow to the head. This had been no innocent, fatal misfortune.

What poor Derman's murderer had done to him was one of the most furious, frenzied onslaughts it has ever been my bad luck to witness.

It took all four of us to pull him up out of the water. It was as if the fen did not want to let him go and, when finally we wrestled his dead weight up on to the planks, the black mud gave out a last bubble of stinking gas as if to spite us. We were filthy, our hands, arms, bodies coated with muck, and Sibert was soaking wet, for at one point, frustrated at our lack of progress, he had armed himself with a stout stick, jumped down into the water and tried to lever the corpse up from beneath.

Edild spread out the blanket, and we laid Derman on it. We each took firm hold of a corner and, with a huge effort, lifted him off the ground. Then we set out across the mile or so of difficult terrain back to my aunt's house.

Edild and I live on the edge of Aelf Fen, well away from the rest of the village. We prefer it that way, and so, I am sure, do the villagers. Healers are very welcome when people need us, and indeed our patients and their relatives are always grateful and fulsome in their praise and their gifts when we make someone well again. However, in most people's minds healing is next door to witchcraft, and they are all more than happy that we don't live right on top of them.

As we approached the path up to the house, we could see that Edild's patients for the day had already begun to arrive. Fortunately, there were only two so far: an old man, and an even older woman. Edild gave a small sigh and indicated that we should lower our burden.

'William and his old mother,' she said quietly. 'She is dying, and William will miss her very much when she goes. There is very little I can do, but he appears comforted by the tonics I prescribe for her.' She frowned, then turned to me. 'Lassair, go on and speak to them. Tell them to go home, and say to William that I'll come to see his mother later.'

I ran on up the path and delivered the message. William looked at me worriedly and whispered, 'Mother may not last till later,' to which I could think of no answer except to agree with him. His mother looked as insubstantial as a piece of dandelion fluff, and I was amazed she'd managed to walk up from the village. I could not, of course, say so. I watched as they shuffled away and, when they could no longer see the house, went back down the path to summon the others.

We carried Derman's body into the house, laid him very gratefully on the ground – he was extremely heavy – and Edild secured the door. There was no sign of Haward, and I hoped he was even now at home in the stoutly reassuring company of our parents. Working very swiftly, Edild removed Derman's garments and studied the body. We all knew how he had died, and I turned away as she and Hrype studied the devastating wounds on the back of his head. Sibert, I noticed, had retreated to the furthest corner and was busy inspecting his hands.

He, however, was not an apprentice healer; I was. All too soon my aunt's autocratic tones sang out: 'Come here, Lassair, for it is rare that we have the chance to see what is inside the skull.'

With the utmost reluctance I did as I was told. Stepping forward, I made myself look at the great crater on the right side of the back of the head. To begin with, I had to fight the urge to be sick, for the bloody, oozing, waterlogged mess was a hideous sight. But then, listening to Hrype and Edild speculating on the brain as the source of all we do, all we are and all we think, revulsion turned to interest, and then to fascination.

'Is his brain different from ours?' I asked after a while.

Hrype turned to me, his eyes alert. 'Why do you ask?'

'Because he was simple,' I replied. 'He may have grown into a man, but he didn't act like one. Everyone said he was like a child, but that's not really right either. He was just . . .' I searched for the right word, gave up and said, 'Just *different*.'

Hrype nodded. 'It is an enigma, isn't it?' he agreed. I was not sure what an enigma was, but I said yes anyway. 'Here we have the brain of a man who was different, as Lassair says –' he paused to prod at the white matter – 'yet, for all that is visible to our eyes, it looks just like any other.' I wondered how many brains Hrype had studied, but quickly decided I did not wish to think about that. 'What happened, Derman?' Hrype asked softly. 'Were you born this way, and if so, why did the gods choose to make you as you were?'

Nobody answered him. I'm not sure any of us knew how.

Edild was inspecting the rest of the body. I moved closer to her, watching as she ran her hands over the stiffening limbs. I found myself looking at the genitals, blushed furiously and then sternly reprimanded myself for my coyness. Healers, as my aunt repeatedly tells me, treat every part of the human body with the same dispassionate interest, even the bits normally kept modestly out of sight. I stared at the penis and testicles beneath the fine downy body hair, noting their lack of development. Derman was a man, yet his genitalia were like those of a small boy.

I suddenly remembered something Zarina had said: *He is not as other men, and he does not begin to comprehend the true nature of how a man and wife live in intimacy together.* And, later, *The idea of any sort of physical closeness is just not possible.*

Staring down at Derman's body, I wondered how she had known. At the widow Berta's cottage, Derman had slept in the lean-to, but then these two had grown up together and travelled with the troupe of players for a considerable time; it was only to be expected that Zarina would have observed her brother's naked body on occasions. All the same, there was something about this that bothered me . . .

I did not have the chance to think it through because just at that moment Edild, who had been inspecting the large, flat feet and was now running her hands up the lower legs, gave a soft exclamation. 'Look,' she murmured.

Hrype and I edged closer to her and stared down at what she was indicating. I could see it immediately: across the front of both shins there was a red mark, a deep indentation that in one or two places had cut into the thin flesh.

'That must have hurt,' I said, wincing in sympathy.

'It perhaps explains the sequence of events,' Hrype said thoughtfully. 'It would appear that he slipped, or tripped, and somehow as he fell he managed to bark his shins on the planks of the causeway. Perhaps he landed in the water; perhaps on the causeway. Either way, he was down, no longer on his feet, and, since he was a tall, strong man, I believe that is relevant.' He paused. 'Let us say that he landed, either on the planks or in the water, face down. It would then have been relatively easy for his assailant to raise their weapon and bring it down repeatedly on the back of his head.'

We all thought about that; even Sibert who, now that we were no longer talking about brains and poking at what was left of Derman's, had crept forward to join us around the body.

It was he who voiced what I'm sure we were all thinking. 'It wouldn't have taken a man to kill him, then,' he said slowly. 'Even a woman could have done it.'

Although none of us said the words aloud, *a woman like Zarina* seemed to echo through the little room.

SIXTEEN

Hrype straightened up and said, in a tone that seemed to reject any contradiction, 'I shall go and tell Sir Alain what has happened.'

Edild and I looked at each other. In her eyes I read compassion, and she waited for me to say what I'm sure both of us were thinking. 'But we can't!' I whispered urgently. 'If Zarina did this, he'll take her off to be penned up in some horrible cell and she'll be tried and they'll hang her, and Haward really loves her, it'll break his heart and he'll never find anyone else!'

The flow of words left me exhausted. I found I was crying, tears rolling steadily down my face.

Hrype said, very gently and kindly, 'I understand how you feel, Lassair. But listen to what I say: for one thing, it is not at all certain that Zarina had anything to do with her brother's death. Sir Alain does not strike me as a man to make a hasty judgement, and I—'

'He fathered Ida's baby!' I hissed, trying and failing to whisper and shout at the same time.

'You don't know that!' Hrype flashed back. 'All we can be certain of is that he visited Lady Claude at Heathlands during the period when Ida became pregnant.'

He was right. I had to admit it, despite my own certainty. Glumly, I said, 'What was the other thing?'

'Hmm?'

'You said, for one thing. That implies there's something else.'

He gave a swift, bleak smile. 'Indeed there is, although you, passionate defender of what is right that you are, will not like it.'

'Tell me anyway.' I felt so weary, so tired with all the emotion, that I could hardly bring myself to care very much.

He thought for a moment, then said, 'Lassair, it is impossible for us to dispose of Derman's body in secret. This is a small village full of people all too ready to discuss and dissect their neighbours' business, usually making wildly inaccurate and damning assumptions along the way. We were very lucky to bear him back to this house without anyone seeing us, and I do feel very strongly that we should not take that for granted.' He paused. I had a fair idea of what he was going to say, but did not interrupt. 'Everyone knows Derman went missing; many of the men of the village have been out searching for him.' That gave me an idea but, again, I kept silent.

'We could, I suppose, try to bury Derman's body by night in some out of the way place and keep up the pretence that he never came back,' Hrype went on. 'That way, we would make quite sure that no suspicion will ever fall on Zarina and Haward.' This time I couldn't prevent my gasp of horror, but he held my eyes and I did not speak. 'But think, dear child, *think* what would happen when our deception was discovered, as it would almost certainly be!' He grasped me by the shoulders, his face so close to mine that I read the strength of his feelings.

I thought. I saw in my mind the four of us – Hrype, Sibert, Edild and me – sneaking out of the village on a moonless night bearing a large, heavy body in a blanket. I saw us walking for miles, right away from Aelf Fen. I saw us work through the hours of darkness to dig a deep hole and bury the body. I saw us return. Then I saw a band of men out searching for a fugitive, and I saw them discover the recently-disturbed earth. Derman had lived in Aelf Fen, and so they would come here looking for those who had killed and buried him.

I said, although I think I knew it was hopeless, 'Wouldn't Sir Alain and his officers assume that some of the village men had killed Derman? Enough of them have been threatening what they'd do to him if he ever turned up, and—'

Slowly, Hrype shook his head. 'That would not be right, Lassair. We must not point blame where there is no blame.'

I remembered what had suddenly occurred to me a moment ago. 'But it might be exactly what *did* happen!' I protested.

He studied me. 'Do you really think so?'

I thought. I thought for some time, trying to persuade myself. Eventually, I shook my head. This was, I felt quite sure, an intimate crime; Derman's killer was far more tightly enmeshed in his life than a handful of angry villagers. Anyway, I had noticed that, as the tally of days since Ida's death and Derman's disappearance increased, so the number of voices baying for justice steadily lessened. People are fickle, really, their attention quickly diverted. We in Aelf Fen live hard lives, and it was understandable that private concerns should have slowly and surely overcome the brief excitement of a murder in our midst.

'If we covered up Derman's murder and tried to hide his body,' Hrype said quietly, 'we would never be sure that we had not been observed. We would wait, all four of us, for the tap on the door that brought the force of the law to us and our loved ones. We would already be guilty of covering up a murder and hiding a body. How quickly, do you think, would other accusations fly to stick to us?'

He was quite right. I thought of Zarina, of Haward. If we did as I wanted and tried to hide what had happened, the suspicion I wanted so badly to divert from the two of them would land square on their heads. They would suffer, my parents would suffer, and so would my siblings. Oh, and what about Froya? If Hrype and Sibert were dragged off in chains, what on earth would happen to her?

I felt myself slump as the fight went out of me. 'Very well,' I said. 'Go and find Sir Alain.'

Hrype did not waste another moment. On his feet in the blink of an eye, he paused to rest a hand briefly on Edild's shoulder and was gone.

Sibert rose, more slowly and reluctantly. 'I'd better go home to my mother,' he said wearily. 'She'll be worrying.'

That was an understatement. As he passed me I whispered, 'Good luck,' and he gave a quick quirk of a smile.

Alone either side of dead Derman, Edild and I looked at each other. She reached out for the blanket and draped it

over the body. 'I will wait with him,' she said, tucking in
the folds of the heavy material as if soothing a sleeping
baby. 'Go where your heart is, Lassair.'

For a moment I thought she was referring to my Norman.
My Rollo. He had been much in my mind that morning,
and I had wished I had his strength and resourcefulness to
help and support me. But quickly I realized that Edild meant
my brother.

'Send for me if you have need of me,' I said as I, too,
got up.

She looked up and smiled. 'I will.'

The scene into which I entered when I reached my parents'
home was touchingly tender. My father stood just inside the
door as if to proclaim his right to defend his loved ones. My
two younger brothers sat beside the hearth, Squeak looking
belligerent, little Leir puzzled. Zarina sat on Haward's bed
with Haward on one side and my mother on the other. Each
held one of her hands, although she had to keep detaching
one or other of them to dry her tears.

I stared at Zarina, willing her to meet my eyes. After a
moment she raised her head and looked at me. 'You went
to the island before dawn, didn't you, Zarina?' She made
no response. 'Haward followed you, searching for you, and
he met you coming back. You were weeping.'

Still she did not reply. My mother tightened her hold on
Zarina's hand and glared at me, although I couldn't help
noticing that Haward did not – could not? – meet my eyes.
My father, picking up on the sudden tension, came to stand
beside me. 'What are you suggesting, Lassair?' His tone
was guarded. My dear father is a very fair man. He is deeply
protective of those he loves, yet always insistent that we
must look for the truth . . .

I turned to him quickly, trying to reassure him, then back
to Zarina. 'You claim you didn't see Derman, yet when Haward
got to the causeway not long afterwards, he spotted the body
straight away. Didn't you, Haward?'

My brother looked so wretched that I hated myself for
what I was doing. But I had to know! He looked at Zarina,

then at me. 'It was only j–just light when I got there,' he hedged. 'Zarina could easily have f–f–failed to—' Honesty fought with loyalty. Loyalty won. 'She w–wouldn't have s–s–seen him down in the w–water while it was still dark,' he said firmly.

Oh, Haward. 'She had gone specifically to *look* for him,' I said. 'There is starlight and usually moonlight except on a cloudy night, and last night was clear.'

I did not need to say more. I found it inconceivable that Zarina would not have noticed what Haward so clearly saw not long afterwards. Looking at her, I said, 'Zarina, why did you lie?'

My mother cried out in protest, but Zarina, turning to her, whispered something and gently touched her cheek. Looking back at me, she said simply, 'Because everyone knows I couldn't marry Haward all the time there was Derman. Of all people, I had the motive to kill him.' Her eyes filled with tears again. 'I cared deeply for him, like I'd have cared for a child wholly dependent on me. He saved my life. I would not have hurt him.' She turned to Haward. 'I would have given you up, for all that I love you, rather than harm Derman.' Then she threw her arms round my brother's neck, pressed herself to him and sobbed as if her poor heart would never heal.

My mother looked up at me with a curt nod as if to say, *There's your answer!*

I wanted to believe Zarina. I knew she loved my brother. In addition, she had sounded very plausible when she had spoken of her own brother. Yet there was something . . . I knew we had not got to the bottom of this.

'You'd better get your story ready,' I said unkindly. I was angry, with her, with myself, and it spilled over into my speech. 'Hrype's gone to inform Sir Alain de Villequier that Derman's been found dead.'

Nobody protested. Perhaps they were all so much worldlier than me that none of them had even contemplated my silly idea of concealing Derman's murder and hiding his body.

My father said with dignity, 'We shall be ready.' He glanced

at Zarina, a worried frown making deep creases in his forehead. 'I think,' he went on, 'we had better tell the truth and
say that you *did* see him in the water.'

Zarina's head shot up, and the shock made her face go
white. '*No.*' Then, quickly: 'They will not believe that I
didn't kill him. They'll say I needed him out of the way
and that I—'

I went to kneel in front of her. 'They won't believe you
if you say you didn't see him, Zarina,' I said gently. 'None
of us really did, and we're on your side.'

She looked wildly round at my father, my brothers, my
mother, and finally at Haward. She said in a pathetic little
voice, 'Didn't you?' and slowly they all shook their heads.

I thought she'd be furious. Instead, an expression of such
intense love spread over her face that I, too, felt like crying.
'And you still took me in and looked after me, even though
I'd lied to you,' she said wonderingly.

My father said, 'That's what families do.'

There didn't seem anything else to add.

I left them soon after that. I would have to speak privately
to Zarina some time soon; the conviction that she was still
hiding something just would not go away, and I cared far
too deeply for my brother's happiness to ignore it. With
Derman dead, there was no longer any impediment to the
marriage. Always assuming, that was, they didn't come along
and arrest Zarina for murder.

Had she killed her brother? No, came the answer, but it
was tentative, and I wished I could have been certain.

I wandered back aimlessly through the village towards
Edild's house. As I approached the path up to it, I remembered what I had intended to do today: I had promised to
pay another visit to Lady Claude. I had my satchel with
me – I rarely go anywhere without it – and so I changed
direction and headed on along the track out of the village
towards Lakehall.

I was ushered into Lady Emma's presence with such urgency
that my immediate thought was she herself was unwell.

Unfastening my satchel even as I hurried towards her, she saw my anxiety in my face and said quickly, 'No, Lassair! I am well, thank the dear Lord, and –' she lowered her voice to a whisper – 'the baby thrives.'

'I am relieved to hear it, my lady.' I tried to catch my breath. Bermund had been standing by the gate as if he had been waiting for me; he had grabbed my arm and made me move so fast that my feet had hardly touched the ground. Now I realized why. 'You sent for me.' It was not a question, for I knew she had.

'I did.' She frowned, looking puzzled. 'You arrived very quickly, I must say.'

I smiled. 'I was on my way here already, Lady Emma. I have another patient here besides you and, when I came to see her three days ago, she was not in her room.'

'Of course,' Lady Emma murmured. 'Well, Lassair, it is indeed on Lady Claude's behalf that I summoned you.'

'She is unwell?' In my head I ran through the symptoms she had complained of when I'd first seen her, recalling the remedies I had suggested and the doses I had prescribed.

Lady Emma put her head close to mine, although the only other people in the hall were a group of servants too far away to overhear. 'She is anxious about the coming wedding,' she whispered, 'and, indeed, she was already tense and nervous on her arrival here a month ago. Then poor dear Ida died, for which Claude blames herself since it was she who brought Ida here.'

'No blame can attach to her for that!' I exclaimed. 'The servant goes where the mistress bids.' I imagined – although I did not say so – that, while Lady Claude might have been a hard taskmistress, nevertheless Ida would have been the first to appreciate that she could have done a lot worse. In an uncertain age when starvation was always lying in wait for most of us, a good job where the work was not too arduous and, above all, was indoors, was not to be sniffed at.

'Yes, yes,' Lady Emma was saying, 'and both Lord Gilbert and I have repeatedly said as much to Claude.' Her frown returned, deepening. 'Now this morning we hear the dreadful news of the death of the simpleton. We tried to keep it from

Lady Claude, but unfortunately she was entering the hall as Sir Alain was told the news.' She sighed deeply. 'Poor Claude begins to speak of this being an accursed place –' she looked slightly indignant, as indeed she might – 'and I do fear, having listened to her wild talk, that her very reason is threatened by these foul deeds.'

I would not have been at all surprised. My impression of Lady Claude was of a driven woman, fierce in her desire to do her duty, intolerant of sin and of sinners. I sensed that there was something . . . not quite right about her, was the best way I could describe it to myself. Well, the poor soul had been thwarted of her vocation. Perhaps this reaction to the horrors she perceived around her was a symptom of a woman in torment.

'Shall I go to her?' I suggested. Lady Emma clearly meant well, for hadn't she just sent for me? However, there was little good I could do for Lady Claude standing there chatting in the hall.

'Of course, of course!' She shook her head at her own thoughtlessness and, gathering up her skirts, hurried away, with me on her heels. We left the hall, went along the passage and up the steps to Lady Claude's room, where Lady Emma tapped gently, listened for a moment and then carefully opened the door.

I followed her into the room. Lady Claude sat straight-backed on a stool, dressed as before in black, the stiff white linen framing her face covered by a long black veil. She looked more nunlike that ever. Her face was deadly pale, her mouth was a small, tight line, and her eyes were dull: the grey semicircles beneath them seemed to extend halfway down her cheeks. There was a young woman attending her – one of Lady Emma's maidservants – and, with an imperious wave of her hand, Lady Claude dismissed her. 'Go,' she said. 'The healer is here now.'

The maid scuttled out. I caught sight of her face as she passed me. She was young, not much more than twelve or thirteen, and it was clear from her expression that she couldn't wait to get away.

Studying Lady Claude, I didn't blame her.

Lady Emma bent over her guest. 'Would you like me to stay, Claude dear?' she asked.

Claude shook her head.

Lady Emma followed the maid out of the room, and I sensed it was only her good manners that stopped her relief from being equally visible.

I approached my patient. I knew how much pain she was in, and I was already calculating potions and proportions. 'I will give you a mixture for your headache,' I said, keeping my voice low and even. I have often heard skilled grooms soothing restless horses, and I sometimes think a healer speaks in much the same tone.

Lady Claude looked up at me. I read horror in her eyes, and I wondered how I could best reassure her. It was an interesting phenomenon, I thought absently, how her distress at the death of her seamstress and, now, of some man she didn't even know, had somehow got tangled up with the abrupt end of her hopes of being a nun and her fears concerning her impending marriage, knotting her up so tensely that the searing pain in her head was the result. I realized that her life just then must be all but unendurable. Edild and I often talk all evening about the human mind. All we ever resolve is that its mysteries are so far beyond us that the solution might as well be hidden away on the furthest star.

My present task, however, was not to speculate on the workings of the mind, but to alleviate my patient's agony. Quickly, I set up the tools of my trade on a small side table placed against the wall, going over in my mind what else I needed. I put my head out of the door and, seeing Bermund hovering in the passage below, asked him to send up both the hot water I would need for mixing certain ingredients and also some very cold water, with which to make a compress for Lady Claude's head.

While I waited, I suggested she lie down on her bed. To my surprise, she agreed. I helped her, for she staggered as she stood up, and took her hands. They were icy-cold and shaking. I supported her while she lay down, then covered her with a soft woollen blanket. As I straightened up from my ministrations, my eye caught something different in the room; something that I knew had not been there on my previous visit.

Behind the wooden bed head a small square of embroidery had been pinned to the wall. I peered closer; Lady Claude had closed her eyes, probably from the relief of lying down, and would, I hoped, not notice my curiosity.

I thought at first that it was another in the Seven Deadly Sins series, for some of the figures were recognizably similar: Lust in her scarlet gown, Wrath with his furious, cruel face. Then I noticed that the intricate, beautifully-worked border was made up of tiny letters. Concentrating hard, I began to make them out, and then I knew the subject of this little piece that Lady Claude had chosen to hang over her bed. She had embroidered the Ten Commandments.

My first reaction was a stab of pity for Sir Alain, who was to take as wife this peculiar, fanatical, devout woman. My second thought was that the pity surely belonged rather to Lady Claude.

The hot and cold water arrived, brought by a manservant under the watchful eye of Bermund. I needed privacy now. I thanked the servant, nodded to Bermund and, as they left, firmly closed the door. Then immediately I bent to my task.

We call the extraordinary substance that leaks out of the white poppy *lachrima papaveris*, for it does indeed resemble the poppy's tears. It can be found in our country, although it is rare, with nowhere near the spread of its cousin the red poppy. Only the white poppy will do in cases such as the one I now tackled, and healers generally conserve their supplies of its tears jealously, for it is costly and hard to come by. I mentioned this once to Hrype, and he went off into a sort of trance and told me an extraordinary tale, of traders from the east who brought with them out of the mysterious lands there great blocks of a magical substance that took away pain, brought beautiful dreams and, if taken to excess, brought about a sleep from which you didn't wake up. Edild, when I told her, sniffed and warned me never to experiment with this miraculous substance, although she refused to say why. Pressed, she merely said that repeated use would give me diarrhoea so badly that I would not dare to venture more than five steps from the jakes.

That was back in my early days as a healer, before I understood that one of our basic rules is that we never use our precious materials for anything but the desire to heal. That was what I was doing now: with careful hands I prepared the raw drug, then mixed it in hot water with a little honey to sweeten it and took the cup to my patient. Hardly aware now – I sensed her pain from two paces away – she obediently swallowed the drink and slumped back on her pillows.

The poppy juice itself induces sleep, but I added one or two other ingredients that take effect more swiftly. Lady Claude needed rest; I fervently hoped I had just given it to her.

I stood by her side for a while, watching the steady rise and fall of her narrow chest. I wondered, looking at her, if she had bound her breasts or was naturally flat. Her waist was insignificant, her hips angular and jutting under the soft, silky folds of her black gown. I eased the veil away from her headdress, careful to stick the pins that had secured it into the little pincushion by the bed. Then, gently turning her head, I undid the ties that held the stiff white wimple in place and removed it. She would sleep more peacefully without it. I noticed how tightly she had fastened it; no wonder the poor woman had a headache.

Her light-brown hair was greasy and smelled slightly unpleasant; the odour was a little like rancid lamb fat. I fetched a bottle of blended lavender and rosemary oils from my satchel and, mixing some in the hot water – still warm – I shook some drops on my hands and spread the liquid through the thin hair. Lady Claude stirred in her sleep, and I thought I saw a fleeting smile on her narrow mouth.

I retreated to the stool and sat down. I would watch over her a little longer, then leave her sleeping. I could soon be back if I was needed; Lady Emma knew where to find me.

A deep peace descended. The chamber was pleasantly cool, and I felt myself drifting into a doze. I shook myself

– it would never do for Lady Emma, or even worse, Bermund, to discover the healer as deeply asleep as her patient. I stood up, quietly gathered my bottles, jars and potions together and slipped out of the room.

SEVENTEEN

I t was late afternoon by the time I was back at Edild's house. I was physically exhausted, and I realized, with mild surprise, that I had not had any food all day. I pushed the door open and went in, the thought uppermost in my mind that I must find something to eat.

Edild was not alone. Hrype sat beside her and, seated on a stool with his back to me, I recognized Sir Alain de Villequier. On hearing me come in he stood up, turned and gave me a brief bow. Amazed – it was so extraordinary for a man of his stature to bow his head to someone like me – I managed to stammer out a polite greeting.

The reason for his courteous gesture became apparent as soon as he spoke: 'You have been looking after Lady Claude, Lassair, and I have no doubt that you have eased her pain. I thank you.' He hesitated, and I sensed there was more he wanted to say.

'I was pleased to be able to help her,' I replied. Then I added, 'She is troubled, sir. The violence of these two deaths has deeply disturbed her.' *Especially*, I could have added, *since she was already so distressed.* That distress, however, was caused by having to give up her vocation and instead marry this man, and since it would have been tactless to say so, I didn't.

'I cannot reach her,' Sir Alain burst out. 'We are shortly to be man and wife and, for all that it suits us and our kin that this union be brought about, still there are other considerations.' He paused. 'I would have her happy,' he said simply.

And you wish to be happy yourself, I thought. It was understandable – who did not seek earthly happiness, no matter how unreachable it sometimes seemed? – and I did not think the less of him. 'I believe,' I said, 'that her mind may be easier once Ida's killer has been found.'

He nodded, slowly sinking back on to his stool. I went to crouch beside my aunt, who met my eyes briefly. I thought I read warning in her eyes. I resolved to keep my peace and let the rest of them speak.

'We have been discussing the death of Derman,' Hrype said after a moment. 'Sir Alain has seen the body, which Edild has prepared for burial.' I had noticed as soon as I had come inside that Derman was gone. I looked at Hrype, raising my eyebrows in enquiry. 'He is in the crypt beneath the church,' he murmured. 'He will be buried tomorrow.'

'Sir Alain suggests that the death might well have been accidental,' Edild said, her tone giving nothing away. 'He observed marks on Derman's shins –' I noticed she did not say that we had also remarked on them – 'and proposes that Derman tripped, caught the edge of the causeway planks across his shins and, as he fell into the water, hit his head on one of the supporting posts.'

I opened my mouth to protest – there had been many more than one blow! – but Edild's eyes flashed an urgent message, and I kept silent. Swiftly, another thought blasted inside my mind: *Why was Sir Alain so eager to attribute the death to an accident?*

The answer came hard on the heels of the question: *Because he killed Ida and Derman saw him do it, so Derman, too, had to die.*

I lowered my head, hoping that Sir Alain had not seen the shock in my face as realization dawned. My mind was in a frenzy. Hrype must have picked it up, for I felt his hand reach out and take hold of mine. His was cool, and he began to stroke my fingers with his, the rhythm fast at first but gradually slowing. I felt my racing heartbeat begin to slow too, and soon I felt in control of myself. Gently, I disengaged my hand, turning to give him a quick smile of thanks.

I said, my voice quite calm, 'Lady Claude will be very pleased to hear that Derman was not the victim of another murder. She did not know Derman, so will not grieve for his death. Perhaps she will be able to put the matter from her mind now.'

Sir Alain's swift nod of agreement suggested that he hoped so too. He started to say something, but I did not hear; it had just occurred to me that if indeed he had killed Derman and had decided to adjudge the death an accident, then it surely meant he would not accuse Zarina of murdering her brother.

My thoughts were whirling once more. Was Sir Alain guilty? If he was, then it meant my liking and admiration for him were unwarranted, that my instincts were wrong, so badly wrong that I could barely bring myself to believe it. If he had killed Derman, then why was I so sure that there was something very dark that Zarina was keeping from me? Were my instincts about her wrong as well?

I wanted to talk to Hrype and Edild. I desperately wanted Sir Alain to go and, clamping down on the wild confusion in my head, I turned all my thoughts to willing him away. Quite soon I had my reward; relieved that all my powers hadn't abruptly deserted me, I stood up as he rose to leave and wished him a polite farewell.

Hrype stood in the doorway and presently said, 'He's gone. Heading for Lakehall, I should think, to visit Lady Claude.'

Edild was busy preparing food and I went to help her. 'Derman didn't die like he said,' I said quietly. 'It's quite impossible, and I can't think how Sir Alain hoped to convince us. We're healers!' I added resentfully. 'Does he think so poorly of us as to believe we cannot tell one accidental blow from many savage and deliberate ones?'

'Hush,' Edild said mildly. 'Use your energy setting out the bowls and the mugs.'

Hrype closed the door and went back to his seat by the hearth. 'Now there is nothing to prevent Haward and Zarina's marriage,' he remarked.

Amid all the other emotions, I felt a stab of pure joy. But swiftly it was obscured; my brother might very well be marrying a murderess . . .

I looked at Edild and at Hrype. Both appeared serene, although I knew from long experience that they were very skilled at not allowing their emotions to show. If they were anything but happy at this prospect, they were concealing it very well.

The food was ready: Edild must have been as hungry as I was, for she had set out a simple but very generous meal. The bread was fresh, and the cheese tangy, and straight away the three of us began to eat.

Up at Lakehall, Alain de Villequier tried to comfort the woman who was so soon to be his wife. He had arrived to find her sitting stiff and straight-backed, barely responding to Lady Emma's attempts at conversation. Her face was a deathly white mask, her small eyes sunk deep in her head. She was dressed in her usual black, the veil drawn forward so that it all but covered the starched white that so tightly framed her face. She smelled slightly unpleasant, although the odour was masked by a more wholesome perfume. Sniffing discreetly, he thought he smelt lavender and rosemary.

Of course, he thought. *The healer girl was here.*

It was late by the time he succeeded in reassuring Claude – if, indeed, he had, and her apparent quiescence was not just a pretence – and Lady Emma persuaded him to stay to supper and accept a bed for the night. Claude forced herself to sit at table for the evening meal, although Alain wished she had not. The sight of her pushing food around her plate and nibbling at the tiniest mouthfuls was singularly irritating, although he told himself repeatedly not to be so hard on her. The meal proceeded on through several courses – Alain could well appreciate why Lord Gilbert was the size he was – and finally, as the last platters were cleared away, Claude stood up and announced she was going to bed. Alain felt relief race through him.

What am I to do? he wondered. *She is soon to be my wife and, although I try, I cannot truly make myself like her, never mind love her.*

He sat twirling the stem of his wine goblet, listening to Lord Gilbert and Lady Emma's voices beside him, quietly discussing some small domestic matter. Did they love each other? He believed they did. He wondered if love had been there from the start; like him and Claude, their marriage had been arranged to suit their families and not themselves. Would love grow similarly between himself and Claude? He hoped so, but in his heart he had his doubts. *The trouble is*, he reflected, *I know what love can be.*

His grief threatened to overcome him. Desperate, he raised the goblet and drank down the contents, swiftly, eagerly. Lord Gilbert, attentive host that he was, noticed and made a discreet sign to a servant, who came forward and refilled Alain's goblet. Alain drank again. The wine was good. If he could have no real hope of happiness, then he would lose himself in drunken oblivion.

Lord Gilbert's wine, however, had failed to bring about the desired result. Now, late in the night, Alain was out of bed and pacing the deserted hall. He had a great deal to think about. He had done wrong, terribly wrong, and his sins played on his mind and would not let him rest.

The hall seemed to confine him. It resembled his own, although it was considerably larger and much grander. *We shall live in a house like this one day, Claude and I*, he mused silently. *Perhaps the grand manor of her family; perhaps a place that I shall win through my own efforts. As man and wife, it shall be our home until death separates us.* The thought threatened to choke him, suffocate him; he had to have air. The hall had been secured for the night, but the bolts and the heavy wooden bar that slotted between iron brackets on the doors were kept in prime condition, and he drew them back without making a sound. He opened one of the doors just enough to slip through the gap and sped down the steps and across the courtyard. The gate, too, had been secured; with barely a pause, he climbed over it.

He knew where he was heading. Instead of going down the track from Lakehall and turning right along the road into the village, he struck out across the open ground. Lakehall was built on the better-drained land to the south and east of the village; on the far side of the road, his feet would soon have blundered into wet, boggy ground, but up here he could remain dry-shod. Lord Gilbert worked these acres – or, rather, his peasants did – with some success.

He saw the outline of the church rise up ahead of him, a darker shape on this dark night. He clambered over the fence into the churchyard, skirting other graves until he came to the one he sought. Then he sat down beside it. 'I'm sorry,' he whispered. There were tears on his face. 'I'm so sorry.'

He sat there for a long time.

The sound, when it finally penetrated his consciousness, seemed like something that belonged to the night. It began so quietly, so subtly, that it was almost as if a soft little breeze had sprung up to bend the tall reeds and grasses and make them flute a gentle melody. Whatever it was, it was a sad sound; achingly sad. Alain's sore heart gave a throb of pain, and he bowed his head, accepting it as his punishment.

The sound grew louder and, disturbed now, Alain raised his eyes to look around. He realized something: there was no wind. The night was absolutely still.

Where, then, did those uncanny sounds originate?

He rose to his feet, remaining in a crouch as he stared into the darkness. His heart was thumping hard as he sensed danger. He was poised for flight, yet his feet remained fixed to the spot. The sounds went on, then suddenly stopped.

He sensed movement, quite close. He spun round, eyes wide: nothing.

Then the sounds started again, far louder now, as if whatever unnatural force was making them had sneaked right up close. Then abruptly they altered, and now Alain knew that they came from a human throat, for he heard *words* . . .

'Where are you?' he cried, panic in his voice. 'Show yourself!'

Again, nothing.

Then he remembered who he was, and a small amount of courage came back. 'I am Alain de Villequier,' he said, trying to stop the tremble that was audible in the words. 'I am the justiciar! I say again, show yourself!'

Then, horribly, there came a cruel laugh. A harsh voice – a man's? A woman's? – said, 'I know who you are.'

The sounds began again, right behind him. But he heard them only for an instant. Then there came a high-pitched whistle, something hit him very hard on the back of the head and all went black.

I was awake early, for Edild had told me before we went to bed that I would have to check on Derman's body that morning. Her work is always faultless, but she has her reputation to think of; if any smell had sneaked up out of the crypt and into the church, word would soon have spread that the healer did not know her own business. I loaded my satchel with fresh supplies of sweet-smelling herbs – bay-laurel leaves, mint, sprigs of rosemary – and Edild gave me several of the special incense cones she makes, the ingredients of which remain a secret that she promises one day to reveal to me.

I slipped into the church, relieved to see that there was nobody there. Closing the door behind me, I walked up to the altar, my eyes on the wooden cross. My senses alert, my skin tingling, I sensed the presence that is always there. I let my mind reach out, opening myself at the same time so that I was receptive. On occasions, I have felt such a jolt of power in the church that I have staggered, but today there was nothing. The presence was still there; of that I had no doubt. But it was quiet, its attention far removed from me.

I bowed low, muttered a few words and backed away.

I walked over to the low door that opens on to the steps down to the crypt. So far I had detected no aroma that should not be there. The little church usually smells of damp, with the lingering memory of incense and of stale sweat. I pushed the door open a crack and sniffed. Now I could smell Edild's incense. She must have left some burning yesterday, and the smoky perfume had been trapped behind the door. Encouraged, I hurried down the steps and emerged into the low-ceilinged crypt.

I know about the strength of a vaulted roof, for Hrype has explained to me that the arch is a wonderful concept and can bear vast weight. Nevertheless, I am always uneasy

in the crypt, especially on my own. I crossed to where the
wrapped body lay, on boards stretched across two trestles.
The head was bound in many layers of cloth. Presumably,
Edild had wished to cover up that terrible wound so that
no blood showed on the outside. The legs were less thoroughly wrapped, and I saw faint blotches where blood from
the cuts on the shins had leached into the material. Cuts . . .
I thought about that. If you fell against the edge of a plank,
would it cut you? It might bruise you and give you a deep
graze, but surely you needed something sharper to give cuts
such as those on Derman's shins?

I pictured the causeway. And I realized that the death
couldn't have happened the way we had thought, for the layout
of the place meant that it was all but impossible. For Derman
to crack his shins against the causeway, he would have had
to be running through the shallow water *towards* it, not along
it, and he would surely have fallen on to the planks that had
just tripped him up, not off them into the water . . .

I was going to have to revisit the scene of his death.

Swiftly, I walked round the body, sniffing as I went. The
stench of death was there, of course it was, but so far the cool
air in the crypt and my aunt's care were keeping it at bay. I
arranged my fragrant herbs around the corpse, lit three more
incense cones and then went back up the steps.

The priest had arrived, and he turned to stare at me as I
emerged from the crypt. He is wary of Edild and, by asso-
ciation, of me too, for like many men, especially men of the
church, he does not approve of a woman who lives by her
own wits, independent of any man. However, like most of
the village, he has had occasion to ask for her help, and she
always responds with her usual generosity and competence.
He is, I suppose you could say, carefully neutral regarding
my aunt and me.

'Good morning, Father Augustine,' I said, making a
respectful bow. Edild always says that it is best to treat potential enemies with courtesy, thus giving them no excuse for
releasing whatever malice they may have towards you.

He returned the greeting. 'You have been tending the
body?' He jerked his head towards the crypt door.

'Yes.'

'Does it – er, is it all right?'

The morning was already warm, with the promise of a hot day. I knew what he meant. 'So far, yes. If I might suggest, you should not delay in putting him in the ground.'

'No, indeed.' He frowned. 'I have told his sister that he will be buried this morning.' Looking up, briefly he met my eyes, and I was surprised to read emotion in his. 'There will be few other mourners, I fear,' he said.

'People are afraid of what they do not understand,' I said softly. 'Derman was not like the rest of us.'

'No,' Father Augustine said. Then, abruptly: 'There was much talk concerning the dead young woman. They would have it that Derman had some hopeless love for her and killed her when she turned him down. I do not believe it is true,' he said fervently.

'No, neither do I.'

He seemed surprised; perhaps I was the only villager to freely admit seeing it the way he did. 'I would not bury a murderer in sacred ground,' he said.

'Of course not.' I was suddenly filled with relief for Father Augustine's conviction of Derman's innocence. I was quite sure Zarina would have been devastated if Derman had been refused a proper burial. Perhaps the priest might even have been reluctant to marry her to my brother had he believed she was sister to a murderer.

Zarina. Not, perhaps, sister to a murderer. But what of she herself?

As if he, too, were thinking of Zarina, Father Augustine said, 'Derman's sister is now free to marry your brother Haward and, indeed, Haward has already spoken to me of his hopes.'

'Yes,' I said. 'It would make Haward very happy.'

My words were automatic, the natural, polite response to what the priest had said. My thoughts, however, were far away.

I was on my way across the churchyard when I glanced across at Ida's grave.

There was something wrong with it; the humped earth that covered her was higher than it ought to have been. My satchel banging against my side, I raced across to look more closely.

He lay face down. The back of the skull had borne the same savage attack as poor Derman's. There was blood; a lot of blood. On the left, where the head curved out above the neck, there was a huge swelling about the size of my clenched fist. Crouching beside him, I put my fingers to it, feeling for the same devastating crushing of the bones that I had witnessed in Derman.

The swelling made it impossible to tell. I reached in my satchel for a piece of clean cloth and wiped away the blood, my eyes straining for fragments of bone. Instantly, the blood welled up again, lots of it, and impatiently I mopped it up, still searching for what I was almost sure I would find.

Then I gave myself a mental kicking for being so stupid; I could only think that the shock had affected me. The blood was flowing; *he was still alive*.

I took another pad of cloth and, swiftly finding the source of the bleeding, pressed it to the wound. I began to tuck his cloak around him – he felt terribly cold – but then I thought that I'd only be keeping the cold *in*, so I dragged it off him and lay down beside him, pressing my warm body against his cold one and pulling the cloak over us both. I dared not leave him. All my training told me that his life hung by a thread.

I opened my mouth, drew in the deepest breath I could manage and yelled at the top of my voice for Father Augustine.

EIGHTEEN

We thought he would surely die.

I have rarely seen my aunt fight so hard to save a life. I did not believe him to be a murderer and nor, I think, did my aunt. At the very least, she seemed to be giving him the benefit of the doubt. It was, of course, still possible, still plausible, that he had quietly dispatched Ida so that she did not reveal their secret and prevent his marriage to Lady Claude; that he had been forced to seek out and kill Derman because Derman knew what he had done.

But if that was how it had happened, who had attacked Sir Alain and left him for dead?

To begin with, Edild required two pairs of hands, and I had no choice but to swallow down my squeamishness and do as I was commanded. The swelling on the left side of our patient's skull had grown alarmingly large now, as fluid of some sort leaked out of his head. Edild applied successive cold compresses, under which she laid a layer of fresh, crushed comfrey leaves and the flowering stems of water pepper, but it was clear she was losing the battle. The bleeding that had so worried me seemed to have lessened, but I could tell from Edild's grave manner that this was not necessarily a sign that Sir Alain was going to live.

I plucked up my courage and, hoping I was not interrupting some intricate thought process, said, 'What are you trying to do?'

She wasn't angry with me; far from it. She turned, gave me a quick smile and said, 'I am sorry, Lassair. I have been so preoccupied that I had forgotten, for the moment, that a part of my duty is to teach you.'

'It's all right, I—'

She ignored the interruption. 'I have often spoken with Hrype concerning wounds such as this one. It is our conclusion that when someone is hit very hard on the head, there is swelling on the outside of the skull cage, which with luck can be alleviated, but there is also similar swelling inside the head bones.' She shook her head in frustration. 'If only we could look and see what causes it! But, of course, that is impossible with a living man . . .' Her words trailed off. She knelt in silence beside her patient, looking at him with an anxious frown. Then, once again turning to me, she said, 'There is a procedure called trepanation. Hrype has told me of it; he has seen it done.'

Uneasiness crept up on me. I had never heard the word before and had no idea what it meant, but there was something in her voice that told me she, too, was disturbed. 'What is it?' The words were barely a whisper, for my mouth was suddenly too dry to speak.

She took a breath, straightened her back and said, 'It involves making a hole in the skull to allow whatever is causing the swelling inside the head to escape. According to Hrype, relieving the built-up pressure frequently restores a patient to consciousness and quite often they live.'

Frequently. Quite often. It sounded as if this operation was by no means a certain cure.

I said, horrified as the realization swept over me, 'You're not thinking of doing this to *him*?' I indicated our comatose patient.

Edild, too, looked at him. 'If there is no other way, I may have to,' she said gravely. 'We are healers, Lassair. We have given our solemn oath to save life.'

'What – how would you do it?' I asked. I didn't want to know – the dreaded queasiness was building up, and I was seeing black spots on the periphery of my vision. There was a thundering, drumming sound in my head. But I, too, was a healer; my aunt was an excellent teacher, and it was my duty to learn from her all that I could.

'Trepanation involves the removal of a piece of the skull,' she said, her voice eager, as if it was a relief to speak with authority after facing up to her inability to help her patient. 'You remove the flesh that covers it, then you scrape, saw or bore through the bone and cut away the firm white skin that covers the brains.'

I concentrated on thinking about the healed patient following this dreadful operation. I told myself that the discovery of how to do it was a gift from the spirits to mankind, a gift that allowed lives to be saved.

Some lives . . .

'Hrype has seen this done?' I asked.

'So he says.'

'Did the man live?'

'The patient was a woman, and yes, she did.' Her eyes looked suddenly unfocused, as if her thoughts had gone far away. 'She kept the piece of her own skull as an amulet, and now Hrype has it in memory of her,' she said softly.

I thought about that. I wondered who the woman had been, but I knew I could not ask. Hrype's secrets were sacrosanct and, even if he had confided in Edild, she would not tell me. 'Should I go and fetch him?'

It was her turn to consider. She removed the compress on Sir Alain's head and put her hand on the swelling. 'I think—' she began. But then her frown lifted and her expression changed. She shot me a swift glance of triumph and said, 'No need. The swelling is going down.' She grabbed my hand and laid it very gently on the lump on Sir Alain's head. 'Feel,' she commanded.

I let my hand rest softly over the area and then, to confirm my initial impression, felt around the lump with my fingertips. Edild was right. I looked up and met her eyes. I felt like cheering, and not only because I had just avoided witnessing – perhaps helping with – an operation that would have seemed more like torture than healing.

'What's happened?' I asked.

She shrugged. 'I cannot say. Possibly the cold of the compresses and the power of the healing herbs has done the trick.' She glanced around and then, lowering her voice, whispered, 'We should thank them.'

I spun round to look where she had looked. I thought I saw movement, and for the blink of an eye I could see a silver wolf and, right up close behind me, a red fox.

I should have known they were there. They are our spirit guides; my Fox is often with me, and I have almost – but not quite – learned to accept his presence. It was, however, a rare privilege to be allowed to catch a glimpse of Edild's silver wolf. I have only seen him twice before, and the first time I thought he was a fox. When I told my aunt I had seen him she told me I had been imagining things. I was young then, and I almost believed her. I know better now.

I whispered to Fox, telling him how much I appreciated his presence, especially when I hadn't been conscious of asking him to come, and for a moment he stood beside me, mouth stretched in what looked very like a grin. Then he faded away.

It was as if the presence of the spirit animals had brought a special, precious mood inside the little room. While they were there, everything had a shine to it; scents were intensified, colours were brighter. With their departure, life returned to normal and, just for a moment, I saw how uninspiring *normal* actually was.

Then Edild commanded me to go outside and fetch fresh water, and I remembered with a jolt that this was no time for meditating on the spirits. We had a job to do.

Some time later, Edild said there was no need for both of us to watch over our patient, because, with any luck, he would wake up soon and in the meantime it was only a matter of keeping him warm and regularly renewing the compress. 'We have almost used up our supplies of water pepper,' she said. 'Go and gather some more.'

I hastened to obey. I would have to walk right down to the fen edge, but I was glad of it. My mind still kept going back to the images of that terrible operation, and I knew that what I needed was a good, hard walk in the sunshine. I fetched my basket and set off.

I was surprised to see by the sun that it was still only mid-morning. It felt as if my aunt and I had been battling for our patient's life for days. I turned my face up to the sun's warmth and silently expressed my gratitude to the spirits who had come to help us. Later, I knew, Edild would slip outside and perform her ceremony of thanks, and I would join her. She frequently reminded me that she and I were but the instruments through which the spirits did their healing work. The power came from them.

I made my way along the water's edge, gathering as I went. I found that my steps had once again led me to the island, which was hardly surprising since it was there, a presence in the back of my mind, all the time. Putting down my basket, I stepped on to the planks of the causeway. I remembered those cuts in Derman's shins. I recalled my certainty, earlier that morning, that they had not been caused by his falling against the planks.

I stopped above the place where his body had been found. I stared down into the black water, then I looked at the planks on which I stood. Just beside me there was one of the upright posts that supported the causeway. This one was quite thick – about as wide as my palm – and stuck up about a foot or so above the planking. Could it be this that had caused the cuts on Derman's shins? I bent down and felt its edge. It was not very sharp, and surely it was too narrow to have wounded *both* shins. I straightened up again, puzzled. Something had tripped him; the evidence was there on his body. Unless, of course, the trip had happened some time earlier in the day that he had died . . . But he had fallen into the water, and how else had that happened? Had he been pushed?

I looked from one side of the causeway to the other, trying to decide if it was wide enough for a man to have got up close enough behind Derman – a big man himself – to push him in. It was, but surely Derman would have seen or at least heard his assailant's approach?

'*Oh!*' I cried out aloud in frustration.

Then I saw it. My eyes flashed to the other side of the causeway – and I could have cheered.

On each of the two upright posts, right at the spot where Derman fell into the water, there was a faint mark. Each mark was an indentation in the wood, more pronounced on the outside edge of each post, and about three or four hands' breadths above the planking.

Someone, knowing that Derman visited the island and the place where he believed his beloved Ida still lay, had been waiting. This someone had fixed a trip wire between the two posts. They had hidden until Derman arrived; then, perhaps, had spooked him, so that when he crossed towards the island, he was hurrying. Perhaps in his haste to get to her he always hurried.

The trip wire caught him across the shins, and he fell, down into the mere. His assailant had then leapt out from his cover, raised his weapon and, as Derman lay in the water, the breath knocked out of him by his fall, had brought it down savagely and repeatedly on the back of Derman's head.

Who was it?

I had thought it was Sir Alain, but now that he had been attacked, bludgeoned in exactly the same way, I knew I was wrong. Was it someone who believed Derman had killed Ida?

I thought about the day I had discovered Ida's body. Derman had been hiding in the clump of willows that stood on a small area of higher ground between the island and the village. He had been weeping. He must have just seen Ida, dead in Granny Cordeilla's tomb; I was sure of it. I was equally sure he had put her there. I had talked with Zarina, and she'd told me how her brother had killed a man who was hunting for her.

Derman killed him and hid his body where it would never be found. He put it in a—

In a grave, I'd thought then. Derman was of very limited intelligence, but one thing he would surely remember was killing a man and hiding the body in someone else's grave. I had wondered – believed – that Derman had killed Ida and then used the same clever ploy – the one clever ploy of his entire life – again.

What if he hadn't killed her? Now, all but sure he hadn't, I thought about it again. What if, having sneaked away from Zarina's vigilance one night and gone off wandering on his own – perhaps to sit out under the stars and think about his beloved – he had come across her dead body? Oh, poor,

poor Derman. My heart filled with pity for him. If it had indeed happened like that, what ill chance that he should have been the one to find her.

I pictured him as I had seen him that morning, his face red, his eyes swollen from weeping. I pictured him some time earlier during that long night, stumbling on Ida as she lay dead. I saw his disbelief turn to certainty; saw him pick her up as easily as if she had been a child, cradling her to him in death as he surely never could have done in life. I saw him bear her to the island, where he knew there had recently been an interment. I saw him place her carefully on the ground, then push aside the heavy stone slab and place her in the ground beside my Granny.

How long had he sat there sobbing? Had it been the first lightening of the sky which heralds the dawn that had finally driven him away, into his pathetic and inefficient hiding place among the willows? I thought of his pain, his grief. It was all but unbearable.

I let myself into the house carefully and quietly, anxious not to disturb Sir Alain. Edild looked up from her place beside him. She smiled at me and said, in a voice only a little softer than usual, 'Did you find any?'

The water pepper. Of course; that was why I had gone out. 'Yes, the basket's half full. I left it outside by the outhouse.'

'You covered it? The stems should not be left out in the sunshine because—'

'Yes, I covered it, and anyway it's in the shade.'

'Good.'

I crept towards Sir Alain. 'How is he?'

She glanced at him. 'Much the same.'

'Will he live?' I breathed the words so quietly that Edild must have read my lips rather than heard what I said. If he were conscious, I did not want him to hear the question, which might have sounded callous. On principle, too, it's usually best not to let a patient know how ill he is.

Edild shrugged. 'I hope so.'

I sat down beside her, desperate to share my new thoughts with her. 'Edild, what if it happened like this?' I began, my voice low. 'Someone killed Derman's beloved Ida, and he found the body and put it in Granny's grave. Someone else saw him do so and, believing Derman had killed her, they killed him too, so that Ida was revenged.'

Edild nodded slowly. 'And who do you think this second someone might be?'

I had been thinking of little else all the way home. There was really only one possible answer. He had told me he honoured her far too much to try to seduce her when he was bound to a wife he loathed. Then, suddenly and unexpectedly freed by that wife's death, he had hastened to find Ida, declare his love and ask her if she would be his. Except he was too late, because Ida was in her grave – my Granny's grave – and he witnessed the moment when a big, shambling, simpleton of a man put her there.

I said, 'Alberic.'

Edild considered that. Then she said, 'You may very well be right, Lassair. It would explain, I think, why Alberic also attacked Sir Alain.' She glanced down at her patient and, as she spoke his name, I thought I saw the tiniest of movements behind his closed eyelids. I watched carefully to see if he would stir, but he lay still.

I believed I understood what Edild had said. 'You're suggesting,' I said slowly, thinking as I spoke, 'that somehow Alberic discovered that Ida was pregnant. Perhaps he saw her from a distance and noticed she looked different? Perhaps he *spoke* to her!'

I realized, with some surprise, that it was perfectly possible. When I had met him in the graveyard, I had been so busy trying to prove I'd been right and he had fathered Ida's child that it had blinded me to everything else. Suddenly, I remembered how he had looked at me when I'd asked if he had been her lover. His expression had been a wild mixture of emotions and, picturing his face now, I wondered if the anger I had seen was because, aware *he* had not been her lover, he knew that someone else had been. He had told me himself that Ida had admitted no village lad to her bed; the only man who could possibly have fathered her child had to be someone she had met after she went to work for Lady Claude at Heathlands . . . *He knew who it was.*

'He killed Derman, and he tried to kill Sir Alain too because he knew Sir Alain had seduced her, left her pregnant and abandoned her to marry his rich Lady Claude,' I said, breathless as the words tumbled out, 'and—'

'I did not abandon her,' a husky, tremulous, but determined voice said. 'I would never have done that.'

Edild jerked as if someone had stuck a pin in her. Her attention fully on her patient, she crouched over him, her hand on his forehead. 'How do you feel?' she asked anxiously. 'Are you in much pain?'

He was trying to put his hand to the bump on his head. Gently, she took hold of it and replaced it on top of the blanket tucked around him. 'Better not to touch,' she said. 'I have a draught ready for you which will ease the pain. Lassair!' she said curtly, turning to me and bringing me out of my amazed state of shock. She nodded in the direction of the cup she had set ready, and I reached for it and handed it to her. She raised his head a little, supporting it with one arm, and held the cup to his lips while he drank, making a face at the bitter taste. He drained the cup, then she helped him lie back on his pillow.

Edild was watching him. He glanced at her, then up at me. He said, 'I will tell you the story of my love for Ida, then you shall judge for yourselves.'

Edild opened her mouth to speak – probably to tell him he ought to sleep, not talk – but he made a small gesture with his hand and so she didn't. I turned to look at him, and he began.

'My family has long wished for a union by marriage with the de Seés of Heathlands,' he said, 'for money is little use without position and influence, and the converse equally applies. It is true that, in the end, money can purchase position, but these things take time, and Claritia de Seés is not a patient woman. The better way, in her eyes, was for her daughter to marry into the de Villequier family, riding high, as we do, in royal favour and destined for great things.' He paused, drew breath and then said, 'I was not averse to the match, for, like the rest of my family, I saw the advantage of a sudden influx of wealth into our coffers. I agreed to visit Heathlands and, when I was presented to Lady Geneviève, the elder of Claritia's two daughters, I saw no reason not to agree to our betrothal. She is very lovely, prettier than Claude and with something wistful in her face. I did not know then, of course, about—' He broke off. 'I must tell the story as it happened,' he muttered.

He paused again, for longer this time. Then he said, 'Ida sewed for the de Seés family before she was engaged to help Claude, although only on occasions. One day I met her as she was hurrying home to the village. Typically, Claritia had detained her, and it was already growing dark. Ida was scared, although she tried to hide it.' His expression softened. 'I saw her to her home. Once she got over her shyness at being with Lady Claritia's future son-in-law, her true, delightful personality emerged. We started talking. She made me laugh.' He smiled. 'I think I fell in love with her that first evening. I give you my word that I did not seduce her –' he looked up at me – 'although, in truth, I know I was wrong to allow our love to develop, bound to marry as I was. But –' he made a small, helpless sound, as if at a loss to explain – 'I could not help myself. I loved Ida, she loved me, and when the opportunity arrived for us to become lovers, neither of us hesitated.'

Two tears spilled over his eyelids and slid away down his face. 'I must tell you now of Geneviève,' he said, 'for of all the tragic things that have happened, it is the suffering that I caused to her that bites the most cruelly. As the days went by and I grew to know her better, I realized with dismay that she was a chronically shy woman, modest in the extreme and very frightened at the prospect of matrimony.'

Suddenly, it was not his voice I was hearing but Gurdyman's. I was back in the little enclosed Cambridge garden, and the wizard was speaking. *Geneviève was an innocent. She had been told by her mother what a wife is to expect on her wedding night – knowing Claritia, who is a somewhat coarse and insensitive woman, I do not imagine she spoke gently or cautiously – and she was fearful and apprehensive.*

Poor Geneviève. I was sorry for her – what woman would not be? – but I could not see why Sir Alain should feel responsible for her state of mind. He was speaking; I listened.

'Geneviève saw me making love to Ida,' he said baldly. 'Ida and I used to meet in a glade on the edge of the forest. We thought it was sufficiently far from the house for us to be undisturbed, but it seems that, as her fears and terrors had grown, Geneviève had taken to going out for long walks by herself. By sheer bad luck, she found her way to our grove. She heard Ida's cries of pleasure, but mistook them and thought I was attacking her. She screamed and screamed.' His face looked grey. 'I have never heard a sound like it,' he muttered. 'I leapt up, still undressed, and hurried over to her. She was staring at my – at me, and then at Ida, lying naked on the ground with a white shift pulled up over her face to disguise her identity. She wouldn't stop screaming. I knew she must not be allowed to tell, so I did a terrible thing.' He paused, drew breath and went on. 'I told her that the thing lying on the ground was no human woman, but a spirit. A night hag, a succubus.' He shuddered. 'Oh, dear Lord above, how many times have I regretted what I did! I told her I had been attacked, wrestled to the ground, my manhood roused by this foul forest spirit. God help me, I played on Geneviève's frail mental state. I was well aware she was already deeply disturbed about sex and having to be married to me, and to save my own skin I used that knowledge to cover up what Ida and I had been doing.'

He stopped talking. The silence seemed to hold the shadow of his words. I risked a glance at him. He was still deathly pale, his face full of pain, grief and, I now knew, guilt.

'My shameful ruse worked, too well,' he muttered, 'and she never really recovered. I thought for one wonderful moment that I might not have to go ahead with the marriage to unite my kin and the de Seés. I dared to hope that, somehow, somewhere, there might be a chance for Ida and me. But I reckoned without Claritia. As soon as she realized there was no hope for Geneviève, she came up with another plan.'

No hope for Geneviève. Once more I heard Gurdyman's voice, speaking sadly of the poor girl. *She was found one morning wandering outside in the cold dressed in nothing but a thin shift. She had seen something that had terrified her, but she was unable to say what it was. Her nervousness concerning the proposed marriage turned to abject horror. Then, when her mother attempted in her robust way to bring Geneviève to her senses, the girl fainted dead away and could not be revived for two days. Since then she has been a slight, silent shadow who flits on the periphery of her family's life and, in the main, is left alone.*

'I know what she did,' I whispered. 'She made Lady Claude give up her vocation to be your wife.'

'She did, she did,' he sighed heavily. 'And, weakling that I am, I agreed. But you must believe what I said just now: in truth, and I swear it upon what little honour remains to me, I would not have abandoned Ida. I could never have done that. Ida and I have always been discreet; Claude knows nothing of what we are to each other, and I would have made sure she never found out. I had formed a plan to acquire a little cottage for Ida where she could bear my child and raise it in safety, where I would have visited when I could.' He turned to Edild, sitting so still and silent as she listened. 'I would have supported them, my Ida and my child!' he said urgently.

'On your wife's money,' Edild said neutrally.

She was right, and there was no denying it. All the same, I felt a stab of pity for Sir Alain, for as my aunt spoke those four damning words, he flinched as if he had been stabbed.

I said, wanting, I think, to save him further pain, 'Alberic's motive for attacking you must, then, have surely been jealousy, for Ida, whom he adored, had given her love to you and not to him.'

He frowned. 'Yes. Perhaps, yes.'

I thought of something that might confirm that it had undoubtedly been Alberic who hit Sir Alain. 'Did you notice anything unusual just before the attack?' I asked.

The frown intensified as he tried to remember. 'I heard something very odd,' he said eventually, and I knew I'd been right. 'It was a sort of humming, and the very notes were enough to make a listener feel so sad, as if all the happiness had been sucked out of the world.' I sympathized; I, too, had suffered the same reaction.

Unless there had been two men skulking around and humming in the graveyard, we had our proof of Alberic's guilt.

I thought about it, extending the image of Alberic's furious attack to encompass another killing. 'It must have been Alberic who killed Ida,' I said slowly, for all that I knew I had originally decided he was innocent. 'He came here full of hopes to claim her and marry her, now that his wife's death had left him free, and when he approached her, she told him she was pregnant by another man who loved her, and she loved him too, so there was no hope for Alberic, after all he'd been through, and he strangled her. Then he had to kill Derman because he thought he'd witnessed the murder, and then finally he tried to kill you, Sir Alain, for despoiling Ida.'

My tumble of words was followed by utter silence. Edild was studying me closely, but her expression told me nothing, and I did not know if she agreed with my suggestion of what had happened or if she believed I was quite wrong.

Tentatively, Sir Alain said, 'It could, I suppose, have been as you say . . .' His voice tailed off as if he could not quite convince himself.

The silence fell again, enveloping us all. Then at last Edild spoke. 'Perhaps,' she said. 'But consider this.'

She stood up, gracefully, in one single movement. She crossed to the place in the corner where we store firewood and, selecting a length of birch as long as her arm, held it in both hands. She swung it through the air, first from right to left, then from left to right.

'I am right-handed,' she said, 'and it is natural for me to swing a weapon this way.' She swung the wood again from right to left. 'My right hand and arm are the stronger, because habitually I use them more, and swinging this way lets the stronger arm dominate.'

She put the wood tidily back in its place and sat down once more beside Sir Alain. She reached out and touched the swelling on his head, hidden under its compress. 'You were hit on the back of your head on the left side,' she said. 'Derman, whom Lassair suggests was felled by the same man, was hit on the right side of his head.'

She looked at me, at Sir Alain, and then back at me. Neither he nor I spoke, so in the end she did.

With a faint sigh, she said, 'One attack was by a right-hander, the other by a left-hander. You and Derman, Sir Alain, were assailed by two different men.'

NINETEEN

The effort of talking seemed to have exhausted Sir Alain, who was lying back on his pillows with his eyes closed. 'He should sleep,' Edild whispered to me.

I nodded. 'Can you spare me for a while?' I asked.

'I can, yes. If you are going out, you can take this tonic round to William for his old mother.' She took the small vessel down from the shelf and handed it to me.

I put it in my satchel. 'What's in it?'

Edild gave a wry smile. 'Little that will do her any good, I fear, for she is dying. It is mainly honey and water, with some cleansing herbs that will give a bitter tang and make the medicine taste sufficiently unpleasant for the old soul to believe it must surely be beneficial.' She had suggested to me before that even a mixture that was mainly water might persuade a patient that his symptoms had been reduced if the healer presented it with sufficient conviction.

I was turning to leave when my aunt caught my sleeve. 'Don't accept anything in payment,' she said. 'It would not be right, for what I am sending is worthless.'

I nodded my understanding. *Worthless*, I thought as I strode away. I would do as my aunt commanded and take no payment, but I did not agree with her assessment of her remedy. She may not appreciate it, but the people of our village believe in her, and indeed they are right to do so. Even a bottle of water has worth when it comes from Edild's hands.

I made my way to William's tiny house and, when he came to the door in answer to my soft tap, I gave him the remedy. He stared at it as if I had presented him with a magical elixir – which, in a way, I suppose I had.

'Thank you,' he breathed, his eyes moist. 'Thank your aunt, please. I know how much this will help Mother.'

It did not seem right to allow him to hope. I said, as
gently as I could, 'Do not expect a miracle, William. She
is very old and frail, and it may be that her time on earth
is drawing to its close.'

He looked at me. 'I know,' he said simply. 'But I am not
sure she does. If I can keep her spirits up, it helps.'

I reached out and took his hand. His words had moved
me, and I admired him for his selflessness. That it came at
a heavy cost to him was evident in his face and his bearing.
I could think of nothing to say, so presently I let his hand
drop and, with a brief farewell and a reminder to call on
us if he needed anything, I left.

I could stride away in the sunshine of a lovely day.
William, poor man, had to shut himself up in the frowsty
darkness with a very old woman. I asked the spirits to
support him and give him the strength he needed.

William's house was on the far side of the village, near
the spot where the road diverges and paths strike off
towards Breckland to the north-east and Thetford to the
east. Instead of returning along the bend of the track that
runs through the village, I cut due south across the higher
ground that lies to the east so as to approach Edild's
house from the back. The land was much drier up here
above the marshes, but even so it did not yield much.
There was some pasture, cropped close by the nibbling
teeth of Lord Gilbert's sheep, and an area of strips was
under the plough. As I walked I nodded to some of the
villagers working away there on the upland. There were
never very many of them. Most of the labour force of
the village was down on the fen cutting reeds and sedge
and carving out peat for fuel. It was hard work; few men
or women in Aelf Fen made old bones.

Directly ahead of me was an ancient oak tree, a rare
enough specimen in our area for it to be a landmark, and
indeed I had been using it as a marker, for when I reached
it I would turn right and come out behind Edild's house. I
was preoccupied, thinking that William's mother was probably the village's oldest inhabitant and wondering just how
old she was, when I sensed movement among the thick

foliage of the oak and, almost simultaneously, someone dropped out of its lower branches and called out to me.

It was Alberic.

'What do you—' I began, before he shushed me violently and beckoned to me to join him in the huge tree's deep shadow. 'What are you doing here?' I hissed as I approached him.

'Is he dead?' he whispered urgently. 'I couldn't help it – I saw him there by her grave, and I went wild.' The words were tumbling out of him. 'He seduced her and made her pregnant, and all the time he knew perfectly well he was going to wed that whey-faced woman who would far rather be a nun, but I didn't mean to kill him, and I shouldn't have hit him like I did! He—'

I put my hand on his arm, trying to quieten him. 'Sir Alain is alive,' I said clearly and calmly. 'My aunt is a healer, and she has tended him.'

I watched as Alberic absorbed the news. Then, predictably, he said, 'Does he know who hit him?'

'He heard you singing,' I replied. 'Besides, it is, I think, fairly obvious.'

The dread and the terrible anxiety seemed to leach out of him, and he slumped against the broad, accommodating trunk of the oak, sliding down until his buttocks rested on the ground. 'I shouldn't have done it,' he muttered. 'I'm not a violent man.'

I sat down beside him. 'Why don't you tell me about it?' I suggested.

Alberic slowly shook his head, but not in denial. 'I don't think there's much to tell,' he said. 'I attacked him, right enough. He was kneeling by her grave with his back to me. I'd been sitting there all night, singing my song to her, and I think it was all too much.' A sob broke out of him. 'I knew he'd always had an eye for Ida, but I didn't really think anything of it because, from what I'd seen of him, he was like that with all the pretty girls. Funny thing is, they must all have realized the sort of man he was, but it didn't seem to make any difference. They all liked him.' He shook his head again as if in puzzlement at the incomprehensible ways of the world.

I pitied him. Married to a jealous and possessive dragon of a woman, the one ray of light in his wretched life had been a girl whom he did not dare approach and with whom all he could share was the occasional song. What a contrast with Alain de Villequier who, as I had observed myself, did indeed have a way with women . . .

'They were that discreet, it didn't even occur to me there was anything going on between them,' Alberic said sadly. He glanced at me. 'I – I thought better of Ida,' he said, shamefaced. 'I believed she was too good, too pure, to give herself to a man betrothed to another woman. But then, what do I know?' he added bitterly.

'When did you find out?' I felt hugely sorry for him. Yes, he had just attacked a man and left him for dead, but I was beginning to understand what had driven him to it.

'When I came here to Aelf Fen to seek her out,' he replied. 'I discovered that Lakehall was nearby, and I reckoned I'd be able to live rough, it being summer and the weather good, while I found her and told her I was now free.' He laughed shortly. 'Fat lot of good *that* did me, I can tell you. She looked at me out of those lovely eyes of hers and said she was honoured by my affection for her, but she loved another. When I pressed her, when I told her about my tidy little cottage and the decent living I make with my flint-working and the music and that, she said she was very sorry, but she could never be mine.' He paused, and I saw tears in his eyes. 'I went on at her, demanding to know who the other man was, and in the end she took pity on me and told me she was carrying this other feller's child.'

'She didn't mention Sir Alain?'

He smiled grimly. 'No. But now she'd told me there was someone else, I thought back, and I saw what I should have seen all along. She loved him all right. I knew then it was hopeless.'

I reached for his hand, then, pitching my voice so he would realize it wasn't a serious suggestion, said, 'You didn't kill her in a fit of jealousy?' I already knew the answer.

'No,' he said, his gentle face full of emotion. 'I had to face up to the fact I had lost her, but I knew I just had to let her go.

I loved her. It was not in me to take her life because she did not love me. I told her I wished her well, and in my heart I made myself believe it.'

That was true love indeed, I thought, that a man would place a woman's happiness so far above his own, even though she would enjoy it with someone else.

'I believe I know who put her in my Granny's grave,' I said. 'I believe it was Derman.' I explained my theory.

'Derman?' Alberic said when I had finished.

I explained about Derman too.

'Didn't know about *him*,' Alberic muttered. 'Someone else who couldn't keep their eyes off my Ida.'

I was just thinking that, unless he was a very good liar, it didn't look as if Alberic had killed Derman, when he spoke again. 'Reckon I know who you mean, though,' he said. 'Big, awkward sort of feller, large head, big, floppy mouth.'

'That was Derman, yes.'

'Hmm.' I waited. 'Saw him talking to a woman,' Alberic went on after a while. 'Or, I should say, *she* was talking to *him*, standing there in front of him wagging her finger at him, giving him a right ticking-off.'

I stiffened. 'What did this woman look like?'

'She was a right looker. Black hair with a bluish sheen, lovely golden skin, and she moved like a dancer.'

Zarina.

'And where did you see this exchange between her and Derman?'

'Down one of the tracks that leads out to the fen edge. I reckon they thought they were alone out there – it's a desolate spot.'

There spoke a man who didn't live in the fens, I thought. I pictured the scene. I imagined Derman returning from some hopeless mission to spy on Ida. Perhaps she had been out collecting the wild flowers she had reproduced so beautifully and faithfully in her embroidery on Lady Claude's bed sheets, and he had followed her. I pictured Zarina, angry because he'd been neglecting his duties and she'd had to do all the hard work. I heard Zarina's furious, scolding voice in my head: *Leave her alone! She's no good for you!*

Then, sliding into the corner of my mind so subtly that at first I didn't notice, I thought of something else. I saw a passionate and beautiful young woman who had fallen in love with a village man and wanted more than anything to marry him. I saw her despair, because she was tied to a simpleton of a brother and, as he had saved her when she'd needed him, owed him far too much to allow herself to abandon him.

My excitement mounting, I wondered if I'd got it all wrong and Zarina had been reproving Derman because he was making no progress in his courtship of Ida. Perhaps she had been trying to encourage him, for if by some miracle Ida had taken pity on her unlikely suitor and accepted him, Zarina would have been free to marry my brother.

When it became clear that Ida, kind though she was, had gently turned Derman down, had Zarina's frustration and rage got the better of her? Had she lost her temper and strangled Ida?

I pictured her hands, rough and very strong from the endless wringing of heavy, wet fabric. Before she'd been a washerwoman she'd been a dancer. An acrobat. I'd seen her perform with my own eyes, and I understood the power there was in her muscular frame.

Out of my memory I heard Zarina's terrible cry: *You know nothing about me!* Oh, *oh*, had she been trying to tell me that the reason she couldn't marry Haward was because she was a killer? And then had she, as I had suspected, gone on to kill Derman, not because he had stood in her way, but because he knew she had strangled Ida?

I had to find out.

Alberic was studying me. 'Important, is it, what I just told you?'

The answer was *yes*. But I could not admit it. The woman I was prepared to welcome as my sister-in-law might well have committed two murders . . . and, if she had, I was going to have to decide what to do about it. For the time being at least, the possibility had to remain a deadly secret. 'Oh, I don't know,' I said, my tone casual. 'Probably not.'

I sat with him for a while longer. I did not want him to remember later that I had rushed off in a lather as soon as he'd mentioned Zarina and Derman. I waited, even hummed a little tune, then eventually I stood up and remarked that I ought to be getting back to my aunt.

Straight away he looked anxious again, and I guessed he was thinking about Sir Alain and wondering how he was. 'Don't worry,' I said. 'He seems to have a hard skull.'

Alberic managed a weak smile. 'What's he going to do? I'll be arrested, won't I? I tried to kill him, after all.'

I thought about it. Alain de Villequier had rather a lot on his conscience; too much, perhaps, to leap to accuse a man who had attacked him for the sake of the woman both men had loved. 'Maybe,' I said. 'Maybe not.'

Hope leapt into his eyes. 'I was thinking I should get away from here,' he muttered, 'much as I want to stay.'

To be close to Ida, I guessed. 'You can't stay for ever,' I pointed out gently.

He looked at me sadly. 'For a while longer, at least.' It sounded as if he were pleading with me.

I bowed my head. 'As you wish.'

Then I hefted my satchel on to my shoulder and left him.

I didn't return to Edild's house. Instead I doubled back and slipped along under cover of the scrubby hedgerows, dipping back into the village close by the widow Berta's house. She was within – I could hear her arguing with someone – but I caught sight of Zarina's slim figure down by the water.

I approached her and, as she heard my footsteps, she paused in her work and looked up at me. I studied her. She had rolled up her sleeves, and her hands were red and raw. She wore her usual heavy sacking apron, and her hair was covered by a white kerchief. Her face was sweaty with effort.

I did not allow the stab of sympathy I felt for her to take hold. I said, 'Zarina, you must tell me the truth.'

Emotion flashed in her golden-green eyes, and I sensed that she was tense with apprehension. Or – the thought was alarming – with anger.

'About what?' she said cagily.

There was no point in anything but a direct assault. 'You told me once I know nothing about you,' I said. 'You have explained certain things concerning your past, but I am convinced that you have omitted more than you have revealed.'

Her cheeks were flushed, and her eyes seemed to snap at me. 'What right have you to know?' she said in an ominous whisper.

'You are to marry into my family,' I snapped back. 'That gives me the right, for I would not see my brother wed to a—' I bit back the word. I would not yet accuse her. 'To someone who would bring him wretchedness and unhappiness,' I said instead.

She sank back on to her heels, considering me. 'And why do you think I would do that?'

'There are secrets you keep that, when they are known, will ruin Haward's life, for if you are condemned he will suffer almost as much as you, so dearly does he love you.'

Her lovely face was the picture of puzzlement. I was just beginning to wonder if I was mistaken, when I recalled what else she had been before she was a washerwoman: she had been a performer, skilled, no doubt, in taking on a different persona when it suited her.

I would not, I told myself firmly, be fooled by her.

She was still looking perplexed. I said impatiently, 'Don't pretend you don't know what I'm talking about.'

She smiled fleetingly. 'But I don't. Really, Lassair, I don't.'

'Then I will put it into words.' I was furious now, all caution gone. 'I know you argued with Derman over his love for Ida. I thought at first you were cross because all the time he was mooning after her, he wasn't helping you, but then I realized the truth.'

'And what was that?' She spoke guardedly, and her tone gave away nothing.

'You were beside yourself because his pathetic attempts to court her were failing!' I cried. 'If she had taken pity on him and accepted him, married him even, you would have been free. She would have taken your lifelong burden away from you, and you could have married Haward without having to bring your brother into the family too.' I paused for breath. She said nothing, merely watched me closely, and I plunged on. 'But Ida turned him down, and you were so angry that you killed her. Derman saw you do it, and so he had to die too. That's why you slipped out by yourself that night to look for him. You had to find him, discover how much he had seen and, if he threatened to expose you as a murderer, you had to silence him. Which you did – you set a trip wire on the posts beside the causeway out to the island and, when he fell into the water, you crushed his skull.' I paused again, panting hard. 'Didn't you?'

I stared down intently at her. I had expected angry denials, violence, a cat's claw, hissing, scratching attack on my face. But Zarina stayed there, quite still, her expression impassive.

Then two tears spilled out of her eyes and rolled down her cheeks.

I did not know what to do or what to think. Desperate now, I said, 'Are you left-handed?'

She looked up at me in amazement. 'Why on earth do you—? No. I favour my right hand.' As if to demonstrate, she dipped into her pocket and extracted a torn piece of thin linen, with which she dried her tears. She held it in her right hand.

Slowly, I lowered myself on to the ground beside her. Our eyes met and held. I sensed her reaching out to me. I said, 'Zarina, won't you confide in me?' Realizing that, bearing in mind the dreadful accusations I had just thrown at her, I was probably the last person on earth she would trust, I gave her hand a squeeze. 'Whatever you've done, I'm quite sure you had your reasons,' I said softly.

After what seemed a very long time, she removed her hand from mine and started to speak.

'I related to you how I had to flee from Haglar,' she began.

'The man your father was trying to make you marry,' I replied. 'Yes. I remember.'

'I told you, too, how he sent a man after me and Derman killed him?'

'Yes.'

She nodded. 'Good. Then you will understand, perhaps, if I explain how I never felt safe, even with the troupe of entertainers. We travelled all over, this country, that city, and always the fear lurked that, having sent one man who managed to track me down, Haglar would do so again and this time I would not be so fortunate as to have Derman on hand to conveniently remove him.' She paused, her eyes full of the memory of that constant dread. 'In the end I confided in one of the older women in the troupe,' she went on. 'Knowing what Derman was like, you will, I am sure, understand that it was not much comfort to talk to *him*. He would kill for me – he *had* killed for me – but his comprehension was severely limited. As long as he was well fed, warm, and the sun shone, he was happy. Until he met Ida,' she added under her breath.

'So,' she continued after a moment, 'I opened my heart to Mathilde. She listened in silence, although I could sense she understood and sympathized. When I had finished, she said that she, too, had been threatened with a marriage she did not want, and her way of avoiding had been simple: she had married someone else.'

As the surprise faded, I saw the sense of it. Haglar might still succeed in tracking Zarina, and he would no doubt try to have her abducted, but even if he did, she would be able to hurl in his face the fact of her being legally married to someone else and, unless or until he could contrive to have that marriage annulled, he would be powerless.

'I was desperate,' she went on. She was looking at me, her face flushed with embarrassment. 'I was young, I was out of my mind with worry, I was alone –' *you had your brother*, I wanted to say, but then, remembering what sort of man he had been, I realized she was right – 'and I did what I did with barely a thought. Before I knew it, I was married and –' her blush deepened, turning her cheeks to scarlet – 'and because I was well aware that an unconsummated marriage can be dissolved, I did my utmost to make that marriage one of the flesh.' She dropped her head. 'I failed,' she whispered.

I wondered what he had been like, this man from the

troupe who had agreed to marry the young Zarina so as to keep her out of another man's clutches. Why had he not succeeded in making love to her? Had he been very old, perhaps? I found it hard to imagine any other reason for a man not to leap at the invitation into Zarina's bed. Or – I recalled something Edild had told me – perhaps this husband had been one of those men who are aroused only by their own sex, as the rumours said our reeve, Bermund, was.

Could I ask her? I waited, not speaking, and after a while she raised her head again and looked at me. To my surprise, she was smiling.

'You do not know, do you?'

'How could I?' I flashed back. 'I only saw your troupe on one occasion. How do you expect me to guess which man was your husband?'

Your husband.

The words sank in at last, and I understood. I stared at her, horrified. 'You're married!' I whispered. '*That's* why you can't marry Haward!' I saw my dear brother's face, imagined him having to say goodbye to his hopes of happiness, and something in me broke. 'You're married,' I repeated numbly. 'Your reluctance had nothing to do with Derman.'

She reached out and took my hand again, holding it so tightly that I could feel the cracked, rough skin of hers. I felt a wave of emotion coming off her – a wave of love? – and I did not know what to do. I saw again the fall of my runes, that time I had tried to read the future for this extraordinary woman and my beloved brother. I remembered what I had seen. A very small, very faint hope began to shine.

Zarina put her face close to mine and whispered, 'It has *everything* to do with Derman. Lassair, dear Lassair, he was already with the troupe when I ran away and joined them. He wasn't my brother, he was my husband.'

I believe I knew it a blink of an eye before she told me. Nevertheless, her words still rocked me to my core. It all fell into place: *You know nothing about me*, she had cried. How right she was.

'I regretted it almost straight away,' she was saying softly. 'My terrible attempt to make him consummate the marriage is something for which I can never forgive myself. He didn't understand, you see, yet somehow I fear I planted in him the seed that would lead to his infatuation with Ida.' She paused. 'He was not formed as most adult men are formed,' she said delicately.

'I know,' I said dully. 'I helped my aunt lay him out, and I saw his body.'

'Of course you did,' she breathed. I sensed she was relieved. 'Well, then.'

I could think of nothing to say. After a moment Zarina spoke again. 'Life was not so bad,' she said. 'I loved the travelling, and I enjoyed my work as a performer. I learned to tolerate Derman and forgive him his shortcomings, which, indeed, were no fault of his. I knew that I could trust him, for he had already proved that he would do almost anything for me. In a way, I grew fond of him.' She hesitated. 'Then one Lammas time we came to a small settlement in the fen country and I fell in love with your brother.' She glanced at me.

'I didn't kill Derman,' she said after a while. 'It would have been like killing a child. I swear to you, Lassair, on all I hold dear. I wanted him gone – of course I did – but I took no step such as you suggest to rid myself of him. He saved my life,' she reminded me. 'What vengeance would I have brought down on to myself, had I murdered my saviour?'

Slowly, I nodded. I understood. Some things in this world are simply unforgivable, and the retribution would have been terrible.

She was still holding my hand, and now I placed my other hand over hers. 'I am sorry I accused you,' I said humbly. 'I know I was wrong.'

My head was down, and she bent so she could look into my face. '*Do* you?' She spoke with sudden fervour.

'Yes.' I smiled. 'Really, yes.'

Her tense expression relaxed. She smiled. 'I'm very, very glad to hear it.'

'Why?' I was smiling too.

'Because I've just told your brother I'm going to marry him.'

The runes had been right. My heart began to sing.

TWENTY

E dild looked up with her finger to her lips when I went in. 'He's sleeping,' she whispered, indicating Sir Alain. Quietly, she got up and crossed the small room to the door, leading the way outside. Pulling the door almost closed behind her, she said, 'Lord Gilbert has heard that Sir Alain was attacked. He sent a messenger to ask after our patient's state of health – no doubt Lady Claude is very anxious – and I told the man to say that he lives and I expect him to recover.' She bit her lip, looking back towards the room she had just left. 'I ought, I suppose, to report in person,' she added slowly, 'although in truth I do not want to leave him.'

'I'll go,' I offered. Just then I was so happy that the last thing I wanted was to sit perfectly still in Edild's small room, not even allowed to talk.

She looked at me, apparently only then really seeing me. 'What are you so cheerful about?' she demanded. She, too, was smiling. She's like that, Edild; she seems to catch other people's moods, which is fine if they're good moods, but not so great when they're bad.

I said, 'Zarina has just told me she's agreed to marry Haward.'

Edild did not appear nearly as amazed and delighted as I had hoped. 'Well, of course,' she said. 'With poor Derman dead and no longer a problem, I'm sure she wouldn't hesitate.'

'But—' I stopped.

Zarina's confession regarding her true relationship to Derman had emerged with considerable pain and shame; that had been very evident. I could fully appreciate why she had been driven to such a desperate measure, and indeed, as she'd pointed out, she had been very young and extremely worried for her own safety.

Was there any need for anybody else to know? Haward, perhaps, although from what Zarina had said, it sounded as if Derman had only been her husband in name. Anyway, I did not agree with what I perceived as the usual male attitude: that it was fine for a man to have sown plenty of wild oats and slept with any number of women before marriage, yet for a woman to behave in the same way was almost as bad as if she'd cut several people's heads off. I reckoned that Zarina had every right to keep that particular aspect of her past to herself. If she chose one day to confide in my brother, that was up to her. I wasn't going to tell him.

Which meant, I realized, that I shouldn't really tell anybody else . . .

Edild was looking at me curiously. 'But?' she prompted.

'Oh, nothing,' I said.

'Nothing?'

It is very difficult to hide your thoughts from my aunt. But she would, I was sure, be the first to agree that another's secret is sacrosanct. I held my head high, looked her in the eye and repeated firmly, 'Nothing.'

She raised an eyebrow, then, apparently accepting that the matter was closed, smiled at me very sweetly and said, 'Thank you for offering to go and speak to Lord Gilbert. I accept. Oh, and Lassair?'

'Yes?'

'You could look in on Lady Claude while you're there. Take some more of the medicaments you prepared for her, in case she needs them.'

I slipped back inside the house and fetched what I needed. Sir Alain, I observed, was still sleeping soundly. He had turned on to his right side, and I could see that the wound on his head was now uncovered. The swelling had gone right down; with any luck, he would be left with no permanent effects once the headache had gone.

It was good to have encouraging news to report up at the hall. As I set off up the track, I thought about what I would say. Lord Gilbert and Lady Emma would be relieved; Lady Claude too, I hoped. But something was niggling at me. I wondered if she really would welcome the news. If Sir Alain had died, she would not have to marry him and could revert to her true desire, to enter a convent. Maybe, when I reported that he was well on the way to recovery, Lady Claude would not be able to prevent the sneaky, evil little thought that if only Alberic had hit him slightly harder, she could even now be making her plans to take the veil.

Instantly, I reprimanded myself. The little I knew of Lady Claude told me that she was a God-fearing, devout woman, ever mindful that temptation was all around us and that we had to be on our guard all the time not to fall into sin. Even if she did entertain a fleeting regret that her future husband had survived the attack, she would no doubt instantly fall on her knees in prayer, begging for forgiveness and offering all sorts of dire, unpleasant and probably painful things in penance.

They were not really like us, the lords and ladies. I reflected as I walked along just how different my life was from Lady Claude's. She had wealth; she was about to marry into a powerful and influential family; she would live in the most comfortable home that money could buy and probably want for nothing all her long life. None of which, I reminded myself, would really mean much to her when all she wished to do was answer her God's call and be a nun.

I would not, I decided, have changed places with Lady Claude for anything.

I was shown into the hall, where I found Lord Gilbert, Lady Emma and the two children preparing for an outing. The nursemaid was in attendance to take care of the little girl, and the boy was sitting up on his father's shoulders, kicking him with small, sharp heels and saying, 'Come on, horsey!'

Lord Gilbert flashed me a slightly embarrassed glance, but Lady Emma, serene and more than equal to the moment, said smoothly, 'Lassair, it was good of you to come to see us. What news of Sir Alain?'

I told her, and she expressed her relief. 'Please, do go up to tell Lady Claude,' she said. 'She is in her sewing room.' She glanced at her husband, who shrugged – as well as a man can shrug with a small boy on his shoulders – as if to say, *You tell her.*

Lady Emma turned back to me. 'We had promised the children that we would all go out this afternoon. The weather is so lovely, and they have been indoors too long. I did try to encourage Lady Claude to join us for the midday meal – and, indeed, to accompany us on our outing – but she refused.'

I felt she was waiting for me to comment, so I said, 'She will have been very worried about Sir Alain, no doubt. I expect she felt she would be poor company.'

Lady Emma's face cleared. 'Yes, yes, I'm sure that is so.' She sounded relieved to have her guest's awkward manners explained. I remembered how I'd wondered if Claude was wishing Sir Alain's injury had been more serious; fatally serious. Was Lady Emma thinking the same thing?

I could not, of course, ask her.

'I will find my way up to Lady Claude's room,' I said.

'Will you? Thank you, that means we need keep the children waiting no longer.'

'Come *on*, horsey!' yelled the little boy, heels flailing, and I heard his father emit a grunt of pain.

I watched as they all trooped outside. Out of nowhere, I had the sudden wish that I was going with them. They all looked so happy, so carefree, and here I was about to shut myself up with a nervy, brooding, sickly woman with whom I had not one thing in common.

I am a healer, I reminded myself. *I do not have to like my patients; I just have to help them.*

I straightened my shoulders, hitched up my satchel and strode determinedly towards the doorway leading to the steps and Lady Claude's rooms.

I tapped on the sewing-room door and, after quite a long wait, I heard her voice say, 'Come in.'

She had shut herself up tightly in there, and even the tiny window set high up in the wall was fast closed. The sweet summer air outside had been firmly forbidden entry.

There was an unpleasant aroma of bad breath and stale sweat, and it was not only that which made me stop on the threshold; for an instant I sensed that an invisible barrier stretched across between the door posts. All my senses – steadily becoming more highly attuned, thanks to my rigorous sessions with Hrype – were shouting at me, *Keep away!* I paused, uncertain what to do. Then I gave myself a mental shake, commanded myself not to be so fanciful, and stepped into the room.

Without looking up, she said, 'Close the door.'

She sat crouched on her little stool, hunched over a large piece of stout canvas stretched on the wooden frame. Beside her on a small wooden table was the black velvet bag that she normally wore hanging from her belt. The drawstrings at its neck that normally kept it closed had been loosened, and the contents were laid out on the table. She was, I saw, embroidering yet another picture – hadn't she run out of Deadly Sins by now? – and the needle was threaded with a length of dark brown wool. The small, careful stitches were outlining a sinister figure that appeared to have wings. I watched as her hand stabbed firmly through the canvas, the needle disappearing only to emerge again almost instantly from beneath, always in exactly the right spot. She was, I realized, a true craftswoman.

Inspired by her skill to a genuinely admiring comment, I stepped forward and said, 'You embroider most beautifully, Lady Claude, and the images are so very artistic.'

Her only acknowledgement was a faint sniff. Did her stark and loveless view of the world disapprove of praise? She would probably disregard it as some machination of the devil, I reflected, designed to make a person so swollen-headed and pleased with herself that she stopped striving to do better.

I felt very sorry for her, stuck in that fetid room all by herself while everyone else was out in the sunshine having fun and Lord Gilbert was pretending to be a horse to amuse his little son. Crouching down close to her, I said, 'Sir Alain is sleeping, Lady Claude. He was hit very hard, but fortunately there appears to be no permanent damage.

He was awake earlier, and he spoke to my aunt and me perfectly rationally.'

She went on sewing.

I cast around for something to say that would draw her out. I thought I knew something of her turmoil. She wanted to be a nun, not a wife; she was extremely devout, perhaps to the extent of viewing the intimate life of husband and wife as a sin; she felt very guilty because her young seamstress would not now be dead had she not brought her here to Lakehall; and now, as if all of that were not enough, the man she was betrothed to had suffered a violent attack. No wonder the poor woman was suffering from headaches and insomnia.

I looked up at her, carefully at first, for I did not want her to know I was observing her. I realized quickly that she was totally absorbed in her needlework; I could stare as much as I liked. I studied her face. The stiff, white wimple seemed to have been drawn even tighter, its harsh edges biting into the flesh. The black veil looked as if it had been arranged with a meticulous, almost fanatical hand, so evenly did the folds hang around her. She was pale, so pale, and her skin had a sheen of grease, or perhaps sweat, for it was hot in that desolate little room. Her small, light eyes were deeply circled in grey. I knew without asking that she was not sleeping well, and I guessed she was in pain.

I closed my eyes and opened myself to her.

Instantly, her turmoil reached out and hit me, with a force so violent that it seemed almost physical. I endured it, concentrating on analysing what ailed her and what I could do to help. I gritted my teeth and tried to call up all I had been taught, but quite soon I had to accept that Lady Claude was beyond my aid.

Very tentatively, I reached out and lightly took hold of her flying hand. 'Lady Claude?'

At first she resisted, trying to pull her hand out of my grasp. I held on tightly, and finally she gave a click of irritation, raised her head and looked me in the eyes.

Hers seemed to burn, glittering so fiercely in the dim light that, had my hand on her skin not told me otherwise, I would have said she was feverish.

'*What?*' she snapped. 'I must get on!' she muttered. 'There is so much still to do –' she cast fearful eyes round the little room, taking in the untouched canvases and the piles of coloured wools – 'and I have little time.'

'You are not well,' I said, trying to keep my voice low and soothing. 'I have brought more of the draught that reduces pain, and also some medicine to help you sleep, but I sense that you are distressed beyond my power to help you. Will you allow me to bring my aunt to see you? She is very skilled, and she—'

Lady Claude's eyes boring into me silenced me. 'Your aunt is an attractive woman,' she stated.

For the life of me, I could not see the relevance. 'Er – yes, indeed she is.' Edild has green eyes in a lovely face, and a tumble of glorious reddish-blonde hair that she normally restrains under a neat white cap.

Lady Claude was still fixing me with that imprisoning stare. 'You, too, have the promise of beauty, although you are too thin, your figure boyish and lacking seductive curves.'

I know my own shortcomings perfectly well, and I did not need anyone pointing them out to me, especially a woman who looked like Claude de Seés. 'Quite so, my lady,' I said curtly.

It was a mistake. Her eyes narrowed, all but disappearing, and she snapped, 'None of that insolent tone or I'll have you whipped!'

Two thoughts struck me simultaneously: one was that Lord Gilbert would not allow anyone to be whipped for such a dubious offence; the other was expressed by a small, wailing voice inside my head that said plaintively, *I'm here to help you!*

I waited until my anger had subsided and then said, 'Shall I fetch my aunt, my lady? She is at present watching over Sir Alain, for when he wakes there will be matters for her to attend to, such as feeding him, encouraging him to drink, bathing him and—'

With an action so sudden, so violent and so totally unexpected that it shocked me to my core, Lady Claude leapt up, flung her embroidery frame across the room and grabbed me by the shoulders.

Her fingers dug into me, and she shouted right in my face, so that I smelt her stale and foul breath, '*Be quiet!* I do not wish to be told of such things! Has your aunt no shame, that she is prepared to remain alone in the company of a man in such a state? Prepared to *touch* him?'

Angry in my turn, I stood up and tried to remove her hands. Her fingers were very strong – all that embroidery, no doubt – and she would not let go until I wrestled myself away and out of her reach. 'My aunt is a healer,' I said icily. 'She cannot care for her patients without touching them.' I backed away to the far corner of the room, only stopping when I was immediately beneath the window, high above me, and my back against the stone wall. I felt safer there, although I could not help wishing that Lady Claude was not standing between me and the door.

Making sure I spoke calmly, I said, 'I will send for hot water, my lady, and make up a soothing draught for you to ease your pain and help you to rest.' I was edging along the wall as I spoke, moving in front of the Deadly Sins embroideries hanging suspended side by side. She was watching me, and I felt her tension across the distance between us. 'Lord Gilbert and Lady Emma will be back soon –' I prayed that was true – 'and I will explain to them that you are unwell.'

I was standing opposite to her now, and the door was to my right. I had closed it, as she had commanded when I'd arrived. 'I'm sure it will be all right for my aunt to leave her patient and come to you now,' I went on, 'and if Sir Alain still needs care, I can give it.' I watched her carefully for signs of renewed fury, but my suggestion did not seem to disturb her. 'Edild could stay here with you, if you would prefer her not to remain with Sir Alain,' I offered. I knew full well that it was against everything Edild honoured in her calling to even think about taking advantage of a helpless male patient, but I did not think Lady Claude was open to reason just then.

I tried to think of encouraging things to say. 'Sir Alain

will not lie abed any longer than is necessary,' I went on, still in the same carefully calm voice, 'for he is justiciar here and still has two crimes to solve. I am quite sure, being the man he is, that he will soon pick up the trail that leads him to the killer's door.'

She was observing me intently, her eyes slits in her pale face. Her hands were twitching, the fingers opening and closing as if she were still engaged on imaginary sewing. Out of nowhere I had a sudden image of Ida's hands, her needlewoman's hands, and I remembered that this pathetic woman in front of me had suffered a loss that was probably affecting her more than she would admit.

'I know you were fond of Ida,' I said gently. 'Everyone who knew her seems to have loved her. You must miss her very much.' I edged closer to her. It was surely not helping to restore her equanimity to have me drawing myself so obviously away from her. She needed to see that I was happy being close to her; that I did not find her repulsive.

Which was difficult, because just at that moment I could hardly bear to be in the same room as her and she was making me feel sick.

'Her killer will be found,' I said confidently, although I was not at all sure this was true. 'Sir Alain, I'm sure, has ideas of his own, and others of us in the village might be able to offer suggestions that may help.' Warming to my theme, I hurried on. 'I do not believe that her killer put her in my Granny's grave,' I said eagerly. 'I think Derman found her – you know, he's the simpleton who had been following her about – and he carried her out to the little island where my ancestors lie buried and put her in the grave because he cared about her and believed that was the right thing to do. But the man who strangled Ida must have been watching and, believing Derman had seen him, thought he had to kill Derman to keep him quiet.'

'Derman,' Lady Claude breathed. 'Was that his name?'

'Yes,' I said, pleased that she was responding. 'Did you see him lurking about when you were out with Ida collecting the flowers?'

'The flowers?'

'Yes, the ones she copied in her embroidery work on your sheets.' I tried to recall what they had been, looking round to see if the sheets were to hand. I saw them neatly folded and stacked on top of a chest beside the door. 'Here,' I said, stepping over and picking up the top sheet. 'Flag iris and—'

But she had leapt across the room, and now she grabbed the sheet out of my hands. 'Leave that alone!' she commanded coldly. She refolded it, put it back on the pile and smoothed it, her hands shaking.

Of course. It was Ida's work, and therefore no doubt precious to her. 'She sewed so beautifully,' I said. 'How lovely for you, that you will have a permanent reminder of her on your sheets, before your eyes every night when you go to sleep.'

Lady Claude gave a moan, grasped the sheet again and, before my horrified eyes, bit into the edge above the embroidered panel with small, sharp teeth. Then, holding it in a grip so tight that her knuckles were white, she tore it apart. The tear made a violently loud noise in the small space, and I watched as it snaked down through the cloth, ripping right through Ida's delicate work. She tore off one long strip, then another.

Lady Claude threw the ruined sheet on the floor. 'She fetched those flowers to give herself an excuse to go out alone,' she said in a low, harsh voice. 'She was always going out. Out to flaunt herself before that great shambling idiot, with his loose, wet mouth and his hungry eyes! Out to meet—' She broke off, squeezing her eyes shut as if the gesture would blank off the things she could not bear to see.

Out to meet who? Oh, surely she hadn't been about to say Ida had gone to meet Sir Alain. He had told Edild and me that Claude did not know about him and Ida. What if he was wrong?

Her face was working, and her eyes held a look in which there was more than a hint of madness. Her pale face had flushed, suffused with a sudden rush of blood. If she did not try to regain control of herself, I truly feared she might fall dead at my feet. I had to distract her.

I stepped forward, holding out my arms. 'Lady Claude, sit down,' I said gently. 'Rest, and I will make you a soothing drink. Soon this business will be resolved and you will be able to put it behind you. Ida's killer will be caught and—'

She acted so fast that it happened before I had time to react. She swooped down to gather up one of the long strips of linen and, in the same movement, grabbed my hands, twisted me round so that I had my back to her and bound my wrists together. Then she shoved me down on to her stool and tied the linen binding my hands to the leg of the stool.

She stood before me, and I stared up at her. I dared not speak. She was on the very edge of sanity, and I did not know how to bring her back.

Having restrained me, she appeared to relax a little. She began pacing up and down the room, pausing to rest her hand on her embroidered panels. 'Ida,' she murmured, 'always Ida. She was lovely, wasn't she?' She glanced across at me. I had only seen Ida in death, and I did not reply. 'Oh, yes –' she resumed her pacing – 'everyone adored Ida, everyone told me how lucky I was to have such a skilled seamstress to help me, and what good fortune it was that she was such a delightful person as well, for she was kind, cheerful, and at ease with everyone from the smallest baby to the oldest grandfather or grandmother. Oh, everyone loved Ida, and they never stopped telling me so.'

It was the impression I, too, had received. I didn't think I had heard one person speak ill of her. 'She had the gift of making people like her,' I said quietly.

I didn't think Claude heard. Now she was nodding to herself, muttering under her breath, and I had to strain to hear her. I'd inadvertently roused her to fury with what I'd said about Ida, and now I was paying the price. Surreptitiously, trying not to make any noise, I wriggled my hands, testing the linen strip that bound me. If I could just manage to loosen the loop that tied me to the stool, I could make a lunge for the door and get away . . .

'Of course,' Claude said, her voice louder now, '*he* had to take just one look at her to fall under her spell. I knew it would happen – he was betrothed to my sister, you know, before my mother arranged his marriage to me. It must have started right back then,' she added wonderingly, 'and nobody realized, clever little vixen that she was.'

Vixen. My Fox is male, but all the same his image sprang into my mind as Claude spoke the word. I closed my eyes and, with all my strength, pleaded with him to come to me.

'I hated Ida,' Claude was saying calmly. 'I loathed her, with her dimples and her smiles and those sweet, round breasts that the men couldn't take their eyes off.' She nodded, smiling grimly. 'But I was too clever for her, oh, yes!' Now her expression turned crafty. 'I used her own deceitful ways against her. I said, *Ida, let us both go out together to the place where you found those pretty flowers. It is a fine day, so we shall take our work bags with us and sit out in the sunshine to sew.'* She glanced at me. 'We went across the marshland until we reached the fen edge. She showed me where the pretty flowers were, in a place near to where the island lies close to the shore. Ida picked some flowers, and then I told her to get out the pieces of fabric she had brought in her basket. She sat there – I can see her now – starting to tear up a voluminous old linen shift to make strips on which to practise the new designs.'

She paused. I waited, hardly daring to breathe.

'I had to be sure, although in truth I already knew,' she went on softly. 'So I spoke of him, Alain de Villequier, the man I am to marry. I spoke his name, and I watched her eyes light up, for she could not help herself.' A spasm of pain crossed the thin, white face. 'I looked at her, and I saw the signs. She was pregnant! She carried his child.'

She was panting from the raw emotion. 'I did it,' she said, eyes imploring as she stared at me. 'I wrapped the plaited cord of my velvet bag around her throat, and I pulled it, pulled it, *pulled it*, until I could pull it no more.'

She fell silent, and I heard the echo of her terrible words sound again and again, diminishing until it was gone.

'I came back here to the hall. I thought they would soon find her and realize what I had done,' she said. She gave a little laugh; chilling, horrible. 'But the idiot man found her first and put her in the grave. They thought he killed her, you see. I wanted them to go on thinking that, and so, before they found him and questioned him, he had to be removed.'

'You tripped him up,' I whispered. 'He fell into the water, and you found a weapon and hit him on the head again and again till he was dead.'

'Quite dead,' she agreed. 'I used a heavy piece of dead wood that I found floating on the water.'

And then, far too late, I realized what I should have been looking out for from the first moment I walked into the room. I saw her as she had been when I came in: sitting on the stool to which I was now bound, bent over her embroidery, her needle in her hand.

Her left hand.

She was walking slowly in front of her panels, her hand caressing the image of Lust. 'They were fornicators, you know,' she said. 'Ida and Alain were sinners, and they had to be punished. *She* had to be punished, for it was her plump body and her pretty smile that seduced him, and he could not help himself.' Her face twisted with contempt. 'She was carrying his child, and that child died with her, so Alain, too, will suffer,' she went on. Then, her strong fingers suddenly clutching at the scarlet-clad woman in the panel, crushing her image as if she were caught in an eagle's talons, she whispered, 'Lust. Lust. *Lust.*'

I could bear no more. 'They loved each other,' I protested angrily. 'It wasn't lust, and their feelings for one another went far beyond the hungry passion of a moment. Sir Alain would not have abandoned her – he told my aunt and me what he planned to do, how he was going to set Ida up with the baby and—'

It was not a tactful or sensible thing to say to the woman before me, already dangerously unbalanced, who was to be Sir Alain's unwilling wife. But I was beyond tact and sense.

Straight away she had her revenge. She spun round and, before I could duck, her left hand flew down in a vicious backhand swing and caught me on the cheek.

My left cheek, where I bear a scar like the new moon.

I had won that scar as I'd fought side by side with Rollo. I bent down low, my arms straining painfully, pretending to be more badly hurt than I was. I needed time . . . Briefly, I closed my eyes, my soul crying out to him, wherever he was.

I saw him. He was standing on a rocky outcrop, and he had a sword in his hand. He wore a heavy leather jerkin, open to the waist, and his shirt was stained with blood. He looked exuberant: whatever fight he had just been in, clearly he had won.

He was out there somewhere in the world, and in my bones and my blood I knew that a part of him was with me, just as a part of me went with him. Silently, I made a vow: *I will not die here before we have a chance to be together.*

I took several deep breaths.

Just as I opened my eyes to face her, I saw Fox. Well, I didn't really see him; he was no more than a flash of red on the edge of my vision. I shut my eyes again and saw him clearly. He was standing by the table where Claude had laid out the contents of her sewing bag and, as if the part of me that was Fox had seen what I should have noticed for myself, I saw the object at which his twitching black nose was sniffing.

Claude raised her hands and launched herself at me. She clutched at my arms, but I was ready for her, and I wrestled myself out of her hard grip. The stool fell over, and I landed on my right arm, crushing it to the stone floor with my own weight. I stifled a cry of pain. Claude was beside herself, striking out blindly, trying to pin me down as I wriggled and twisted beneath her. I could not see the table, but I knew where it was. With a lurch I threw myself against it, and it toppled over.

I needed my searching hands on the floor beneath me, and I had no choice but to turn on to my back. She was on me, a cry of triumph roaring out of her wide open mouth as she landed on top of me. Praying to my guardian spirits that I would find what I sought before she killed me, I scrabbled with my fingers across the floor . . .

. . . and the edge of my hand touched cold metal.

I grasped Claude's small sewing knife and found the blade; it sliced into my thumb. Ignoring the pain, I grabbed the bone handle and pressed the blade against the linen strip that bound my wrists. I cut myself several times – the blade was very sharp – but the fabric gave way.

With my hands free, I levered myself off the ground and, lowering my head, butted Claude very hard in the stomach. She gave a grunt as the air was forced out of her body and slumped, winded, against the wall.

I hurled myself at the door, raised the heavy latch with bleeding hands and raced out into the corridor and down the steps. I flew out into the hall, crying, 'Help! Help! Is anyone there? I need help!'

I heard running footsteps, and Bermund appeared through another doorway, two startled-looking women servants behind him.

There was no time for detailed explanations, and I just said, 'It's Lady Claude. She's had a fit.'

One of the women caught sight of my hands and rushed towards me, her kind face full of sympathy. 'She's attacked you!' she gasped. Then, with a scowl that I knew was not directed at me, she added, 'I always thought it was only a matter of time before someone got hurt.'

'Enough!' barked Bermund. He was already halfway across the hall, racing off to Claude.

I had to warn him. 'Be careful,' I shouted. 'She is not in her right mind.'

He paused, just for a moment, and looked back at me. He too, I realized, knew the true nature of Lady Claude de Seés. Was it only her equals who were so blind?

The servant with the kindly face had wrapped her apron round the worst cut, on the back of my left hand, and, thanking her, I said, 'We should go with him.'

She looked very reluctant, but, brave soul that she was, she nodded. 'Come along, Tilda,' she said to the other woman, and the three of us hurried after Bermund.

My heart was pounding. Each beat was sending a huge throb of pain through the blow on my cheek; I could feel it swelling up, and briefly I put my hand to feel it. I wondered if she had broken the bone.

We reached the doorway to Claude's sewing room. Bermund was standing there, so still that he might have been turned to stone. I rushed up to him, about to speak, to demand he go inside to help her, to restrain her . . . I did not know.

And I saw why he was so still.

She was sitting against the wall, her back resting on the Lust panel. The woman in the scarlet gown still lay there in her abandonment, her mouth open, her bodice splayed wide to show the pale breasts. Now, another patch of scarlet echoed the vivid gown; another gaping mouth parodied the woman's arousal.

Below her, Claude de Seés lay with her head fallen back against the colourful wools of the panel. Her mouth was open, and her dead eyes, half-closed, stared accusingly out at us. There was a deep cut right beneath her chin, narrow where it began under her right ear, wide and bloody as it slashed down across her neck. In her left hand she held the knife from her sewing bag.

She had drawn it across her throat.

TWENTY-ONE

Bermund had sent men out to find Lord Gilbert and, as soon as he came puffing and panting back to Lakehall and heard what had happened, he ordered one of the men to take me home. 'You have had a dreadful shock,' he said, looking anxiously at me, 'and you are hurt.'

'But you have to know what happened, what she did!' I protested. 'I've got to explain!'

He hushed me, kindly but firmly. 'Bermund has already told me. He relayed to me all that you told him, and I will take what action is necessary.' He sighed. 'To think she has been living here, right here under my roof, with my wife and my children, all this time!' He gave a shudder.

I said quickly, 'I don't believe you or your family were in any danger, my lord. Lady Claude's madness was limited and—' I stopped, suddenly seeing again her eyes narrowed in hate and terrible vengeance. I couldn't prevent the violent shudder that ran through me.

He looked at me. 'Don't think about her now,' he advised. 'Go home, girl. If there are matters concerning her that I need to speak to you about later, I will send for you.'

I bowed my head. I wanted desperately to get away and was more than ready to obey his command. 'Very well, my lord.'

I remembered then who was lying asleep in my aunt's house. I think Lord Gilbert had forgotten, in which case it would not have occurred to him that I would have to break the news of Claude's death to the man who had been going to marry her.

As I hurried away from Lakehall and headed for home, I wondered what he would say.

Of all the sad moments that followed on from what Claude had done, the worst was when I explained to Sir Alain de

Villequier that his bride-to-be had murdered the woman he had loved.

He was awake when I opened the door and went into the house, and I told him straight away. His eyes registered his shock and his horror. Then, covering his face with his hands, he wept.

'I was out looking for her, that morning when you came to the hall to tell Lord Gilbert you'd found her body,' he sobbed. 'We'd arranged to meet in our usual trysting place, but she didn't come. I waited all night, and I thought Claude must have caught her slipping out and locked her back inside that damned sewing room.'

'I thought she was locked in every night,' I said. 'How did she get out?'

He grinned briefly, the expression there and gone in a heartbeat. 'She had a second key,' he said. 'She wheedled it out of old Bermund. She said it was in case she wanted to get on with her work when Claude wasn't there. That night when she didn't come out to meet me, I thought Claude must have discovered Ida's key and confiscated it.'

Edild was watching him. I was very afraid she would try to stop him talking, convalescent as he was, but she said nothing.

'When you took so long to answer Lord Gilbert's summons that morning, you said you'd gone hunting,' I reminded him. 'I, for one, believed you.'

'I *was* hunting,' he said softly. 'I was looking for Ida.'

My thoughts ran on. I remembered the day Ida was buried and saw in my mind's eye the figures of Lord Gilbert, Lady Emma, Sir Alain and Lady Claude up on the low rise above the grave. 'She was looking at you, when Ida was buried,' I murmured. 'Lady Claude, I mean. I was touched because I thought she was looking to you for the strength to get her through the ordeal of burying the girl who had been her seamstress.' I knew different now; Claude, I had no doubt, had been watching Sir Alain like a hawk to see if he gave away his feelings for the dead girl.

'Claude didn't need anyone else's strength,' he said wearily. 'She had more than enough of her own.' Then, in a burst of

passion, 'I wish I'd realized that she was in the habit of
sneaking out of Lakehall! I thought, just like everyone else
did, that she locked herself away all day and every day
working on her sewing, but she didn't.'

'No,' I agreed. 'She went out with Ida the day of Ida's
death, and she went out again to set the trip wire that
Derman ran into. Then, when he had fallen in the water,
she beat him over the head with a piece of wood and killed
him.' I thought of something. '*I* knew she used to slip out,'
I said quietly. 'I was treating her, you know, for her
headaches and her insomnia. One day when I went to see
her she wasn't there. Lady Emma was quite upset, because
she'd invited Lady Claude to go on an outing with her and
the children and she'd said no, and then she went out by
herself.'

I felt Edild's hand on my shoulder. 'None of this was
your fault, Lassair,' she said firmly. 'It was impossible
for you to have realized the significance of Lady Claude's
absence.'

Perhaps it was. It didn't stop me feeling guilty about it.

Silence fell. After a while I looked at Sir Alain and said,
'What will you do?'

I have rarely seen anyone look so hopeless, so bleak. He
gave a deep sigh and said, 'I shall have to make my report
for the king concerning the three deaths here.' He looked
at Edild, then back at me. 'Unless you two have told anyone
else, only the three of us know what Ida and I were to each
other.'

'Alberic knows,' I said.

Sir Alain smiled grimly. 'You can safely leave Alberic
to me.'

Edild said thoughtfully, 'You will keep the fact that Ida
was pregnant with your child when she died a secret.'

He held her eyes. 'I will. And you, will you do so too?'

'Lassair and I are healers, and as such we are privy to
many people's secrets,' she said. 'We do not tell.'

His relief was evident. 'Thank you,' he said.

'What will you give as Lady Claude's reason for killing

herself if you withhold the true one?' I asked. It was forward of me, I dare say, but after what I had suffered at Claude's hands, I felt I had a right to ask.

Evidently, he did too. 'I shall explain discreetly, first to her mother and then to the king's officials, that Claude's frustrated desire to enter the convent finally overcame her, and she decided that life other than as a nun was not worth living.'

'Won't that make her mother feel very guilty?' I asked. 'It was she, after all, who proposed that one of her daughters should marry you.'

'If it does, then she deserves it,' he said harshly. 'God knows, I have my own guilt to bear, over both Claude's death and poor Geneviève's withdrawal, but it was not I who made the sisters what they were.'

I thought he was letting himself off lightly, but I did not say so. I met Edild's eye and guessed she was thinking the same.

I looked down at Sir Alain. His face was pale, and his eyes were closing. 'He's almost asleep,' I whispered to Edild.

She nodded. 'We will leave him to rest.' She got up, and so did I. We stood over him for a few moments, watching as his breathing deepened.

He would go away and make his report to whoever it was waiting to receive it, I thought. He was our justiciar; he could reveal as much or as little as he wished. Three people were dead, two of them killed by the third, who had died by her own hand. Alain de Villequier could, if he so wished, attribute all three crimes to Claude's extreme reaction to the thwarting of her ambitions to take the veil, a reaction that had driven her to insanity. He could, and he probably would. Because of who and what he was, no doubt he would be believed.

It wasn't really fair. But that was the way life usually was.

We never found out whether Sir Alain's face-saving version of the events at Aelf Fen that summer was accepted. We heard no more of it – nor, indeed, of him. I was sorry, in a way; he was a likeable man, and we could have done worse in a local officer of the law. Especially since my aunt and I knew his most carefully-guarded secret . . .

He went away, and he didn't come back. Lord Gilbert seemed more than ready to forget all about Lady Claude and her seamstress. The summons to return to Lakehall and give my account of what had happened the day Claude died never came. We concluded, my aunt, Hrype and I, that Lord Gilbert, too, might have known more about what had been going on than he wanted to reveal.

I do not know what became of poor Alberic. I never saw him again after that day I encountered him beneath the oak tree and, for a while, I assumed he had returned to Brandon. He hadn't. Sibert was sent to the village on some business of Lord Gilbert's, and he reported that Alberic's little house was standing empty. I like to think he went away from the scene of his unhappiness and settled elsewhere, finding a measure of contentment, but it isn't very likely. With the death of Ida, his hope had died too, and when I look into my heart, I sense he is dead.

Our return to normal life was helped and hastened on its way by a happy family event: Haward and Zarina were married. They do say that we value a wonderful gift even more when we have feared we would never receive it, and such was the case with my brother and his new wife. Joy seemed to shine out of them, as everyone who witnessed them on their wedding day agreed. My brother, straight-backed and handsome in his best tunic, was so relieved, so proud, that as he spoke his promise to take Zarina to be his wife, to love her and honour her, his stammer disappeared, and it has not come back. As for Zarina, she looked so beautiful that she might have been a spirit out of the blessed realm, her golden skin glowing and her eyes full of magic.

They moved into my parents' house, and there they will stay until Haward can build them a little place of their own. I have a feeling that day won't be very long in coming. Zarina is pregnant, although she does not yet know it, and I think the three of them will want to be on their own.

The picture that I saw in the runes has proved to be right.

As for me, I am forging ahead with my studies. New roads are opening up before me, and I am both excited and apprehensive. Hrype has spoken to me several times about Gurdyman and the drawings he is trying to make to show the route to faraway places; for some reason the two of them believe I may have an aptitude for the work Gurdyman is trying to do, and there are suggestions that I should go to Cambridge to study with him.

I worry about leaving my home and my family, and also about where such studies will take me. I worry, absurdly, that if I leave Aelf Fen to go to Cambridge, Rollo may come back and not know where to find me.

That, I know, is foolish. If – *when* – Rollo comes back, he won't let a little thing like half a day's journey keep him from me. I wonder what he and Gurdyman would make of each other?

Sometimes I can't sleep. Then I pick up my bag of runes, slip outside into the night and, once I am far away from the sleeping village, light my little fire and see what the stones can tell me. I still suffer afterwards, although I am learning how to lessen the effects. Perhaps that's something Hrype will help me with, once I pluck up the courage to ask him.

Tonight is such a night, and I sit here alone in the darkness looking back at the village. My fire has died down, and I shall not replenish it, for soon I shall return to my bed. I look up into the sky. It is autumn now, and if I wait a little longer I shall see the Huntsman over in the south-eastern sky: his belt shining like precious jewels, and his faithful hound at his feet.

I love the stars. I heard them singing, one summer night, or I thought I did. I still remember Alberic's beautiful, heart-breaking lament for Ida. When I visit her grave, on his behalf, wherever he is, I sing it to her.

Oh Ida, can you hear this sad refrain?
Can notes of music pierce your damp and peaty frame?
And would you hold me close if I were lain
Beside you? Could we sing the happy songs again?

I think she would be pleased.